Ghost
EVA SIMMONS

Copyright © 2024 by Eva Simmons

All rights reserved.

No portion of this book may be reproduced in any form without written permission from the publisher or author, except as permitted by U.S. copyright law.

No part of this book may be used to create, feed, or refine artificial intelligence models, for any purpose, without written permission from the author.

This novel is entirely a work of fiction. The names, characters and incidents portrayed in it are the work of the author's imagination. Any resemblance to actual persons, living or dead, events or localities is entirely coincidental.

Published by Eva Simmons

Editing by Kat Wyeth (Kat's Literary Services)

Proofreading by Vanessa Esquibel (Kat's Literary Services)

Model Cover Photography by Wander Aguiar

Model Cover Model: Gianni M.

Alternate Cover Artwork by: Atik Sugiwara

Cover Design by Eva Simmons

Model Cover Paperback ISBN: 9798300439538

Alternate Cover Paperback ISBN: 9798300440022

Content Note

This is a dark MC romance series with **graphic on page violence and explicit open-door scenes**. The characters in this series make morally gray decisions that are not always redeemable. Hard topics will be discussed that may be sensitive for some readers. Content warnings (which contain spoilers) can be found on my **website**. Please review before reading.

https://www.evasimmons.com/contentwarnings

When you like him tall, tatted, morally corrupt...
and always watching.

Ghost

Albuquerque

Fourteen Months Earlier

HACKING IS ART, AND with every stroke of the keys, the person on the other side of the screen lets me know who they really are. They give themselves away bit by bit until I see their truth.

Some hackers are easier to detect than others. They storm in, and I catch them when they hit the first tripwire. Others are quieter. They're careful. They get deeper before giving themselves away. Weaving a careful web as they roam my network, thinking they're getting somewhere when I've made sure they still have far to go.

It's artwork that I appreciate, even if I ultimately lock them out before they can get anything from the Twisted Kings. I admire them for trying.

Whoever I'm up against now knows what they're doing. They're almost as good as I am as they tiptoe through my system, sneaking around.

Almost.

No one gets through without me knowing about it.

Sitting back, I watch the hacker work. I'm familiar with the patterns of most of our rival club's tech specialists, so this person must be new. If it were Richter or Snake, they would be barreling in. Both tend to take a hard and fast approach. They'd plant a virus in an attempt to cripple the system before I could shut them down.

This person operates differently. They're barely a whisper, sneaking through the firewall. Every movement is delicate. They're cautious with their approach but bold in what they target, as they immediately seek out files with our bank account information.

They won't find anything in there. It's a dummy folder set up to distract them when they get this far. I lean back and smirk as I watch them take the bait, but I don't shut them down just yet.

They hacked me, but they don't seem to have any sense of direction with their random strings of code. At first, I thought they were planting a virus because that's the easiest way to get in and get out, but if that was the plan, they've yet to do it.

The hacker breaks through another firewall, and it would be impressive if I didn't already know they were there. Their skill level far surpasses anyone I've seen try to break into our system in the past year, which has me curious about who I'm dealing with.

My fingers fly across the keys, and I divert them again, watching to see what they'll do.

When faced with a wall, they work around it. When given an obstacle, they weave.

They still haven't realized I fed them into a backup server ten minutes ago, so anything they find won't compromise the club, but I use the time to study their movements.

Glancing at my second screen, their location finally pings. As talented as they appear to be, they must be new because they left their network open. It took less than five minutes to trace where they are, and, as it turns out, they're at a coffee shop less than three miles away.

Opening another browser, I break into the city's transportation department to pull footage off the nearest traffic camera, but it's no good. I can only make out the corner of the shop.

Closing the traffic camera, I dive back into the backup server and retrace the hacker's footsteps, being bolder this time because I have no choice.

The Merciless Skulls have been relentless since the Twisted Kings arrived in Albuquerque to help the Road Rebels defend their territory. They've been hitting us from every angle, and when the Iron Sinners showed up to help them, they became even more persistent.

I have no choice but to connect directly to the hacker's server if I'm going to report back to Steel about who is trying to strip financial information from our records.

Eyeing the clock, I set a mental timer. I'll have no more than sixty seconds before their system detects my presence.

Luckily, it doesn't take that long.

A few more keystrokes, and I'm in their settings, feeding the laptop's camera view directly to my second screen. It blinks, and the face of the person walking around my system comes into view.

I expected someone like me—a biker.

A recluse.

Someone who hides in the shadows, protecting the club without being seen.

Instead, I'm met with the image of a girl who beams as bright as the sun. Her black-rimmed glasses frame her bright-blue eyes, and they're the color of the sky on a perfectly clear day. They narrow as she continues to type, and she's biting the inside of her cheek.

The girl's hair is blonde at the roots, but the rest has been dyed a pale lavender. She has it tied up in a loose ponytail with a few pieces falling around the sides of her face.

She enters another string of code, frowning when it gets her nowhere she hasn't already been.

She's lost in thought, and I'm lost in her.

How she fights against my firewalls.

How she wets her lips when she's thinking, and how her eyes light when she breaks open another file.

The faintest hint of a smile curls up in the corner of her mouth, but it's immediately followed by her eyebrows scrunching when she finds the file empty.

A constellation of freckles dusts the apples of her cheeks.

She's an entire universe wrapped up in one body.

Her blue eyes scan the screen, meeting the camera lens.

Just for a second.

Just long enough that it feels like she's looking into my eyes.

Shutting down the feed, I try to digest whatever is stirred in my gut. I pull out of her system and sync my phone to my laptop so I can keep an eye on her chasing her tail while I'm on the move.

Once I'm connected, I walk out of the office and down the hall.

We're only in town for a few weeks, helping the Road Rebels defend their territory, but their old equipment and dusty office have me missing our Las Vegas Clubhouse.

At least the brunt of the battle is over. After the collapse of the Merciless Skulls clubhouse, the Iron Sinners have started withdrawing their help, and whoever is left is scattering. It's a win for both the Rebels and us since they transport most of our product from New Mexico to Nevada.

But if this hacker is any indication, my work isn't done yet.

The remaining Merciless Skulls might be in the wind, but someone sent this girl after the club.

I make my way down the hall and toward the clubhouse den. The Road Rebels clubhouse is quiet since most of my brothers are still passed out after a late night of celebrating us putting a few more Merciless Skulls in the ground.

Steel looks up from his phone the moment I stop in the doorway.

Like me, he doesn't drink as much as the other guys, so he wakes up early. As our club's president, he takes pride in never getting too wasted and losing his clear head, especially on the road.

"What's wrong?" Steel's gaze narrows.

"Nothing." I rake my hair back.

The lie is out before I can stop it, and it's the first sign I'm fucked. I don't ever lie to my president, but something about this girl grinds against the loyalty that's embedded in my bones.

I don't feel right telling Steel about her until I'm sure of what she's up to because the second I do, she'll be the enemy, and the club will need to handle it.

Handle her.

"I'm grabbing a coffee. Want anything?" I prop my forearm on the doorframe.

Steel lifts his mug off the table and tips it at me. "I'm good, but let me know when you're back so we can talk logistics. You drained the Merciless Skull's assets?"

"All but a couple of accounts I'm still working on. But something's off."

"What?"

"When the Iron Sinners first showed up, we thought it was to help. But they didn't get involved in the shootout, and even if Legacy said it might be all financial assistance, there's no indication Titan transferred funds to them."

Steel's eyebrows pinch. "Why were they here if they weren't helping?"

"Moral support?" I joke.

"It'd be a cold day in hell." Steel shakes his head, chuckling. "Well, if you figure it out, let me know. I don't like how easy it was to take the Merciless Skulls down, especially when their allies were right here to help them."

"Me either."

While it's always a win when we can limit the amount of blood spilled, the Merciless Skulls barely put up a fight, and that hasn't been sitting well with me.

Victor and his Road Rebels are celebrating taking back over the territory, but something feels off.

"I'll be back."

Steel nods, going back to whatever he's working on as I walk away.

Pulling my phone out of my pocket, I check on the little hacker. She's still making her way through my backup server and keeping herself busy. If she's figured out it's a front, she's not showing any indication of it, which gives me time.

I hop on my bike and take the short ride to the coffee shop, parking a block away so the sound of a motorcycle doesn't make anyone scatter if the little hacker has bodyguards. The second a Merciless Skull or Iron Sinner hears me rolling up, they'll get suspicious, and I've already made a mistake coming here alone. The last thing I need is more trouble.

I'm careful as I circle the coffee shop. While her laptop camera had a clear view of her, it showed nothing but windows in the background. There was no view of her table or who might be sitting with her.

Walking into the coffee shop, I spot the hacker immediately. She's sitting by herself at the far side of the shop. Sunbeams shine through the window behind her, drawing out the blonde underneath the purple.

If she is working for the Merciless Skulls, then for the first time in my life, I'm jealous of them. There's something about this girl that is fucking fascinating, and it doesn't make sense for someone with her level of talent to be answering to anyone from our rival club.

Everything about her is captivating, and it isn't just that she's beautiful—which she is. It's those eyes of hers—working as she tries to hack my system. It's her mind turning over as she sneaks quietly into my territory.

She's in my maze, and I'm tempted to watch her fight her way out forever because now that I have her, I don't want to let her go.

Glancing at my phone, I watch her movements on the screen. She's trying to break open another file. There's nothing in there, but I hit a key to shut her out just to see how she'll react now that I have her right in front of me.

She doesn't so much as flinch at the dead end. Instead, she rolls her shoulders back and continues typing in a new string of code that sends her in a different direction.

The smallest smirk climbs up in the corner of her mouth, and it's so gentle I can't stop staring at her.

I'm winning this cyber sparring match, but she's amused, having fun toying with me.

"What can I get you?" A bubbly redhead from behind the counter stops at the register.

Her smile is hesitant as she glances from my tattoos to my cut.

I'm used to it. People see the demons inked into my arms or the bike I'm riding and assume I'm trouble.

Depending on who they are, they might be right.

"Coffee. Black." I slide a twenty-dollar bill onto the counter, and her smile finally relaxes when I refuse the change, motioning to the tip jar instead.

"Your name?" She holds a marker to the empty cup.

"Ghost."

Her eyebrows pinch like she's trying to figure out if I'm messing with her or not as she scribbles it down. "Give me just a minute."

I cross to the pick-up counter, which is next to where the purple-haired girl is still typing away.

From this angle, I get a better view of her screen. Her small fingers dance over the keys as she gnaws at her lower lip. Attempt after attempt, she tries to break through and can't. It's an endless web with nothing at the end but my amusement.

She's good, but I'm better.

Which is why I was given my position with the club when I patched in at eighteen. Before that, I helped with fake IDs and surveillance, and as the years went on, I helped with more delicate things. Computers make more sense to me than people. There's no emotion, just mechanics. I understand the parts and how to manipulate them.

Leaning against the counter, I pretend to stare at my phone while I keep an eye on the purple-haired girl and wait for my coffee.

Her eyebrows pinch, and her fingers fly over the keys.

Precise.

Quick.

Purposeful.

If she were up against anyone but me, I have no doubt she'd have already found everything she was looking for.

Beside her laptop is a notepad and a physics textbook. The name *Luna* is scribbled on the side of her coffee cup, and it's fitting for a girl who doesn't make sense.

Luna's eyes brighten, and I glance at my phone to see what she's so excited about. She's almost made it into a dual-authenticated, password-protected file, and that's when I decide to shut her out. I lock the door and kick her out of my server for good.

Looking up, I see Luna's brow furrow with the sudden defeat, expecting frustration to wash over her face. Instead, a wide smile stretches her cheeks, and she bursts out laughing.

Loud.

Unapologetic.

She laughs so big and bold it fills the silence of the coffee shop.

Nothing about this girl strikes me as delicate, but with one giggle, she has the whole room's attention.

She tips her head back with her laugh, and I know I'm staring at her, but I can't fucking help it. I can't tear my eyes off this girl. Even when her blue gaze meets mine, I can't look away.

"Sorry." She smiles, slapping her laptop shut and shaking her head. "There's nothing like getting caught, right?"

I glance around, and it takes a moment to process she's talking to me.

"Caught?" I play dumb.

Luna brushes her fingers over her closed laptop. "Yeah, *caught*. I know people always say there's nothing like the chase, but they're wrong. Or they're scared, maybe? Who knows. Getting caught is way more thrilling."

Her gaze moves down, pausing as she takes in my leather cut. Unlike the redhead who works at the coffee shop, she doesn't look scared, but I can't read what she's thinking. Knowing I'm in a motorcycle club makes other people look the other way, which is how I prefer it. But Luna doesn't so much as blink.

Her complete lack of fear is probably a red flag, confirming she works for my club's enemies, but my mind struggles to process that as she watches me.

"Ghost?" My name is a question as a guy behind the counter slides my coffee across it toward me.

"Thanks." I take it, popping the lid off to cool it down.

"Ghost, huh?" Luna asks, readjusting her purple hair into a bun on the top of her head. "That's a strange name."

"I could say the same for Luna." I tip my chin at her coffee cup.

She glances down at the scribbly letters and smiles up at me. "I guess you're right. Is Ghost a nickname or something?"

"Or something." I glance down at her books, thinking up a way to divert the conversation. "Are you studying for a test?"

She can't know why I'm here or that I'm with the club.

"Studying?" Her eyebrows furrow as she follows my gaze, spotting her physics book. "Oh, right. Yes, I was. Studying and working."

"What kind of work do you do?"

I shouldn't be entertaining this conversation when I should be reporting her to my president, but I can't seem to help it.

"Research…" She taps her fingers on the table, looking nervous as her gaze drifts off. "I help people find things."

"What kind of things?"

"They don't say, and I don't ask."

I want to believe that's the truth, especially knowing who she's likely working for. She could have been contracted for this job, having no idea she's digging into the original chapter of one of the West Coast's biggest motorcycle clubs. But I doubt it.

"You're not from here, are you?" She glances at my cut again.

I shake my head. "Las Vegas. Why?"

"I've seen some guys around wearing vests like that, but it's a different logo."

Vests.

Maybe she doesn't know who I am after all.

"No, I'm not with them."

"You make it sound so ominous." She smiles up at me. "How is Vegas, anyway? I've always wanted to go."

"Hot."

"Hot?" Her eyebrows pinch.

I nod. "And busy."

Luna smiles, leaning forward on the table as she watches me. "You don't talk much, do you, Ghost?"

"Not usually."

She laughs, but this time, it's quieter. Sweeter. It's half an exhale, and it makes me question everything I'm doing right now.

"Well, people tell me I talk too much, so I guess we balance each other out." She adjusts her hair. "Maybe I should move someplace like Vegas next. It sounds exciting."

"It's not as spectacular as you think."

"Or you're just jaded from being there too long." She shrugs, looking around the coffee shop. "Either way, it seems like a place you can get lost in."

I don't ask her why being lost appeals to her or what she's running from. All I do is stare into her eyes and know exactly what she's talking about.

"Vegas is good for that."

"Maybe if I end up there, I'll look you up."

I smirk. "You can try."

Luna bites her lower lip and smiles. There's something about how she meets a challenge that lights me up inside.

But just as suddenly, we're cut off by her phone pinging on the table.

"Crap." She looks down at the screen and starts shoving her books in her bag.

"Everything okay?"

"Yeah, but I've gotta run." She stands up, which makes her ponytail flop around. "But maybe I'll see you around town again. Or maybe even in Vegas."

"Maybe."

She clutches her bag to her chest, standing in front of me with the sweetest smile on her face. Her head tilts back so she can look up at me, stretching her beautiful neck. A foreign urge to shield her from whatever mess she's blindly getting herself into surfaces inside me.

"If I do, I'll look you up." Luna waves, turning to hurry away. "Bye, Ghost."

I watch her rush toward the door, knowing I need to drive back to the clubhouse and tell Steel everything that just happened—and knowing that I won't.

One moment. One lie.

I'm a smart man. But right now, I'm making a stupid decision for this girl.

1

Luna

Las Vegas

Present Day

PEOPLE ARE MESSY. I play the part for them, but it doesn't mean I understand them. I've always been better with a computer screen between me and whoever I'm dealing with. Which is probably why I'm standing outside Ghost's office door like a frozen, pathetic girl, dreading knocking on it.

This man makes me stupid.

Closing my eyes, I tip my head back and let out a breath.

A little over a year ago, when Ghost offered me a job with the Twisted Kings and I moved to Las Vegas with them, things seemed simpler than they are now.

I underestimated what it would be like working for the tall, tattooed man on the other side of the door. Because any friendliness he showed when we met stopped the moment we started working together.

Now, he acts like I'm more of a nuisance than anything.

Finally finding the courage to knock, I hold my breath and wait for him to invite me in. I close my eyes and pretend he doesn't affect me when I clearly don't affect him. Knowing the moment I step inside, he'll make my insides spin around.

His gaze is trouble.

His tattoos are a path of temptation.

Everything about Ghost screams danger and emotional unavailability. So, of course, my reckless little heart chases after him.

"Come in." His deep voice sends a shiver through my core.

I swing the door open, and I'm met with the familiar, comforting scent of soap and leather.

Ghost is sitting at his desk, but he doesn't look up at me when I step inside. His fingers fly across the keys as he works, and he's so tall, he dwarfs everything in the room in comparison. His eyes are steely cold and focused, and I wish he'd let me help him with whatever he's struggling with instead of sending me on errands and tasking me with boring, simple things like replacing cameras and staring at surveillance footage.

He doesn't trust me.

I might live in the clubhouse and work for the Twisted Kings, but it doesn't make me one of them. They are careful who they let in on their secrets, which is why I'm always tasked with mind-numbing clean-up work and secretarial bullshit.

"You asked for this?" I hold up the flash drive, and Ghost glances up from his screen.

His chilling blue eyes meet mine, and it sends a shiver through my entire body.

"Is that the surveillance from Sapphire Rise?"

"No, it's the footage from Kings Auto right before the fire started. I went back three days leading up to it, and there's nothing useful."

He frowns. "Did you double-check the camera at the main garage? Sometimes the footage is a little pixelated, so you have to refocus it."

"Contrary to popular belief, I know what I'm doing, Ghost." I roll my eyes. "So yes, I tried that and still… nothing. I can handle more complicated jobs than surveillance if you give me a chance."

Ghost leans back in his chair, tapping his thumb on his keyboard. "I don't need your help with anything else."

"Of course not." I breathe out an unamused chuckle and slap the flash drive down on the desk.

Crossing my arms over my chest, I stand up tall.

It wasn't always this infuriating working for Ghost. When I first came to Vegas, Ghost was distant and quiet, but at least civil. He would give me a task, and I'd get it done. Ignoring the electricity sparking between us.

I had a home, a steady stream of income, and a place to finish my degree while I figured out what I wanted. And it was more than enough.

Every city I've lived in before Vegas had been so small and suffocating. But in the desert, possibility was wide and endless.

When I first came here, I had hope, and Ghost was part of making that happen.

But lately, things are changing. Ghost shuts down more every day, and the deterioration is starting to eat away at me. Any little flirtations we shared the first time we met have faded, and I'm lucky if he looks me in the eyes when we talk.

I don't know what I did wrong or why I expect things to get better when all he does is shut me down, but the tension in the room is nearly debilitating.

Staring at Ghost now, I wait for him to reassure me this is all in my head, but he won't.

"Did you need something else?" Ghost hitches an eyebrow.

"Apparently not." Turning, I leave the room, shutting the door a little too hard behind me.

He can't even be bothered with a *Thanks, Luna* or a *You're not imagining we used to have something between us, Luna.*

Nothing.

I do my job without appreciation and pretend I can keep my eyes off the man who brought me here in the first place.

Making my way into the den, a few of the guys have already started drinking. I should probably study in my bedroom, but instead, I've set my books up on the couch in the corner. While the noise and rowdiness might bother some people, the madness of the clubhouse soothes me. It gives me something to listen to other than the doubts running circles in my head.

I pile my books on a cushion and then head into the kitchen to get something to drink that isn't alcohol. I have an online test due tomorrow, and I need to pass it to move on to the next module.

Reina is sitting on a stool at the counter, talking on the phone. She twirls a white-blonde strand of hair around her finger, smiling at me as I walk in.

Opening the cabinet, I reach for my favorite mug on the top shelf, but it's just out of reach. My fingers graze the handle, but I can't quite get it. Planting my palm on the counter to gain some leverage, I silently curse Stevie's height, knowing he must have put away the dishes.

I can almost snag the handle with my middle finger, but it's not enough, so I plant my feet down and sigh.

Right as I'm about to give up and pick a different mug, a body closes in behind me.

Warmth seeps through my T-shirt, and I breathe him in.

Leather.

Soap.

I look up over my shoulder to see Ghost reaching up for the mug, pressing my body into the counter as he does. He was just working in his office, but somehow, he manages to be nowhere and everywhere at once.

Once he has the mug, he steps back, handing it to me, and I wonder if he felt all the air leave my chest just now. Our eyes connect, and I can't help wishing this was different.

"Thanks." I take the mug, trying to ignore that my cheeks feel like they're being eaten up by flames.

He nods, breaking my stare, and leaves the kitchen as Reina hangs up the phone.

No water.

No food.

Did Ghost follow me in here just to get me a mug and leave?

"What in the world was that?" Reina's eyes widen. "Did Ghost just touch you?"

"Touch me?" I turn away from her, hoping the warmth crawling my entire body isn't obvious. "He got me my coffee mug off the top shelf. That's it."

"The man is tall. He could have reached it without feeling up your ass."

I roll my eyes and pour myself a cup of coffee. "He wasn't feeling up my ass. He was helping me out."

"Sure he was." Reina grins, following me out of the kitchen when I try to escape her interrogation. "So you're running from the question now?"

"I answered your question. It was nothing." I shrug. "If it was Venom doing me a favor, then yes, I'd say he's trying to get some, but this is Ghost we're talking about."

"True," Reina agrees, and part of me hates it. "When do you think he's gonna drop the whole celibacy thing? It can't last forever. Did I tell you I wore that red dress around him last week, and he didn't even look at me?"

"Since when are you interested in Ghost?" And why does the thought of that make my entire body light up with rage?

"I'm not." She watches me sink into the couch. "I was just curious what he would do about it since none of the other guys can seem to resist a short red skirt."

Rolling my eyes, I pick up a textbook. "It's not a game to him, Reina. You can't break him by teasing him with your ass."

She smirks. "Clearly, or you'd have done that by now."

"What are you talking about?"

"Come on, Luna. I see how you walk around here in your T-shirts that barely cover your ass." She narrows her eyes. "I'm not the only one trying to see what will break him."

"I wear leggings under them... most of the time."

"Most of the time. Exactly." She grins. "Who knows, maybe someday it will work."

"That would require him to notice."

"Oh, he notices."

"Says who?"

"You're kidding, right?" She hitches an eyebrow.

But right as I'm about to ask what she's seen, Havoc walks into the room, catching her attention.

"Gotta run." She darts off after Havoc, and I watch her go.

Across the room, Ghost is finishing a conversation with Soul. They clink beers, and then he makes his way outside to the patio. He drops into a chair that is directly in front of me but angled so I can't see him straight on.

His strong jaw glows with the flicker of flames from the firepit as he pulls out his phone. And I'm not sure how long I've been staring when he glances over at me.

Immediately, I look away.

The last thing I need is him thinking I'm obsessed and can't keep my eyes off him. It's not true.

At least, not always.

Turning my attention to my textbook, I try to focus on the page and not the tattooed biker sitting across the club. But when Steel steps into the room and the guys all cheer for him, it draws my attention.

I watch Steel say hello as he walks through the crowd, meeting Ghost outside and sitting in the chair beside him. They fall into conversation, and I watch as it slowly turns from friendly to tense.

Something is wrong.

I think I'm imagining it until Ghost hands Steel his phone, and they both glance over at me. For the first time in a year, I feel seen by Ghost, and something tells me that right now, it's not a good thing.

2

Luna

Ghost disappears with Steel, and I'm finally able to focus on the chapter I've been staring at for the past thirty minutes. I finish taking notes when a message pops up from Rider in my online gaming app, asking if I'm in the mood to play tonight.

There's someone else I'd rather be spending time with, but Ghost is ignoring me and MIA as usual, so I take what I can get and let Rider know I'll log on for the raid he's coordinating.

It's better than sitting alone staring at a wall.

I've been lonely lately.

The clubhouse has been quiet since the Iron Sinners kidnapped Steel's old lady and her brother a few weeks ago. They were thankfully rescued without being harmed, but the club has been on high alert ever since. An attack on the president is as bold as it gets, and that means fewer parties, less visitors, and more time to sit and stew with my pent-up sexual tension.

Reina keeps trying to convince me to screw one of the guys and work it out of my system, but that's the problem. I can't, and I won't.

The Twisted Kings are off-limits. The second I fall into bed with one of them, things are bound to get complicated. Besides, the only one I have any interest in couldn't care less about me.

So instead of worrying about getting laid, I focus on work and school. And in my free time, I play my online multiplayer game with Rider, giving me an escape from life at the clubhouse.

Rider joined my guild around the time I first moved to Vegas, and we both enjoyed raiding and player-versus-player gameplay. Slowly, we spent more time together and talked about our lives outside the game. And now, he's more of a friend to me than some of the people I live at the clubhouse with.

With Rider, it's simple. We play and keep each other company. No complications and no strings. He doesn't even know my real name.

It's perfect.

Behind my character, I can be anyone I want. I can hide in plain sight like I do in Vegas. I can pretend my past doesn't exist and just be an elf on the screen, with purple hair that matches mine in real life.

Rider: You're burning through your cooldowns, little owl.

SnoOwl: Are you telling me how to play now? Watch it, or I'll point out that you're running low on mana... AGAIN.

Rider: Isn't that you pointing it out?

SnoOwl: Maybe.

His character stops moving on the screen, and I watch as his mana bar regenerates with the potion he just consumed.

SnoOwl: You're welcome.

Rider: I was already on it.

SnoOwl: I'm sure you were... or maybe you were distracted by my new chainmail dress...

My elf is wearing something short and revealing as always. I enjoy dressing her up, even if this outfit does nothing to protect her. Still, it's a standard piece of gear for my character because God forbid men who play women in game have to look at something *not revealing* while battling monsters.

Not that I mind it.

This outfit shows off my character's glowing, purple runes.

Leaning back in my chair, I kick my feet up on my desk and tap my fuzzy, pink slippers together. My wireless keyboard is on my lap as I kite the boss, moving around him and waiting for my cooldowns to reset.

Rider: With a dress like that, you should hit up Timbershire after this raid and see if you can get some gold.

SnoOwl: Very funny... We both know I'm not that kind of lady.

Rider: Technically, you're an elf.

SnoOwl: I'm not that kind of elf then.

Timbershire is one of the places in game where people gather to strip their characters down to their underwear and talk dirty. Sometimes, Rider and I go there to laugh at how ridiculous it all is, but I never participate.

Rider: Just say the word, little owl, and I could take you on a real date. Or are you still swearing off all men?

I laugh at the fact that he remembers I said that. I was bitter at the time. I'd caught Ghost watching me from across the room, so I took a shot of vodka and figured I'd actually try and flirt with him. He shut me down so fast, my pride hurt for a week from the whiplash.

SnoOwl: You couldn't keep up with me if you tried.

Rider: I'd still try ;)

The boss topples on the screen, his health taking a massive drop.

Rider: Nice hit.

SnoOwl: Thank you.

I do an in-game curtsy before turning my attention to the minions that spawned the second the boss went down.

Rider helps me pick them off one by one, and after we collect our gold, we teleport to a safe zone. I set my character into dance mode while we wait for the next raid queue.

People run past us on the screen, heading to their missions. And I wonder what it says about me that my online elf life is the most normal part of my day. Or that Rider, a man I've never met in person, is one of my closest friends.

The downside of living with a motorcycle club is that it can be isolating and lonely, especially when they're in lockdown.

While many of the girls here are looking for a relationship or waiting for a biker to claim them as their old lady, I'm in limbo.

I'm an outsider in a building filled with people.

When Tempe showed up, she felt like a kindred spirit. She was an outcast, too, since her father was Steel's former VP, and he betrayed the club. We were both here for unusual reasons, and it gave us something in common. But now that Tempe is Steel's old lady, I'm aware there's a difference between her role in the club and mine.

I'd like to think the Twisted Kings are my family, but if my childhood taught me anything, it's that family can be as temporary as friendship.

I bounced around from foster home to foster home growing up, collecting bad memories and non-blood-related siblings. And when I turned eighteen and was no longer worth the checks I used to come with, I was kicked to the curb.

It was just me, alone, in a world that couldn't care less if I found my footing or drowned.

That's why Rider and I get along so well. He doesn't have any blood relatives either. We've both always been on the outside looking in. Seeing what a family is supposed to look like and not having one.

My computer pings, snapping me out of my thoughts.

Rider: You're quiet today. Everything all right?
SnoOwl: I've just got a lot on my mind.

Rider: Like?

I debate not saying anything, when there's nothing that he can do about it, but maybe it will help to get it out.

SnoOwl: Something feels off with the guys.

Rider doesn't know I live at an MC clubhouse. So when I first mentioned *the guys*, he assumed they were my roommates, and I left it at that.

Rider: Are they treating you all right?

SnoOwl: Yeah, they always do. It's not that. I just get this feeling they know something that I don't. Something was off tonight, but I don't know what it is. It feels like everything's about to change.

Rider is quiet for a minute on the other side of the keyboard. A message pops up that he's typing, and I glance around my empty bedroom while the in-game music plays in my ear.

My roommates' beds are empty since Reina and Wren are with the guys at the bar partying. So I have this room to myself at the moment.

It doesn't usually bother me, but tonight, it feels so empty the silence is deafening.

A ping from the computer pulls my attention back to the screen.

Rider: You always feel like that, remember? But from what you've said, they won't let anything happen to you. You can trust them, can't you?

SnoOwl: I think so.

Rider: Everything's going to be okay.

I wish he had the power to make that promise. I wish I could pull us out of the screen and have a connection with a real live person in my life for once.

We get along, so maybe it could be something more. I could move out. I could move on.

I've been in limbo for so long that I'm in a constant state of suspension between who I am and who I want to be. Never quite living in the present when one foot always toes the line with the past.

Rider: It will be okay, little owl. I promise.

SnoOwl: I hope so.

Rider: Hey, I gotta run. Just remember what I said. Everything will be okay. I'll make sure of it. Good game.

Rider logs off before I can respond, and I sit staring at the elf running into the rock wall ahead of me, relating a little too much to how that feels when I keep hitting one myself lately.

Shutting my game off, I place my headset on the desk and lie down in bed. Little glow-in-the-dark plastic stars decorate the dark ceiling, and I trace the patterns with my gaze. Reina told me a previous patch bunny hung them up, and I'm thankful for it because it gives me something to stare up at in the dark of night.

If only plastic stars granted wishes.

I'm halfway asleep when a knock comes at my door, jolting me awake. If it were Reina or Wren, they'd just walk in, and when I glance at the clock, it's one thirty in the morning.

"Coming." I hop off the bed, walking over to swing the door open.

Havoc is standing on the other side with his arms crossed over his chest.

Once more, that sinking feeling I've had all day settles. Last I saw him, he disappeared with Reina, so this can't be good.

"Prez wants to see you." Havoc frowns, but I don't know why.

He's the club's sergeant at arms, so there are very few things that make him nervous outside of threats to the club. But right now, the pinch between his eyebrows tells me he's worried.

I nod, following him down the hallway.

Havoc is a large man, and he takes up most of the space with his wide, muscular shoulders. His long hair is tied back like it usually is, and his thick, tattooed arms are on display in his T-shirt and cut.

It's quiet as we pass the kitchen, which means anyone still awake must be hanging out by the bar up front. And when Havoc leads me to the room where the club holds church, my stomach churns.

No one is allowed in here, especially club girls. This is the club's most sacred space, and the second I walk in, everything feels wrong.

The chairs circling the table are filled with the ranked members of the club, with Steel at the head watching me with a stone-cold expression. At his side is Soul, his vice president. Havoc sinks into the chair at Steel's other side while Legacy and Chaos watch each other like they're having a silent conversation.

Ghost sits back, his expression like ice, and I know in the pit of my stomach this can't be good.

"Have a seat, Luna." Steel waves to the empty chair at the other end, directly across from him. "We need to talk."

3

Luna

IT FEELS WRONG TO sit at this table.

The solid wood is polished so it shines under the single bulb that hangs dimly overhead. The Twisted Kings logo is carved deeply into the center, and the crowned and winged skull stares at me with all its judgment.

My nails dig into the leather cushion I'm sitting on as all eyes are on me, and I've never felt so alone in a room full of people.

No one speaks, and I assume they're waiting for Steel to say something.

Steel is respected in his role as president of the club. He's ruthless but honorable. He's fair.

He'll do whatever is necessary to protect his club, but he's always smart about it. He's known for being decisive but not rash and acting with the intent of justice over brutality.

Still, as he watches me now, I can't help but squirm, wondering why he's looking at me like I'm the enemy.

"You guys are making me nervous." I try to force a smile, but it dies on my lips with my laugh as nerves skitter out.

There's little empathy radiating from the ranked club members in the room, even if I do sense hesitation.

"We need to talk about Albuquerque," Steel breaks the silence, leaning forward and resting his elbows on the table.

"Albuquerque?"

Of all the things he could have said, I wasn't expecting him to say that. There's nothing to note about my time there. It was an escape after I left Glendale. I picked anywhere at least one state away from the foster family that haunted me, and that was it. I worked odd jobs I found on the internet and took classes online.

My time in Albuquerque wasn't interesting.

If Steel was going to bring me in for anything, I expected this meeting to be about the fact that I've been skirting the club's firewalls to play my online multiplayer game, and Ghost must have found out about it.

Worst case scenario, I thought they might have brought me in here to tell me they need my bed for a girl who wants more from them than a place to stay.

But Albuquerque?

I haven't thought about New Mexico since I left.

Steel nods.

"What about it?" My voice pitches, and I hate that it gives away my nerves.

Steel taps his fingers on the table, watching me. "When was the first time you heard about the Twisted Kings?"

There's no friendliness in his tone, and a chill runs through the room. This isn't a conversation; it's an interrogation. And I'm at the center, waiting for the gavel to drop and decide my fate.

I glance at Ghost, who is still watching me, and try to read his expression. But it's nearly impossible. His cool-blue eyes are the gravity in a room that's slowly starting to spin out of control, and I grab it for what it is—something to hold me in place.

A looming sense that everything is about to change settles when I wish my gut hadn't been right about this.

I've been rejected by so many people—so many families—I don't fit anywhere anymore. But I hoped with the club that had changed.

"Luna." Steel's voice snaps my attention back into focus. "When was the first time you heard of the club?"

"When I met Ghost." I glance at him. "We ran into each other at a coffee shop, and I saw the logo on his cut. I asked if he was from somewhere else because it said Vegas on it."

I called it a vest back then because I had no idea how motorcycle clubs worked. A couple of my foster siblings rode, but it was recreational.

My run-in with Ghost was my first official interaction with someone in this world. Over time, I've picked up their lingo, but back then, I was new to all this.

"What were you doing at the coffee shop that day?" Steel continues.

"Drinking coffee." My eyebrows pinch as I think back. "Studying…"

"Anything else?"

My nose scrunches as I think, trying to remember that day. "Working. I was finishing up a job."

It's been so long that I almost forgot about that.

"What job?"

So that's what this is about.

Another puzzle piece clicks in place, but I can't see the full picture.

"I was helping a corporation track down information. Hacking data for them. You know I used to do that. You all did."

My gaze cuts to Ghost before I scan the room. My work before the club is no secret. It's one of the reasons Steel offered to let me stay here while I went to school. He gave me a roof over my head, and I offered my unique skill set. It doesn't make sense why it's an issue now.

"Who hired you for that particular job?" Steel's tone somehow manages to be even colder now.

"I don't know." I shake my head. "Most of the work I accepted back then came through anonymous listings. That was one of them."

Steel hums, but I can't read him well enough to know if he believes me.

Either way, it's the truth.

The type of hacking I performed wasn't legal, so it wasn't unusual for my employers to want to keep their identities hidden. I'd respond to anonymous postings on message boards, and neither party knew who the other was.

"When they hired you, what did they need you to look for?"

"Bank account numbers. Statements. They were looking for a financial trail for a shell corporation." My palms sweat as I rub them on my thighs. "But I couldn't find anything, so they never paid me for the job. Whoever was on the other end shut me down before I could get any real data. I think they knew I was in their system from the beginning because everything I found was nonsense."

Steel hums, glancing over at Ghost.

"Can you just tell me what's going on?" I glance between the two of them. "Did I do something wrong?"

"You tell me, Luna." Steel fixes his gray stare on me. "Did you really have no idea you were working that job for the Merciless Skulls?"

"The—" My eyes widen as I cut myself off. "No."

Panic swells in my chest when I realize what Steel's asking me. When I met Ghost in the coffee shop, I didn't know anything about motorcycle clubs. But after arriving in Vegas, I heard rumors around the clubhouse telling me why they were in Albuquerque when I met them. The Twisted Kings were helping take down the Merciless Skulls.

And now Steel is implying I was helping their enemy.

"I swear. It was like any other job to me. I had no idea who I was doing it for. Or who—" I pause, swallowing hard. "Who was I hacking?"

This time, I look at Ghost because it occurs to me that they already know the answer.

I already know the answer.

I just need to hear it out loud.

"Us," Steel says.

My heart races as I sit back in my chair.

I'm a traitor—an enemy—and I didn't even know it.

My stare meets Ghost's, and he's barely moved. His tattooed hands are resting one over the other on the table in front of him, unsurprised by anything said up to this point.

"Did you know?" I ask, even if I know Steel won't let him answer. "Is that why you came into the coffee shop that day? Were you the one who shut me down?"

I think back to that day, remembering Ghost walking in. He's impossible not to notice, especially when he drew the attention of everyone working behind the counter. Their eyes widened as they watched him.

They were afraid of his tattoos and perma-scowl.

But I wasn't.

I couldn't stop tracking his movements from the corner of my eye, curious about who he was and desperate to know more about him. Ever since that first moment I was face to face with Ghost, there's been an undeniable pull. And even after I told myself I was coming to Vegas for business, I knew the truth.

I'm here because of him.

Ghost might show me breadcrumbs of attention, but I eat each one like a full meal. Desperate to ease the hungering ache inside me.

"Did you know?" I ask Ghost again, tears burning behind my eyes.

Ghost doesn't answer, and it occurs to me that maybe I'm not the only one who is in trouble. While Steel seems surprised, Ghost isn't.

Ghost knew, and he never told them.

He lied for me.

The Twisted Kings are his life. His family. His loyalty is with them, so why would he do that?

"When's the last time you heard from the person who posted that job?" Steel asks, ignoring my pleas to Ghost and continuing his interrogation.

I shake my head. "A year ago. Eleven months, maybe. I argued with them for a while about payment, since I did my part trying, but eventually, I gave up. I haven't heard anything from them since."

"So, you were still talking to them when you came here?"

I swallow hard. "I guess. Yeah."

"Did they know where you were?"

"No. I never shared my whereabouts with my employers. It was better that way in case either of us got caught."

"So no one outside of this club knows you're here?"

I shake my head. "No one knows."

It's mostly the truth. No one knows I'm *here*, at the clubhouse.

Rider knows I live in Las Vegas, but I've never told him my exact location. Technically, we're on the outskirts of town.

Glancing at Ghost, I think about the number of times I've vented to Rider about this man. I've never called him by name, but I had to get it out somehow. Being around him wasn't enough. Watching him wasn't enough.

While I mean nothing to Ghost, I've been obsessed with him since the first time I met him.

Look where it got me. Alone and stepping in a pile of shit as always.

"Good." Steel taps the table. "That's good."

"Am I in trouble?" I'm scared to ask, but I need to know. "Do I need to leave the clubhouse?"

Steel might be understanding with his men, and he might be known for protecting people who need it, but I'm not Tempe. I don't have his heart wrapped around my finger. He doesn't owe me anything.

"No." Steel shakes his head. "We voted before bringing you into the room and agreed that so long as your story aligned with what we've been told, there was no reason for that. But you do need to understand this raises questions."

"I understand." I swallow hard.

"Luna." Steel leans forward, fixing his gaze on me. "I'm giving you my club's trust right now. We all are. I'm giving you that because you've proven yourself to us and been there for us during some challenging times. But if I find out you're lying or keeping something from me—no matter how small it is—you aren't going to like the outcome. Do you understand what I'm saying?"

"I do."

He nods. "Then go get some sleep. In the morning, I need you to sit down with Legacy to go over everything you remember. What accounts they wanted; what information they were after. Every little detail is important."

I glance over at Legacy. "I'll do anything I can to help."

"You're dismissed." Steel juts his chin to the door, and Havoc stands.

He circles the table to usher me out of the room in the same way he brought me in here. And even if it feels impossible, I fight the weight of guilt holding me down and manage to find my way to my feet. I look at Ghost a final time before turning to leave.

I'm free to stay. I'm not a prisoner. Yet, everything has changed. I'm not off the hook, no matter what part I did or didn't play.

Every glance.

Every pause.

They're questioning me.

The men I've put my trust in don't know if it's safe for them to do the same.

My heart cracks at that thought—at another family slowly slipping through my fingers.

I wanted to believe this would be different. That I found a home and people I belonged with. I wanted to believe that even if Ghost was incapable of returning my affection, he cared.

But Ghost lied to me. He brought me here, knowing what I'd done. He put me in this familiar position of being alone.

When I leave the room, they aren't smiling and friendly like we've been this past year. They're cautious. They've lost their faith in me.

I'm a threat.

A traitor.

Ghost probably thinks he was protecting me by shielding me from the truth, but his lies dug my grave with the Twisted Kings. Now, I have no choice but to climb into it and hope they don't bury me alive.

4

Ghost

I DID IT ALL *for her.*

I remind myself of that truth as I walk into the Shack, having broken my oath to my brothers. Guilt overwhelms me, but I'd do it all again if it meant protecting Luna. Which is why I'll accept whatever punishment Steel deems fitting.

I've spent one year in denial. I avoided Luna as much as possible and pretended her purple hair didn't catch my attention every time she walked into the room. I lied to myself and tried to ignore the siren song of her giggle. I acted like her blue eyes didn't alter my brain chemistry, and that one look didn't give her the power to make me betray everything I stand for.

The facts remain.

I lied to my club for her.

I betrayed my president for her.

And I don't regret a thing.

Legacy walks up to me the second I step foot inside the Shack, gritting his teeth. "This is bullshit. We were already at war with those fuckers before she got involved."

"That's not the point."

"You shouldn't have to be the martyr just to prove a point."

Legacy is my brother beyond the patch, so I'm not surprised he's taking it the hardest. We've been friends since birth, and after I lost my family, his parents took me in. They introduced me to the club and showed me family can be more than a room full of broken people using each other like emotional punching bags.

Legacy has been at my side through the worst of times, and I'm closer to him and his daughter than anyone else in this world. But in this moment, that's clouding his judgment.

I made this mess, and it's time I face it.

"Just let me do this." I shrug off my cut, hanging it on a hook just inside the door. "We both know this is how things work, and it's for a reason."

Legacy doesn't relax, but he doesn't argue because he knows I'm right.

At the opposite end of the Shack, Steel, Havoc, and Chaos stand around the pit of red-hot coals.

Physical pain isn't something that scares me when I know there are worse things than flesh wounds. Scars, cuts, and bruises are nothing compared to what marks my soul.

At least the body heals—mostly.

What's rotten inside can never be fixed.

Legacy grabs my shoulder as I take a step forward. "Ghost—"

"I'm the reason the Iron Sinners put a target on our backs after Albuquerque," I cut Legacy off. "You saw the text message. Everyone did. Whoever hired Luna is with the Iron Sinners now, and they want her back. They don't like that I brought her here, and they aren't going to stop. The club is going to pay the price because of what I did. It's my fault."

Legacy releases my shoulder so I can strip off my T-shirt. I hand it to him, and his jaw tightens as he bites back whatever he wants to say.

He knows I'm right, even if our brotherhood makes it hard for him to digest it. The Twisted Kings aren't just biker outlaws; we're a family. We fight for each other. We die for each other. I turned my back on my brothers by not telling them the truth, which means I need to pay for that betrayal.

"Jesse—"

"Go." Legacy takes a step back, not looking any happier than when I walked in here.

Unlike the rest of us, Legacy actually has a heart buried beneath his cut.

I wish I still did.

It's been so long since I've had hope or faith that I don't remember what it's like. All I know is that someday, I'll sacrifice my body and soul for the Twisted Kings, and my job will be done.

There's nothing more for me on this earth. Not even the girl I did all this for.

Luna's too good for a man like me. Too sweet. She didn't even know who she was working for when this mess started, and I didn't want to weigh her down with my secrets, so I kept it to myself.

I don't know what's worse: lying to my president or lying to her. That thought is proof alone I deserve this.

I move to the center of the Shack, meeting gazes with each of my brothers as I do.

Havoc hands Steel the branding iron, taking a step back. Hesitation is thick in the air, but it doesn't change what needs to be done. And when Steel turns to me with the brand in his hand, I'm not face to face with a lifelong friend or a brother. I'm staring down the cold eyes of the club president, out for a pound of flesh.

The Twisted Kings have a three-strike rule for dealing with brothers who've fucked up. The first strike results in a skull brand to the ribs. The second, and you get an X over it. Third, and you're six feet under.

Not that you always get three chances.

Betraying the club usually ends with a grave, but the club voted for the brand, given all I've done for them. It might sound lenient, but it's a mark I'll live with. Proof of what I did.

Taking a deep breath, I accept this for Luna. I give in to the promise of pain as I stand in a dusty shack that's been painted with the blood of our enemies. I set my mind to another place and another time, picturing Luna instead of my brothers circling around.

I imagine how her eyes light when she smiles.

How her hair falls around her cheeks when she tries to tie it back.

Up until a year ago, there was nothing more important than my brothers because they wouldn't let me give up in the darkness. But then there was her.

My light.

So bright I can't risk actually touching her. I can't risk my shadows drinking her glow.

My brothers circle around me, with Steel unflinching before me.

"Ghost…" Steel straightens his spine, taking a deep breath. "You've been found guilty of lying to your club. For welcoming an associate of our rivals and bringing war to your brothers. Let this brand be a reminder I'm not giving you another chance. If you lie to me or the club again, there will be no more mercy. Do you understand and accept your punishment?"

"I do."

Steel glances behind me and nods, signaling Havoc and Soul to grab my arms. I don't plan on fighting them because I deserve what's coming, but that's not why they do it. My body will react whether I accept this or not.

Steel steps forward, and all eyes in the Shack are focused on me. Legacy's jaw ticks as he watches me over Steel's shoulder, while Chaos stands back, indifferent about the situation.

I block them all out and focus on Steel.

The man who handed me my cut when I finished my year as a prospect. The man who gave me the club—a home. The man who reminded me I had a reason to keep fighting when I was ready to ride until my tires found their way off a cliff.

I'm not good at much. I got mediocre grades in school and didn't get a formal education past my senior year. Apart from fixing bikes and working on computers, nothing else really made sense to me.

But Steel saw past my failings and understood my unique gifts. He helped me find a purpose. While most people treated me like a pariah for my lack of social skills, Steel understood me. He handed me the computers to hide behind, and he gave me the club to protect.

Which is what I've done up until this point.

As I stand here, I stand for my president—the man whose trust I broke.

"I believe you." Steel grabs my shoulder with his free hand, squeezing it once as he lifts the brand to my ribs with his other.

The brand meets my skin, and it's so hot it's cold. An icy bite that rips through my flesh worse than any bullet wound. My teeth clench so hard they might crack, but I don't make a sound.

The smell of burning skin floods my nostrils while Soul and Havoc tighten their grip. My body must be reacting, even as I dissociate from the pain, because I'm vaguely aware of the resistance on my arms as the brand eats my flesh.

I close my eyes and try to remember how I ended up here.

Why I'm still here at all.

If punishment is what I deserve for failing people, then maybe Steel should lift the brand and keep going. He could toss my body into the coals so I could finally repent for all the suffering my life has caused.

I clench my jaw, accepting this pain for every person who is six feet under because of me. And when Steel pulls the brand away, there's no relief. Even as my arms are freed and my head swims from the adrenaline and pain, there's no peace to be found.

There isn't enough forgiveness in heaven to grant my soul an escape from hell.

"It's done." Steel looks around the room, still holding the branding iron tight in his grip. "Ghost accepted the punishment of the club, so now we focus on the problem at hand. The Iron Sinners are coming for us—for Luna. We need to figure out why."

"You got it, Prez," Chaos answers, watching me from the corner of his eye.

He's still fresh out of prison after going down for the club, so he isn't as understanding about what I did as some of the others.

Legacy steps forward, handing me my T-shirt. "Go find Patch and get that burn cleaned up before it gets infected. I gotta get home to Bea."

He stalks away, angrier now that I've taken my punishment than he was before. But I can't tell who he's mad at. Me for betraying the club, or Steel for following through on what had to be done.

Soul and Havoc meet Chaos at the side of the room, slowly shuffling out after Legacy, but Steel stays behind with me, setting the iron back in the coals.

The bright orange glow lights his face while he thinks.

I slip my T-shirt back on, and it hurts to lift my arms over my head. Pain radiates through my whole body when the fabric brushes the freshly branded skin. I clench my teeth, and Steel must notice because he finally turns to face me.

"Remember what you said to me a few months ago on that first night Tempe came here?" Steel wipes his forehead with the back of his hand. "You said, 'If she's not involved, she's not safe.'"

"I remember."

When Steel's old lady first showed up at our clubhouse, he didn't want to believe she was just a pawn being used by our rivals. He thought she was guilty, but I knew there was something we were missing, and I was right.

"Same goes for Luna right now." Steel walks up to me. "If she's not involved, she's not safe, and you brought her here, Ghost. You need to face why you did that—why you lied to your club for this girl. Why you took a brand for this girl. Why you betrayed your brothers for this girl."

"I know."

"Good. Because if we really do pull through this and you don't make a fucking move and tell her how you feel, you're a fucking idiot. And you're too good a man to be that, whether you believe it or not."

Steel shakes his head and walks away, leaving me with the pit that's been living in my stomach since I first saw

Luna and knew she was it for me. I'd like him to be right. I'd like to think confessing what that girl does to me would fix this mess. But it won't.

There are worse things for her than the Twisted Kings. Worse than our enemies or anything that came before this.

There's me.

5

Luna

A FEW HOURS AGO, the stars on the ceiling felt less fake.

Hope was more tangible.

My future made more sense.

Now, I don't know what to think as I stare at the fading plastic specks above me. They're losing light at the same rate I'm losing optimism, and I no longer know what to make of my being here.

Ghost lied to me.

Worse, he lied to the club on my behalf.

I've been replaying the first time I met him over and over in my head, trying to see it for what it really was—him doing his job.

While I thought we were flirting, he was watching from the start. He wasn't there getting coffee; he was scoping me out and determining if I was a threat to his club.

His being at the coffee shop wasn't fate. It wasn't coincidence. It was business.

For over a year, I've held onto the idea that there was something between us. I thought this all started with a magnetic pull we couldn't resist. He mentioned Vegas, and when I joked about following him there, he seemed genuinely interested. He vouched for me with his president. He gave me this job.

Now, it turns out, Ghost was keeping me close to confirm I wasn't after his club.

Once again, I'm chasing a man who is incapable of giving me what I need from him.

Still, a nagging thought won't let go. If he didn't care at all, why would he risk it? Why protect me if it meant going against his club?

He could have let me take the fall a year ago when he caught me hacking his system. Knowing what I do now, I'm well aware that he should have turned me over to Steel so the club could decide what to do with me.

He didn't.

Ghost thought I was working for the club's enemies, and he still brought me to Las Vegas. He moved me in with him and has watched out for me ever since.

Ghost ignores me, but he broke his oath to his brothers *for me*. That has to mean something.

I pinch the bridge of my nose, but it does nothing to dull the ache between my temples. Rolling out of bed, I slip into my neon-pink, fluffy slippers and tie my hair up in a ponytail.

The clubhouse is quiet tonight since there was no official party, so I don't hesitate to walk around in a T-shirt and slippers.

As I slip past Reina's bed, she grabs my hand.

"You okay?"

Reina just went to bed a few minutes ago, so she's still awake. She's been spending time with Havoc lately, but never stays the night in his room. While she's having fun with him, it's not the same as it was when she was with Steel, so I've seen a lot more of her lately.

"I'm good." I force a smile and squeeze her hand. "Just need to splash some water on my face. It's hot in here."

She lets me go, and I slip into the hallway quietly. The room I share with Reina and Wren is at the end of the hall, and on either side are doors leading to more bedrooms.

This side of the clubhouse is reserved for patch bunnies, clubhouse staff, and the chef. Meanwhile, the ranked members occupy rooms on the opposite end.

Between this hallway and the guys' is the main body of the building, which consists of the kitchen, two large bars, and a main sitting area. Part of it is open to the public when the club allows it, but the rest is only for those of us who live here.

The bunkhouse is a detached building, and that's where the prospects and newer members live.

For a split second, I let myself think this could be my home—*my family.*

That fairytale is gone now, all because of what I did without even knowing it.

If only Ghost had been honest from the beginning, I could have explained myself. But he hid it, and in trying to protect me, he made a mess of the one place I thought I belonged.

When I reach the bathroom at the end of the hallway, the handle is locked, and there's moaning coming from the other side. There's no shortage of beds at the clubhouse, but it doesn't stop people from fucking on every surface.

I roll my eyes and continue past the kitchen into the main bar. Soul and Chaos are keeping the party going with a few patch bunnies, even though it's already four thirty in the morning.

Chaos watches me with a calculated stare as I cross the room. I didn't know him well before he went to prison, but since he's been out this past month, he's seemed different. Angrier. More closed off.

Soul, on the other hand, is much more relaxed when he smiles at me passing by. Which is probably, in part, due to the fact that he's in the middle of getting a blow job.

I divert my gaze and continue through the room. The open debauchery shocked me for the first week I was here, but now I've seen so many of the guys fucking I barely even notice it anymore.

I've seen too many of their dicks for never having been near one of them.

Continuing to the bar in the front of the clubhouse, I cross the room to the bathroom that sits at this end of the building. It's rarely used when the Twisted Kings aren't throwing a party, so I'm surprised when the door swings open as I reach for the handle, and I almost collide with someone walking out.

"Sorry." I take a step back, looking up into the cool gaze of the one man who makes my heart jump to my throat.

Ghost is in the middle of tugging his T-shirt down, giving me a hint of his tattooed, muscular chest. Ink covers every inch of him—from his knuckles to his neck, and I've always been curious what they mean to him. I'd like to learn the history of a man who is clearly haunted by it.

He winces as his T-shirt brushes his side, but I only get a glimpse of a wound before the fabric covers it.

"Are you okay?"

"Fine." He reaches into the bathroom, grabbing his cut off the hook and shrugging it on.

He barely looks at me as he starts to walk away.

"Fine?" I spin to face him, and he pauses with his back to me. "That's all you have to say? Are you kidding me right now?"

He tips his head back, letting out a heavy sigh. His fingers dig into his black hair as he thinks.

"You knew, Ghost." I take a step closer, immediately realizing my mistake when I get a hit of his warm leather scent. "You knew who I was working for, and you didn't say anything to anyone. Not even me. I was hacking the club, and you vouched for me anyway. Why?"

He doesn't turn around immediately as he dips his hands in his pockets. His thick shoulders rise with every inhale, and I stare at the back of his head, begging him to say something—anything—that explains this mess.

After a long pause, Ghost finally turns to face me. His light-blue eyes are cold and empty, but still, his attention makes goosebumps flurry across my skin.

His gaze skims down to my T-shirt. To my bare legs, prickling at his attention. And when his stare snaps back to mine, I have to swallow to catch my breath.

He's a man of few words because he doesn't really need them. One look, and I'm speechless.

Ghost shrugs. "Did you know who you were working for back then, Luna?"

I shake my head. "I already told you I didn't."

"Well, there you go. Nothing to worry about. I'll deal with it."

"You lied to your club for me."

He doesn't respond.

"You brought me here instead of turning me in." I take a step closer again, and his jaw tightens at the movement. "But you barely pay attention to me, so why would you risk it?"

"Would you rather I have left you in New Mexico?"

"That's not an answer."

Ghost stares down at me silently. The warmth of our bodies nearly touching gives me a head rush, but I don't step back. I look up at him and wish he would stop throwing up walls just so he doesn't have to face what's on the other side of them.

"Please, Ghost." I press my lips together. "Tell me the truth. Why would you do that for me?"

He grinds his teeth, and I sense everything he's holding back when I wish he'd just crack open.

After a long pause, he drops his chin and shakes his head. "You were innocent. I couldn't let them hurt you."

He doesn't clarify whether he's talking about the Merciless Skulls or the Twisted Kings. He doesn't need to.

Ghost was protecting me.

Flirtation might not have brought us together, but I'm not imagining this—he cares. He brought me here to keep me safe, and if he thinks I'll let that go, he's wrong.

6

Ghost

It takes Luna thirty-two minutes to leave the bathroom, and when she finally does, her nails are a shade of lavender that matches her hair.

The patch bunnies hide their nail polish under the sink in the communal bathroom since theirs is packed to the brim with makeup and whatever crap they put in their hair.

Luna purses her lips, walking down the hallway and blowing on her nails to finish drying them. She pauses at the door to my office, and I don't move so she won't hear me.

Clicking the screen, I zoom in to get a better angle of her face, but I can't read her expression. She stares at the wooden door, and I swear the heat of her body radiates through it.

The faint scent of acetone creeps through the crack, and I try to hold my breath and keep quiet.

But I don't close my eyes.

I don't blink.

If I do, I might miss something.

Like how her shoulders deflate with her thoughts. How her eyebrows furrow the longer she stares. How her teeth sink into her plump lower lip, and how her hand hovers when she considers knocking.

If I wasn't paying attention, I wouldn't see the defeat in her eyes as she turns and walks away, starting on the path that leads to her bedroom.

The sadness in her gaze is one more reminder that I'm failing her, and I wish I wasn't.

But tonight, she saw too much, and if I let her stew in that, she'll think something could happen between us. She'll get it in her head that I care about her. Watering those thoughts will only lead to bad things.

People who hang around the club too long get into trouble, and people who associate with *me* end up dead.

I switch cameras and follow Luna through the clubhouse. She ignores Soul fucking a patch bunny on top of the pool table as she makes her way to her room.

I should stop here.

Shut it down and go to sleep.

If I was a better man, I might.

But just because Luna can't know I'm watching her doesn't stop me from actually doing it.

I switch my view to the camera on her laptop, and I'm irritated she left it open. All it would take is one unauthorized intrusion into the wireless network and someone who isn't me could be watching her right now.

Which reminds me, I need to do a sweep of our firewalls in the morning.

Luna lets her hair down, and lavender-blonde hair pools around her shoulders as she tosses her hair tie onto the nightstand. She slips out of her fuzzy, pink slippers and climbs under her blanket, but she doesn't lie down. She leans back against the headboard and bites on the inside of her cheek while she thinks about something.

She stares into the darkness, and when her gaze flicks to her laptop camera, her eyebrows pinch. It's the faintest hint that has me wondering if she senses me.

If she knows I'm watching her.

Those blue eyes are my damnation. One look and my soul takes a bite out of her like she's an apple from Eden.

It takes all I am to stay in control.

To look but not touch.

To keep her but not ruin her like I do everything good that walks into my life.

Luna's eyes get heavy the longer she stares at the camera. Slowly, her body sinks down into the covers.

It takes her thirty-four minutes to fall asleep, and even then, she's restless. She tosses and turns, and I wonder if it's nightmares or something else.

I watch her, and the branded flesh on my side aches, reminding me not to lose focus. Reminding me why I can't give in and that I'm all that stands between Luna and those out to get her.

The club might have agreed that she's innocent, but I sensed their doubt. There was just enough hesitation that

I know I'm the only one who will truly risk it all to keep her safe.

Someone is after her, and I'm the only one who can stop them.

If only I knew who *they* were so I could put this fucking mess to bed once and for all.

Before we left Albuquerque, the Twisted Kings obliterated every trace of the Merciless Skulls, and I thought that included whoever hired Luna to hack my system. It was reckless of me to assume someone smart enough to hire her wouldn't also have the wits to survive.

They must have moved back to Vegas with the Iron Sinners, the same way Luna moved here with us.

I should have realized it a month ago when the Iron Sinners used a flash drive to hack us. I was so busy focusing on our business plans and financial records that I ignored what was right in front of me. Whoever gained access to my private server spent more time in the club's payroll records than anywhere else.

They weren't looking for money or access. They weren't looking for *something*. They were after *someone*.

Luna Cassidy.

While to her, it was an anonymous job posting that led her to hack the Twisted Kings, the person who sent her after us was clearly after more. They knew her. The question is, did she know them?

By the time the sun rises, I'm still at my desk. My untouched bed is becoming a staple lately, and my body drags as I pull myself out of my office.

Luna isn't at the clubhouse, so there's no risk of running into her. I waited until she left to shop with Reina and Wren before stepping foot in the kitchen. After last night, everything is jumbled.

The gap of indifference I've maintained for over a year is blurring, and the only way to keep her away is to draw clearer lines.

I'll keep an eye out, and she'll be safe. She can hate me for ignoring her, and someday, she can move on with her life while I sit in purgatory.

By the time I make it into church, Legacy is already in his seat at the table across from me. He's usually the first here, given he keeps a tight schedule for his daughter, Bea. Apart from the club, she's his priority, and he spends every spare minute he has with her.

He'll do his tasks as treasurer during the day and take breaks to see her for breakfast and dinner. And if the club's having a party, he'll wait until she's in bed before leaving her with the nanny and coming out with us. Even then, he'll try to be home before she wakes up in the morning.

And now that Tempe and her four-year-old brother, Austin, are in the picture, Steel's been the same way.

When I first patched in, Steel and Legacy were known for their reputations with women. They were almost worse than Soul is now. But lately, everything's changing.

It's another reminder of why I don't have any plans for locking down an old lady, much less a family. It's my job to watch out for every member of this club. I can't risk my time or attention being split.

Blink and people end up dead.

Legacy watches me take a seat, lacing his hands behind his head and leaning back in his chair. "You still coming by for family dinner this week? Bea's been asking why you're MIA lately."

Usually, I eat dinner with Legacy and Bea a few times a week, but lately, it's been less and less.

It could be guilt.

It could be fear I'll miss something if I walk away from my post for even a minute.

Either way, Bea doesn't deserve that.

"I'll be there Sunday."

Things are usually quieter on Sundays. The guys party hard on Saturdays, and most of our businesses are closed until late at night. So it's easier to get away.

"Sunday works." Legacy nods. "You talked to Luna since all that shit went down last night?"

"Thought she was supposed to be talking to *you* about bank accounts. I don't have anything to do with that shit."

"We both know that's not what the fuck I'm talking about." Legacy plants his forearms on the table and squares off with me. "Are you really gonna continue pretending whatever's going on between you and her doesn't exist? Even after what you did?"

I sense a hint of irritation in his tone, and I wonder if he's still pissed at me for keeping this from him. I kept the truth from all my brothers, but the difference is that Legacy is as close to a blood sibling as it gets for me, and I lied to him.

"There's nothing going on with me and her," I huff. "If you want to play matchmaker, go find your own old lady. Bea's been asking—"

"Bea's fine," Legacy cuts me off.

I struck a nerve, but I don't take it back because he's going to have to face his own issues for Bea's sake at some point.

When Bea was a couple of weeks old, her mom, Sera, left Bea on Legacy's doorstep without notice. He didn't even know he'd gotten Sera pregnant since she left the clubhouse the second he knocked her up and didn't come back until she was holding their daughter.

Sera wasn't ready to be a mom, so she gave him a choice of raising their kid or letting a stranger do it, and he picked the former because that's the type of man he is. But after Bea's mom abandoned her, he hasn't trusted a woman again.

He fucks around as much as the rest of the guys, but he avoids patch bunnies and never keeps women around for more than a one-night stand.

"The last thing Bea needs is another woman walking out of her life. I'll leave locking down old ladies for the rest of the guys."

"You all need to shut the fuck up with this old-lady talk." Soul stumbles over the threshold to the room because he's probably still drunk. "Steel settling down is bad enough, but that shit's contagious."

"It's not the fucking flu." Legacy shakes his head.

Soul practically falls into his seat beside me, pulling out a cigarette. He balances it between his lips and lights the end.

"Tell that to the Road Rebels." He takes a drag. "After Victor put his name on Tallie's back, it was only a matter of time before they all fell."

"You make it sound like women are a virus taking them out."

He shrugs. "Might as well be. I'm telling you, first it's one old lady, then the place is crawling with 'em. And then, next thing you know, they're getting jealous of the patch bunnies and fucking shit up for all of us."

"Scared some woman's gonna tie you down, Soul?" Legacy smirks.

"Chicks wish they could."

"Like you could get a woman to stay the fuck around." Steel walks in with Chaos and Havoc behind him.

Soul grins at Steel, always amused by a challenge. "Already forgetting our wagers with the ladies, Prez? I seem to remember winning a few over you. And with you shacked up and off the market, I'm having to do double time just to keep 'em busy."

"Finding a woman willing to fuck you and finding a woman willing to love you are two different things." Steel drops into his seat at the head of the table.

I never thought I'd see the day Jameson Steel would be saying shit like that. He used to be as bad as Soul, wanting nothing to do with putting a property patch on a woman's back. Now, all it takes is one mention of Tempe or Austin to change his mood.

Steel pats his pocket out of habit, but he doesn't carry cigarettes on him anymore, so he frowns in disappointment.

"You're outnumbered on this, Prez." Chaos snatches one of Soul's cigarettes as he drops into his seat. "Spend five months in prison, wondering if you'll ever get out, and you'll think a little differently about all these freedoms. Free to go where I want. Free to fuck who I want. No one's locking me down."

Soul chuckles, and they bump knuckles across the table. Steel shakes his head, not bothering to argue. While Legacy and Havoc might eventually get past their shit and put a property patch on some woman someday, Soul and Chaos are like me.

Damaged beyond recognition and better off alone.

"All right, let's get to business." Steel looks at me. "Where are we with the Iron Sinners? Have you figured out which of the Merciless Skulls patched over when we took out their club?"

"I've found a couple who moved to Vegas when everything happened but not whoever we're looking for."

"How do you know?"

"The person who hired Luna wrote the code to the virus in that flash drive, which means they know what the fuck they're doing. Anyone I've tied to both clubs so far doesn't fit the profile."

"If they were so good, why'd they use her to do their dirty work?"

"Distance, maybe?"

Soul chuckles. "Or as a distraction. Pretty faces and all."

"Possibly." My jaw clenches because I don't like thinking of Luna as just a pretty face. "But either way, I don't think they planned shit to go down like it did; otherwise, they wouldn't be trying to get her back."

"If that's the case, why not do it sooner?" Havoc asks. "She's been here for over a year, but they're just now making demands?"

"What are you implying?"

Havoc doesn't immediately answer, and he doesn't need to. I know what he's trying to say. That Luna's been here for over a year with access to the club, operating with our trust. We've seen it before with Reyes hiding in our ranks. She wouldn't be the first person to double-cross us.

"Just asking a question." He crosses his arms over his chest.

"For all we know, they didn't know she was here until they got access to our payroll records," I counter as pressure settles between my temples. "She's clear. I made sure of it."

Soul smirks. "I'm sure you did."

Chaos reaches across the table again, and they bump fists.

"Focus." Steel shakes his head, looking at Havoc. "No one leaves the compound without a guard. Even us. We move in pairs at a minimum. For all we know, they're using Luna as just another distraction so they can keep us busy while they go after something else."

"You got it, Prez." Havoc nods.

"Ghost, I want to know the second you figure out who's pulling the strings. I'm not waiting around again. When they took Tempe and Austin, they declared war. This isn't over until we burn the Iron Sinners infrastructure to the ground. They know too much, which means there's a leak somewhere."

"I'll comb back through the security footage the night of the attack and run facial recognition against the Merciless Skulls roster. See if anything pops."

"Sounds good." Steel's jaw clenches. "And keep looking for Reyes while you're at it. The second I get my hands on that traitor, he's paying for all of this."

Reyes pretended to prospect the club so he could plant the flash drive he used to hack our network, so I don't blame Steel for wanting vengeance.

"And one more thing." Steel glances over at Havoc. "We're throwing a party tonight, so I want security doubled at the perimeter."

"'Bout fucking time." Chaos pounds the table, and Soul grins, nodding in agreement.

"As much as I'd like to keep us in lockdown until this Iron Sinner shit is dealt with, that's not realistic," Steel says. "And I refuse to let them make us seem weak or like we're hiding. We protect our own, and that's what we'll do. Show those fuckers nothing slows down the Twisted Kings."

"Music to my fucking ears." Soul grins.

"And Ghost..." Steel looks at me. "They might see this as an opportunity."

"If they do, I'll be waiting."

An excuse is exactly what I need right now. One Iron Sinner to give me a reason to remind my brothers why I'll always have their backs.

I lied to protect Luna, but she isn't the only one I'm responsible for here.

On this land, it's my eyes that keep watch.

It's my cameras, my trackers, my systems, and my sensors that keep my brothers safe. And nothing is getting in the way of that again.

7

Ghost

Working with Luna used to be simpler.

When she first moved to Vegas with us, we managed to keep our interactions about work. She'd help with small tasks that kept her busy and away from me, and in return, the club gave her a place to stay.

I'd maintain a distance, and she'd leave me be.

Lately, the carefully crafted gap of space between us has been closing.

When I'm working, she finds a reason to need something from my office. When I'm at a party, she orbits. I can't figure out if she's closing in or if I am. But her purple hair is a beacon I can't keep away from.

I've considered assigning her a more complicated task than archiving surveillance footage. She's capable of a lot more than I ask of her, and eventually, she's bound to get bored. But doing so would give her access to information that puts her in even more danger.

Our rivals use our allies against us, and the feds are no better. At least if Luna's in the dark about what she's working on, then she's safe from the club's agenda. I owe her that much after bringing her here and sticking a target on her back.

My office door cracks, and Luna walks back in. She's been messing with camera angles all morning, but she left for a few minutes to replace one that was damaged on the back patio of the clubhouse after Bea and Austin knocked it with a frisbee.

She ignores me as she walks over to the wall of screens on the opposite end of the room, but the ripple of her presence swims through the air. Her haunting honeysuckle scent seeps into my senses.

I watch her back as she starts adjusting the feeds on each screen. Some show angles of the clubhouse, while others are sprinkled around Vegas at our businesses and club-owned properties.

The halo of light from the screens surrounds her as she focuses the new camera and sends it online.

At least that task got her out of the office for ten minutes. Maybe I'll upgrade the entire grid just to send her somewhere I can't look at her or smell her.

Can't touch her.

Can't hear her shuffle around.

Can't see her sway her hips to whatever song she's playing in her head.

One of the screens at the top of the wall blinks, and she lifts onto the balls of her feet to adjust the settings on the monitor. Her baggy T-shirt pulls up with her reach, revealing a hint of the curve of her perfectly round ass, which is on full display in her skintight leggings.

"Need help with that?"

Usually, I'd pretend not to notice what she's doing because the less she knows I'm watching her, the easier it is to keep her at arm's length. But then she bends down, and I strike enter on my keyboard so hard I might break it, and figure the sooner she's done, the sooner she'll leave.

Still bent over, Luna glances back at me. "I've got it."

Her voice is pitched, but it's not nerves. She's just that fucking sweet to everyone—even an asshole like me.

A smile lifts in the corner of her mouth as she gets back to work. It edges the line between sweet and devious, and I'm pretty sure she caught me staring at her ass.

Do I care?

It's not like I'll do anything about it, and she knows that. No matter how much I want to circle the desk and walk up behind her—to sink my fingers into her lush hips and drag my palms up the inside of her thighs until I'm lost in her scalding sunshine—I won't.

No matter how hot my blood runs when she once more starts to sway her hips or how badly I want to break this tension, I can't.

"Done." She snaps to standing, spinning around.

I was a dick to her last night, and I've been a jerk to her all morning, but still, she fucking smiles at me.

I glance at the screen behind her. "Sapphire Rise is still out of focus. I can't read a single license plate in the parking lot."

Luna's smile falls, and her eyes narrow. "I was talking about the club perimeter. I haven't gotten to the Strip yet."

"Hmm." I turn back to my screen, starting another download while Luna's eyes burn into me from across the room.

"Do you even need my help, Ghost?"

"With what?"

"With anything?" She waves her arms out. "Because you sure don't act like it. You know I can do more than adjust cameras and watch surveillance. It's a waste of my skills."

"I know." I avoid her eyes.

"So give me something more challenging."

"I don't need help with anything else." And even if I did, I wouldn't risk her life involving her in it.

"Of course you don't." She huffs, adjusting her ponytail. "You never need me for anything, apparently."

The last part is mumbled, and when I look up, her gaze has fallen, and she's biting her lower lip.

"You help *the club*, Luna, and that's all that matters."

Her jaw tightens. "If you offered me this job out of guilt for not telling me what was going on in Albuquerque, I can just ask Steel for something different."

"Why would you do that?"

"Because lately, all I do is bother you."

"Who said you're bothering me?"

"No one needs to say it. It's obvious." She crosses her arms over her chest, and she might be waiting for me to say something, but I don't. "I'll just ask Steel—"

"No," I cut her off.

She hitches an eyebrow. "No."

"No."

"But why—"

"I've got to go." Anywhere but here.

I stand up so fast that I almost knock my chair over.

Luna is too smart, and the more I say, the easier it'll be for her to see straight through all my bullshit. I've been hiding behind the facade that she's just like any other employee of the club, but now she knows the truth. I risked it all for her, and if I'm not careful, she'll think this can be something it can't.

"Ghost—"

"Lock up when you're done." I storm out the door, slamming it behind me.

I can't have her, but I can't let her go.

I can't be around her, but I refuse to let her work with anyone else.

She's mine, even if it's only in my head.

8

Luna

Spring in Vegas means the clubhouse has already started warming up. It's April, but the back doors have been open all morning, and by afternoon, the fans will be moving air through the building. The air conditioner kicked on twice this past week, which means we're in for another blistering hot summer.

After Ghost stormed out of his office, I finish what I started, adjusting the last of the new cameras, then go to find Legacy to review the bank account Steel wanted my insight on.

Stepping into the main body of the clubhouse, Ghost is nowhere to be found.

I don't know what I did or said to piss him off so badly this morning, but he has no right to be upset. I'm the one who's been lied to for the past year. If he didn't want me around, he shouldn't have invited me to Vegas in the first place.

My nails dig into my palms as I clench my fists, wishing he'd let his walls down for one day and admit what's actually bothering him. Then maybe I'd finally figure him out.

There's still so much I don't know about Ghost.

He's quiet and keeps to himself.

He hasn't laid his hands on a woman in the entire time I've known him, and he rarely talks to anyone but his brothers.

If I were smart, I'd stop hanging onto this hope that someday he'll let me in. Or worse, that this could grow into whatever I thought it was the first time we met.

I keep hoping he'll wake up one day and see me like I see him.

Walking through the clubhouse, I find Legacy at the bar on his laptop. He's typing while Kristen, one of the newest patch bunnies, tries to get his attention. She giggles and smiles, hoping he'll look up and take notice. She's still learning the ins and outs of the guys, so she doesn't realize Legacy doesn't fuck patch bunnies. His bed might not be empty like Ghost's, but he sticks with local girls, tourists, or anyone not associated with the club.

Kristen smiles, messing with her long, blonde braid. She leans forward when Legacy says something, and her cleavage draws his attention, even if he won't do anything about it.

I roll my eyes at the obvious move when I'm no better. I purposely bent over in front of Ghost this morning just to see if he'd pay attention. It worked, but seeing it from the other side makes me wonder if he just thought I was pathetic.

Legacy's attention returns to his computer, and Kristen frowns. Someday, she'll learn she's on a long list of girls who couldn't break him, and she won't be so bothered by it. All the patch bunnies try when they first make the clubhouse their home, so it's nothing personal.

Legacy is the cookie-cutter definition of what most girls melt over. He's tall, solid muscle, and has a smile that's practically cut from a magazine. He's also fiercely protective and the sweetest father, so if his model good looks don't get their attention, Bea's first trip to the clubhouse will. Legacy is everything girls like Kristin seem to find irresistible, and I understand it, even if I don't feel that way.

My tastes have me scanning the room for a different biker. One with more tattoos, more emotional baggage, and one who is not nearly as friendly. But Ghost is nowhere to be found.

I cross the room and slide onto the stool beside Legacy.

"Hey, Luna." Kristen smiles, darting away.

New patch bunnies are always awkward around me at first. They don't know what to make of my role at the club. I'm not a threat to them when it comes to the guys, but I'm not one of them either.

It's the only benefit of being on Reina's good side. She's their unofficial leader, so she bridges the gap.

I glance at Legacy's screen. "Steel said you wanted me to take a look at a few bank accounts?"

He hums, switching browsers. "We need to know if any of these accounts look familiar. They're all inactive now."

Something about how Legacy says *inactive* feels like there's a hidden meaning behind it, whether he intended that or not. He's making it clear where the line is with the club's trust. And while they need my help to figure out what I was hired to find, Legacy is also making it clear that I'm not being given access to anything that could hurt them now.

I try not to let it sting.

"Here." Legacy spins the laptop around to give me a clearer view.

Scanning the accounts, nothing looks familiar. "No. None of that matches."

He turns the computer toward himself again and clicks through a flurry of browsers.

Watching Legacy dig through bank accounts is like watching Ghost write a string of code. Muscle memory. Second nature. It makes me miss my fingers on the keys doing something meaningful.

It's been so long since I've hacked anyone; I barely remember the rush of it.

Legacy opens a spreadsheet and finds the tab he's looking for. "They gave a set of guidelines for what you were searching for, correct?"

"Yes." I reach into my back pocket, pulling out a piece of scrap paper. "But I don't remember much off the top of my head. I tried searching my old emails for our communications, but someone wiped them."

"Ghost can probably dig it out."

"I already tried. It's gone."

Legacy glances over at me, and doubt flares in his eyes at the reminder that the club only uses me for a fraction of what I'm capable of. If I couldn't find the emails, Ghost wouldn't be able to either, and from the look on Legacy's face, that's not a settling thought.

"But…" I hand the piece of scrap paper to Legacy. "I was able to recover this. They had me searching for an account ending in these four digits. They didn't say what for."

Legacy picks up the paper, and his teeth clench.

"That bad?"

"It's not good." He sets the paper down. "What were you told to do if you located it?"

"Nothing."

"Hmm."

"Yeah… I thought it was strange too."

Usually, if I was hired to hack someone, there was an end goal. But this employer made sure I stayed in the dark. They'd only send instructions one at a time, delivering the next set if I made it past the previous one. I never knew what I was after or what they were going to do if I found it.

Legacy closes the spreadsheet, opening a pdf printout of another account. I don't recognize the business name at the top.

"How much were they supposed to pay you for that job?" Legacy asks, scrolling through the withdrawals.

"Five grand."

Legacy skims down the screen. "There's a withdrawal matching that amount on the day Ghost shut you down. But you said they never paid you."

"They didn't."

"Well, they paid someone." He points to the screen, and sure enough, five thousand dollars left the account on the day Ghost caught me hacking the Twisted Kings.

"It could be a coincidence, right? Payment for something else?"

"It could be, but I doubt it. Money always talks." He closes the pdf and slaps the laptop shut. "That's all for now. I'll get this to Steel and let you know if we need anything else."

"Okay." I slide off the stool.

"And Luna..."

I pause, looking back at Legacy. He skims me over, opening his mouth like he's about to say something. But he stops himself, shaking his head.

"Nothing." Legacy grabs his laptop off the bar and stalks away, leaving me wondering what that was about.

Waving at Kristen, I head to my bedroom, wishing I knew more so I could help. The war the club fought a year ago isn't over, and it might be all my fault.

I could leave. Maybe then I'd protect them from whoever is after me. But if I do, I'll be at their mercy without the club's protection, and I still don't know what their intentions are. Besides, the club is my home. The people here are my family. I can't just walk away.

Stepping into my bedroom, I find Reina and Wren styling their hair and painting on their makeup. The guys have been walking around stressed today, so the girls have mostly been staying in their rooms and wasting time getting ready for tonight's party.

"You done with Legacy?" Reina asks as I sit on my bed.

"Yep. You know Legacy... to the point and nothing more."

"What did he want?" She paints a fresh coat of eyeliner.

"Nothing interesting." I shrug. "He just had a couple of questions about a file Ghost asked for."

"Boring." Reina frowns, and I'm glad she feels that way since I can't actually tell her what Legacy wanted from me.

"I wouldn't mind getting to know Legacy better." Wren smiles, tugging her red hair up into a ponytail. "I'd climb that man like a tree. Good lord, he's hot."

"I thought you and Chaos had something going on."

"Chaos is too busy with his precious strippers." Wren rolls her eyes. "I'm keeping my options open."

"And you jumped to Legacy?" I try to picture the two of them, even if I know Legacy wouldn't do anything with her. "Interesting..."

"Why do you say it like that?"

"I guess I just figured that if you were into Chaos, then you were into guys of the tattooed, dark-haired variety."

"Like Luna and Ghost." Reina nudges my foot.

"There is no *Luna and Ghost*," I narrow my eyes, correcting her.

"Really?" Wren's eyebrows pinch. "I also always kinda got the impression that he was yours."

"How?"

She shrugs. "Just a feeling."

"Well, for the record, Ghost is no one's."

"For now…" Wren tugs the hem of her tank top to reveal her cleavage. "We can test that."

My stomach sours at the thought of her trying, but Reina laughs.

"Seriously, that's not going to happen." Reina spins to face Wren. "Ghost is celibate. You'd have better luck chasing a property patch from Chaos. Or breaking a priest."

"A celibate biker? You're joking."

"Not celibate." I shake my head. "It's not like he's a virgin or made some lifelong vow to God or anything. He just doesn't do anything with any of the women here anymore."

"But he used to?"

"I guess. From what the guys have said, he used to be as bad as the rest of them."

Wren frowns. "What happened?"

"That's the million-dollar question." Reina turns to the mirror, painting her lips cherry red. "No one knows what his deal is. But I've been here two years, and I've never seen him with anyone. The girls before me told me the same thing. So, I guess he has his reasons."

"Well, that's too bad for you, Luna," Wren says.

"I don't like him." My eyebrows pinch, and Reina rolls her eyes at me. "I don't."

"Whatever you say, Luna Cassidy."

The two of them giggle, turning back to their hair and makeup, but I'm still hanging onto our conversation.

I don't *like* Ghost. What I feel is stronger than that.

Terminal.

If I don't do something about it soon, that man might be the end of me.

9

Luna

I WAS A TROUBLEMAKER in high school. I partied and experimented. I thought I'd seen it all until I met the Twisted Kings. But if anyone knows how to throw a party that will go completely off the rails, it's them. And when they celebrate, they do it to make a statement.

Music is already hammering through the clubhouse by the time I'm dressed. Reina and Wren are long gone, working on who they're going to claim for the night before any locals arrive. They get territorial on nights like this. Always worried that the guys will brush them aside. And it got worse when Tempe came in and stole Steel's heart.

It wasn't intentional, but now all the patch bunnies are on edge, wondering who will fall next, wishing it could be them. They live with a constant fear of being temporary.

Something I can relate to.

While I'm not a patch bunny, I could be replaced. The only security found between these walls is with a cut or a property patch on your back, and I don't have either. Anyone else who lives here serves their purpose but eventually moves on.

I weave my way to the bar at the front of the clubhouse, spotting prospects guarding every door and hallway. Just because the Twisted Kings are throwing a party doesn't mean they're letting down their defenses. And after a direct attack on the club, I don't blame Steel for being cautious.

If anything, it makes me feel safe.

I spot Tempe through the crowd as I walk into the bar. She's glued to Steel's side, smiling up at him while he says something. Steel has his arm wrapped around her waist, and as much as I'd like to pull her aside to vent about the tension between me and Ghost, I know Steel won't let her out of his sight tonight with outsiders roaming around.

Kristen and Venom, the newest prospect, are working behind the bar, serving drinks. Venom spots me the second I walk into the room and meets me at the end of the bar. His lopsided smile grows at his approach.

Venom is attractive in the way most guys who join the club are. He's tattooed, looks good on a bike, and he's trouble. His brown hair is a shade darker than his eyes, and from what the girls have been whispering about him, he's pierced in places that should make me even more curious to give him a shot.

After all, there's something appealing about a walking red flag.

Still, I can't help that I have no interest when I look past Venom and see Ghost sitting at the other end of the bar, staring at his phone. My frown deepens, and I wish that just once, he would look up and see me. That he'd storm over here and pick me up in his strong, tatted arms and prove I didn't imagine what sparked between us when we met.

Like he senses me staring, Ghost's gaze lifts to mine. His pale-blue eyes meet me from across the room, and goosebumps prickle my skin. We hold the stare for a fraction of a second, and I swear the room silences.

Time stops.

My heart thumps.

His attention is palpable.

This man is pure gravity pulling me in.

But just as quickly as I'm flooded, the dam breaks, and he glances down again.

"Luna Cassidy." Venom stops at the end of the bar, grinning.

Everything from his smile to the way he says my full name is flirty. But I don't know if he actually likes me or if he's just shooting his shot after hearing a rumor that I don't give any of the guys a chance.

"What can I get ya, babe?"

I scan the bottles behind the bar. "Gin and tonic?"

"You got it." He winks. "Anything else? Maybe a nightcap later?"

I laugh at the ridiculously lame attempt to hit on me. "Just the drink."

"You break my heart." He slaps his hand over his chest, taking a step back like he's been hit and stumbling a step.

"I'm sure." I roll my eyes. "Can you bring it over there?"

I point to the other end of the bar, where Tempe is still standing.

Venom nods. "Sure thing."

He turns to start my drink, and I cut through the crowd toward Tempe. It's not my fault she happens to also be standing next to Ghost, who's showing Steel something on his phone.

"Luna, you're here," Tempe cheers, moving to hug me, but Steel won't let her go, so it's sideways and awkward.

My body bumps against Ghost, and the small bit of contact heats my cheeks.

"Sorry." I step back.

Ghost doesn't bother looking up. "You're fine."

Fine.

There's that word again.

Everything is *fine* with Ghost. I'm burning up from the slightest bit of contact, and he's utterly unaffected.

Turning to Tempe, I try to ignore the fact that every person added to this packed room pushes me closer to Ghost.

"You don't have a drink." I look at her empty hand. "Want me to ask Venom to add another one to my order?"

"No, I promised Austin we'd make waffles first thing in the morning, and that's easier when I'm not hung over." She plants her hand on Steel's chest, and her new engagement ring flashes under the lights. "But if you're up early and want breakfast, you're welcome to come by."

"If all goes well tonight, that won't be happening." I laugh.

"Well, have fun for both of us."

"Will do." I grab my drink from Venom and take a sip.

I'm not a heavy drinker. Even when I take shots, I stop after the first one and switch to something lighter. But tonight, I could use something to take the edge off, especially with Ghost ignoring me.

I'm on my second drink by the time Steel and Tempe disappear to meet up with Soul and Havoc, so I slide onto the empty stool next to Ghost. One of the perks of his constant frown and fuck-off glare is that people usually give him space, leaving an empty seat for me to sit down in the packed room.

I glance over at his phone, but he has it angled so I can't see what's on the screen.

"For you, beautiful." Venom slides me a shot. "You look like you could use it."

"You have no idea," I mumble, lifting it to my lips and draining the glass.

From the corner of my eye, I feel Ghost watching me—judging me.

"Thanks." I slide the empty shot glass back to Venom, but he doesn't walk away.

He leans on the bar, bringing himself closer to me. "I'm almost done back here. Ricky's taking over when he gets back from the strip club, so do you wanna hang in a few?"

Venom's gaze skates down my body, making his intentions clear.

"Steel needs you on Shack cleaning duty," Ghost says, still staring at his phone.

"I don't remember—"

"Didn't ask if you remembered," Ghost cuts him off. "If you've got free time, might as well put it to use."

Venom looks between me and Ghost, taking a step back. When he doesn't say anything, Ghost looks up.

"Is there a problem?"

"No, sir." Venom disappears to the other end of the bar, and I turn toward Ghost.

"He didn't do anything wrong."

"Did I say he did?"

"You scared him off." I narrow my eyes. "You don't want him hanging out with me or something?"

"Never said that."

"Of course you didn't. God forbid you pretend to give a shit."

"What are you doing, Luna?" Ghost sets his phone on the bar, angling his body toward me.

His knee knocks mine, and I hate that the simple, accidental moment of contact rattles me.

"Drinking."

"That's your second drink, and now you're taking shots."

"You're counting my drinks now?"

"Just looking out."

"Maybe I don't need you to look out for me, Ghost." I lean forward, realizing I'm too close, but I refuse to let him think I'm weak by backing down. "I can take care of myself."

"I know you can." His glare hardens. "But until we figure out who hired you—*who is looking for you*—I'm just doing my job."

"Your job? Is that what I am?"

We're so close now that I can feel the heat radiating from him. Ghost's knees are kicked open, and mine are between them. Our fingers nearly brush where they're resting on the bar top. My skin prickles with static.

I'm breathing harder than I need to be, but I can't catch my breath. He towers over me in his seat, and his eyes are blue pits I'm lost in.

Swallowing, I shift back and hold my breath.

I can't look at him.

I can't smell him.

I can't have him.

It's all too much.

Ghost doesn't answer my question, which is answer enough.

"Never mind." I shake my head, hopping off the stool.

"Where are you going?"

I force a smile, looking back at him. "To my room. Wouldn't want to make *your job* harder."

I push through the crowd, and the number of people in the room has easily doubled in the last twenty minutes. I can't breathe through the pot and cigarette smoke, and now that I'm walking, the alcohol is swimming through my bloodstream.

My head spins as I slip past the prospects guarding the hallway that leads deeper into the clubhouse.

I need water.

Air.

Space.

The compound has never felt so small until this moment.

"Luna." Ghost's voice makes me jump.

I didn't hear him following me with the music blaring, and when I spin around, he's right behind me.

"You're following me now?" I glare at him.

"I didn't say you had to leave."

"That's the problem. You don't say much of anything."

He steps closer, and I tip my head back to look up at him. His blue eyes burn with something fierce I've never seen.

"What?" My voice stutters, and I hate it.

"You shouldn't be wandering around alone tonight. It's not safe."

"Not safe." I laugh. "And whose fault is that? You're the one who brought me here, remember? You're the one who didn't tell me the shit I'd gotten myself into a year ago so that I could fix it back then. You're the reason I'm in this mess."

He dips his hands in his pockets, looking down at me. He's standing close enough that I can smell his leather cut. I can feel his body heat. I can hear the deep sigh as he looks me over.

"You're right. And now I'm fixing it."

"By keeping every guy in a five-foot radius away from me? We both know I'm not doing shit with Venom, or any of the guys here for that matter. So, I don't need you scaring them off." I cross my arms over my chest, getting the urge to push back to see what he'll do about it. "Or maybe I should…"

His jaw ticks. It's so slight that I almost miss it.

But I don't miss the slow, rough grinding of his teeth as he processes my comment.

Stepping closer, I tip my chin up to face off with him.

Ghost is the one who's been lying to me. He's the one who brought me here because he just couldn't help himself. He might not want to admit why he did it, but every second that passes, it becomes clearer.

He lied to his club to protect me.

He won't let me work with anyone but him.

He scared off Venom at the bar.

He might not want to admit what's changing, but I need answers. And I'm going to get them even if it takes me pissing him off to do it.

Squaring off with him, I narrow my eyes. "I can't just fuck anyone, can I, Ghost? *It's not safe.* So maybe I'll give Venom a chance after all."

"Luna." My name is a threat, rumbling in his chest.

"That's not against the rules, is it?" My voice pitches as I continue to double down. "A girl has needs. And there are plenty of options walking around."

Ghost tips his face to the ceiling. Tension radiates from him, and I've never been so desperate to snap it.

"What do you think?" I take another step closer, officially toeing the line now. "Are you going to continue sitting back and watching? Or are you going to do something about it?"

With a final step, I freeze, and he looks down at me.

Body heat rolls off him, and the muscles in his neck pop with his clenched jaw. There's so much tension; it's palpable. I catch my breath, and my chest brushes against him with my inhale.

I'm too close.

This might be pushing it too far.

I'm on the verge of detonating.

My threats are useless when I know he's the only man who lights me up, but I hold my stance, hoping he'll do something about it.

He doesn't move. He doesn't flinch. His eyes are the ice that makes my skin prickle and my nipples peak.

Shivering, I wish I had the strength to stand under his attention unaffected like he is, but I can't.

I'm not sure what I was thinking trying to play a game of chicken with a man who has resisted all temptation for longer than I've known him, but it's clearly no use.

"Fine, you win." My shoulders deflate.

Wanting him does nothing but eat me up inside, and I can't do it forever.

But when I start to turn, Ghost grabs my arm and spins me, pinning my back to the wall. One hand holds my wrist while the other grabs my jaw. He's so close his lips nearly tease mine. A breath away while his hard body anchors me in place.

His hips hold me to the wall, revealing the proof he's as desperate for me as I am for him, but he doesn't close the distance.

"Marcus." I never use his legal name, but it slips out.

Something about the look in his eyes makes me weak.

"I can't fucking do this, Luna. Don't you get it?"

There's pain in his voice. A cold chill that makes his words crack.

"Why?" Tears sting my eyes with my question.

I'm not sure where they're coming from, but being this close to Ghost breaks me open. He slides through my defenses and reminds me of the things I want, that I've been smart enough to avoid up until now.

Ghost drags his thumb up over my mouth, and I press my lips together. My skin prickles beneath his touch, and my heart races.

When he doesn't answer my question, I dare to reach for him. To plant my hands on his sides and explore him. He might be resisting, but I feel the proof that he doesn't want to as I rock my hips forward.

"Why did you really lie for me?" I tip my chin up so we're almost mouth to mouth. "Please tell me why."

His cool eyes focus on mine as he drags his tattooed fingers into the back of my hair. "Because I'll do anything to protect you."

He leans in, and I lift up on my toes, trying to meet him. But the moment before our lips connect, he pulls back, letting me go. My body deflates against the wall, and the chill of the space between us feels so wide it's infinite. His hands tethered me here, and now he's gone.

"Ghost—"

"I can't." He pops his knuckles, taking another step back. "We can't."

But his words are no longer angry, and I swear there's sadness in his eyes as he walks away.

10

Ghost

Silence is never a good thing. Most of the time, it's louder than words. Especially when war is whispering on the horizon.

I monitor the feeds we set up at our meet point, and there's still no movement. It should be a relief, but history tells me it's a bad omen.

It's too quiet.

We've been waiting for the Iron Sinners to retaliate ever since we rescued Tempe and Austin from their grasp, but they've yet to make a move, leaving the club in limbo as we wait. And it makes me nervous as we head out on something that should be a simple buy.

We hit a bump in the road, and I grip my phone tighter. Vegas is warming up, turning the van into an oven. I'd rather be on my bike than inside this cage.

Feeling the air on the back of my neck.

Hearing every crunch of my tires ripping against the pavement.

Instead, I'm crammed in the back of this van with Soul, Chaos, and Legacy while a few prospects follow us.

I wipe the sweat off my neck and lean back, irritated.

"Heard you disappeared after Luna last night, brother." Legacy knocks me on the arm. "Something you want to talk about?"

I look up and see Soul grinning at me.

"I swear you all gossip like fucking teenagers." I shake my head.

"And you're avoiding the man's question." Soul chuckles.

"Because there's nothing to talk about." I turn to Legacy. "But if we're digging into personal shit, where were you last night?"

"Fuck you." Legacy flips me off.

Chaos laughs, resting his elbows on his knees. "Last I saw him, he disappeared with a fine-ass redhead."

Legacy glares at him. "The bar was out of champagne, and she was celebrating. Helped her find a glass."

"I'm sure you helped her find a little more than that." I chuckle, and Legacy flips me off again.

"Bachelorette party? Birthday?" Soul tosses out guesses.

"College graduation." Legacy tips his head back when the guys burst out laughing.

"Fuck." Chaos holds his fist out, but when Legacy refuses to bump knuckles, Soul does it for him. "College. Fucking. Graduation. Damn, brother."

"Someday, our boy's gonna make a young girl with daddy issues very happy." Soul grins.

"I hate all of you."

I'm sure he does. Especially since Soul is right. Legacy has a type. Early twenties, innocent, pretty, and looking to work out their fucked-up childhood with an emotionally closed-off biker.

"When did this become about me?" Legacy diverts the conversation, looking at me. "Are you fucking Luna now or not?"

"I thought she was fucking Venom."

Chaos's comment drags my attention from my phone, but when I meet his stare, he's grinning. He baited me, and I fell for it.

"Got his attention." Chaos elbows Soul, who's quietly chuckling.

The guys have always given me shit about Luna, but it's worse now that they know what I risked for her.

My resistance is corroding, and my brothers know it.

She knows it.

Last night, she was testing me.

She taunted me with Venom, and when she felt me crack, she broke through my defenses. That was the closest I've come to breaking the promises I made to myself five years ago.

Luna's the perfect combination of heaven and damnation, and when she stood so close her tits brushed my chest, I almost snapped.

Her skintight dress hugged her petite curves and showed off every inch of her arms and legs. Her wavy purple hair framed her face, drawing out the richness in her eyes.

I shouldn't let myself get that close to paradise because I'll start thinking I'm allowed to taste it. But her sharp little exhales drew me in; I was desperate to lean closer. To kiss her neck and see if she tastes like she smells—like vanilla and honeysuckle.

And then she called me Marcus.

She whispered my name, and I was tempted to hear how loud I could make her scream it.

I wanted to know if she's the kind of girl who will bend to my will or beg me for more.

"Three minutes." Havoc yells from the front seat, and it's enough to get the guys off my back so we can get back to business.

I scan the feeds from my phone, double-checking every angle. "Still clear."

Havoc nods, and the guys start to prep.

It doesn't matter how many drops we've done over the years; the edge never wears off. And if it does, that's usually a sign you're no longer sharp. Even something as simple as a buy can go sideways. You can never *not* be on your game.

The van silences, and we all settle into our roles, ready for the moment the doors open.

As the road captain, Chaos will do most of the talking. Havoc will monitor everyone's movements and direct the prospects if shit goes sideways. Legacy will accept the payment transfer after all the product is accounted for.

And Soul will make sure everything goes according to plan and report back to Steel.

Me, I'll sit back and watch.

It's my job to be invisible while having everyone's backs.

If tonight goes well, I won't have to do anything because the critical pieces have already been taken care of. The surveillance is done. The positions are set.

I have eyes in every corner because all it takes is me missing one little thing for this to fall apart.

All it takes is one blind spot, and we'll be mulch by morning.

One mistake, and we could lose everything.

Everyone.

The van rolls to a stop, and I check the perimeter a final time before anyone moves, but there's nothing.

"We're good."

Havoc nods, popping open his door. "Let's do this."

It's been three weeks since our last run, so the club needs this. Legacy keeps the bulk of the club's assets tied up in stocks and real estate, giving us security, but our cash on hand mostly comes from selling guns and ammunition.

With war on the horizon, every little bit helps.

Chaos opens the back of the van, and we all funnel out. Legacy hangs back with me until they need him, keeping watch. His gun is at his side, and he stands alert, ready to use it.

The Road Rebels are already waiting outside their vehicles when we approach. Chaos and Soul meet their VP, while the rest of us fan out. I toggle between the sensors and the nearby traffic cam footage, keeping an eye out for anything that might be out of place.

No movement.

No shadows.

I glance up and see Chaos smiling while Soul shakes their VP's hand, and Legacy steps forward to handle the transaction.

Once Legacy confirms we've received payment, the prospects get to work unloading product and helping a few of the Road Rebels load it into their van.

It's been getting more difficult to traffic guns with Iron Sinners trying to intercept our shipments, so I'm relieved when this goes down without a hitch.

"Good doing business with you." Chaos and Soul shake their hands again, and we all regroup at the van.

Havoc directs the prospects to head back to the clubhouse before climbing in. The van starts, and everyone is quieter than they were when we left. It's already four forty-five in the morning, and we have a three-hour drive back to Vegas.

Soul stretches his legs out, lacing his hands behind his head. "How about it, boys? Want to celebrate?"

"What did you have in mind?" Havoc asks from the front seat.

"Blow. Strippers. Booze. Take your pick."

Havoc chuckles. "Sapphire Rise?"

"I'm down." Chaos grins, always onboard to blow off steam at the strip club.

Strippers at seven in the morning isn't how I prefer to start the day, but there are worse things than tits, ass, and whiskey.

Pulling my phone out of my pocket, I angle it away from Legacy so he can't see what's on the screen, and I flip through the clubhouse camera feeds until I find her.

Luna is still awake, sitting outside with Wren and looking up at the stars. She's playing with the tips of her purple hair when a laugh bursts out of her.

That's all it takes—her smile. My blood run so hot it might melt my fucking bones.

Locking my phone, I rest my head back and close my eyes, burning the sight of her into the back of my eyelids, when I should be trying to forget it.

Maybe strippers at seven in the morning isn't such a bad thing. At least then, I can pretend it's not Luna's face that I see when I look anyone in the eyes. At least then I can convince myself I'm not going to break this girl like I've done everything else good in my life.

11

Luna

Rider: You've been MIA. Everything all right?

SnoOwl: I'm fine. Things just got complicated around here.

Rider: Anything I can help with? Getaway car? Escape plan?

SnoOwl: Maybe. Do you happen to know anywhere with cheap rent and good security?

Rider: You're moving?

SnoOwl: Not sure yet. I might need to.

Rider: I can keep an eye out. And I'm here if things get bad.

SnoOwl: It's not like that. I'm fine. I'm just keeping my options open. But I appreciate you looking out for me.

Rider: Anything for you, little owl. Just give me the word, and I'll come get you.

I close my gaming app on my phone and step outside onto the back patio. It's still early in the morning, so the temperature is perfect. I'm comfortable in a T-shirt and jeans, but the second the sun hits midday, the heat of Vegas will be overwhelming. It's only a matter of weeks before it's too hot to spend much time outside, and I'm dreading it.

But that's not the only thing that has me on edge today.

I've been keeping my distance from Rider because if the club finds out I'm communicating with him, they could kick me out. But I broke down and contacted him this morning because I miss him.

If I were smart, I'd cut ties, but I can't.

Rider is my only friend outside the club, and he might be all I have left if things turn sour here.

"You're here early." I smile at Tempe.

She's sitting at a picnic table on the clubhouse's back patio when I step outside. Her honey-brown hair is tied in a messy bun, and she's wearing one of Steel's sweatshirts, shrinking her already tiny frame.

She smiles when she sees me walking up. "Just enjoying the show."

I follow her gaze across the yard to see Steel, Ghost, and Legacy carrying large planks of wood to the edge of one rock area. Tempe's four-year-old brother, Austin, and Legacy's daughter, Bea, run in circles around them, playing tag.

"What are they building?" I drop into the seat beside her and kick my feet up on the table to watch.

"A mini clubhouse for the kids."

"Making bikers out of them already, huh?"

"Apparently." Tempe takes a sip of her coffee. "I told Jameson it's fine so long as Austin knows he's not getting a cut until he's at least eighteen."

"Does he want Austin to follow in his footsteps?"

"Yes and no." Tempe shrugs. "Jameson's family started this club, so I think deep down it would mean something if Austin carried on that tradition. But he also understands the pressure that creates, so he wouldn't want Austin to take on anything he doesn't want himself."

"How do you feel about it?" I know her father also comes from this world, but that soured her to the lifestyle until she met Steel.

Tempe watches Steel stack wooden planks, wetting her lips. "I'm fine with whatever Austin chooses. I trust Jameson, and I know he's building something different here than what I remember growing up. So if Austin wants to follow in Jameson's footsteps, I'll support him."

"That man better know how lucky he is to have you."

She grins. "He does."

"Austin too." I look over at where Steel is giving Austin a high five. "You guys bring out a whole other side of Steel. A whole other side to this club. You're good for them, and I'm glad you stayed."

"You're partly to thank for that." Tempe nudges my arm with her elbow. "I never really thanked you for how welcoming you were when I first came here. You made this place feel like home."

Home.

That's what this place has been for me, and now I feel it slipping through my fingers.

"You okay?" Tempe's eyebrows pinch.

She must have noticed me flinch at her comment.

"I'm fine." I force a smile. "I'm thankful for you too, Tempe. And I hope you know that even if I'm not here, I'm always here for you if you need it."

"Are you leaving the club?" Her eyes widen.

"Undecided. But it might be time."

"Don't tell me this has to do with whatever has Jameson on edge lately. I knew something was off ever since I overheard him and Ghost talking about you being in church. What's going on?"

"It's a long story."

"I've got time." She smirks. "This mini clubhouse is going to take them all day."

I adjust in my seat, watching the guys across the yard. "You know how I told you I used to do freelance tech work before I came here."

"Yeah."

"Well, apparently, one of those jobs had me hacking the club."

"*Apparently*? So, you didn't know?"

I shake my head. "I responded to an anonymous posting on a job board. I had no idea. I thought I was just digging up some account info for a tech firm. And that's how Ghost found me."

"Found you?" Her eyebrows pinch.

"He caught me trying to break through his firewalls, and he shut me down."

"So, whoever hired you never got the information?"

"Nope." My lips pop with the word.

"So why do you sound like something's still wrong?"

"Because all this time, Ghost knew I was working for the enemy, and he didn't say anything."

"To you?"

"To anyone."

Her eyes widen, and I watch her process what I'm saying. "That's why Jameson's been so upset."

"He lied to them."

"For you," Tempe points out.

"He didn't do me a favor if that's what you're thinking. They brought me in and basically interrogated me. It feels like I'm the enemy, but I had no idea about any of it."

Tempe leans forward, setting her coffee mug down and reaching for my hand. "If the club actually thought you were the enemy, do you think Jameson would let you stay here?"

"I guess not. But still, it feels like everything has changed."

"Nothing's changed." Tempe squeezes my hand. "And I swear if Jameson tries to kick you to the curb, I'm going to be standing right beside you. You're family, Luna. I don't care what brought you here. You'd never do anything to hurt the guys or the club."

"I wouldn't."

"Exactly." She smiles, and I feel pressure building behind my eyes. "We've got you."

Even if I appreciate her trying to mend this situation, there's more to it than that. Like the fact that the person who hired me a year ago is trying to find me again, and

I don't know what lengths they're willing to go to. I'm bringing danger to her, Austin, and the entire club.

I swallow that thought and keep it to myself. She has enough on her plate without adding my problems to it.

"Now that that's out of the way..." Tempe releases my hand and leans back in her chair, eyeing the guys across the yard. "Are we going to talk about the fact that Ghost risked everything for you?"

"No."

"Luna." She glares at me. "That man is obsessed. How do you not see it? And why are the two of you still not doing anything about it?"

"He was helping me out of a bad situation. That's all."

She ticks an eyebrow. "He lied to his club. The club he vowed his loyalty and life to... Luna, that man is in love with you."

I frown, watching him pick up another plank. His arms flex as he lifts it overhead, carrying it across the yard. "Let's say you're right... he still wouldn't ever do anything about it."

"Then why don't *you* do something?"

I think about the party. How he cornered me against the wall. How our lips almost brushed. So close I could taste the whiskey he'd been drinking.

I leaned in, and he pulled back.

"I've tried."

"Then try again." Tempe swats at my arm. "These men are stubborn and difficult, and it makes it hard as hell to get them to see what's right in front of them. But if he was willing to lie to his club—his *president*— for you, then that means something."

"I guess."

"Girl, I have seen you take a punch from a drunk local who was getting too rowdy. You have no fear. Don't start being scared now." Tempe smiles, picking up her coffee and watching the guys.

Austin tags Bea, and she stops in her tracks. Turning, she starts to run after him, but her foot catches on the ground, and she stumbles, landing on her hands and knees.

Tears immediately stain her cheeks as she stands up, clutching her hand.

Legacy turns, but he can't get a good look with the large stack of planks he's holding, so Ghost drops to a knee in front of her to look at it.

Whatever he says makes her smile through her tears. She wipes them away with the back of her hand while he picks her up. Legacy moves to set down the planks, but Ghost shakes his head, carrying Bea toward the clubhouse.

"You okay, Honey Bea?" Tempe asks when they reach us.

"I fell." Bea frowns. "Uncle Marcus is going to fix it."

Uncle Marcus.

Being a mom isn't something I've spent much time thinking about. The concept of building something permanent is terrifying, especially when I know what happens when it all falls apart. But when Ghost looks down at me as he holds Bea in his arms, I can't deny that my heartbeat kicks up a notch. Or that I dare to picture a different world, where we're different people, and we could have something resembling this.

Ghost sets Bea down on the picnic table facing me. "You good with Luna and Tempe while I grab you something to wrap that up?"

She nods, and he wipes a tear from her cheek with his thumb.

Ghost is a man with blood on his hands, but when he leans down to kiss Bea on the top of the head, all I see is a man who cares. I see someone who found a family with Legacy when he lost his own. Someone who treats Bea like his own flesh-and-blood niece. Someone who makes me think love is possible, even if I know better than to think he'd ever hand his to me.

Ghost's eyes meet mine, and my spine tingles. One glance and my entire body is on alert for him. But like always, the moment I feel anything is the moment he pulls away.

Ghost turns, walking into the clubhouse.

Maybe Tempe is right, and he brought me here for a reason. Maybe this isn't one-sided. I need an answer, and I'm going to get it.

12

Ghost

Half of Sapphire Rise is under renovation, but luckily, it hasn't affected our profits. Chaos is picky when it comes to the strip club—from the location to the girls who dance here. He's selective, and right now, it's paying off. Because even if half the club is being renovated, our doors are open, and we're as busy as we've ever been.

The song changes as I make a final adjustment to one of the camera angles, giving a clear view of the VIP hallway.

Once it's installed and in focus, I start recording, setting a sensor so I know if it goes offline.

Unlike Chaos, who is currently auditioning a new stripper by having her ride him topless, I'd rather finish up what I'm doing here as fast as possible so I can get back to the clubhouse. I prefer where it's quiet so I can focus. In my office, I'm in my domain, and I'm in control.

Music throbs through the club. It's packed, making the room feel ten degrees hotter than it is from the bodies alone. Seats around the main stage are starting to fill the later it gets, and the walls start closing in around me.

Twelve years ago, when I patched in at eighteen, I would have been right there with them. Celebrating the start of a new life, trying to convince a stripper to come back to the club with me when her shift ended.

Back then, it all seemed so fucking simple.

I was proving my father wrong and making something of my life, and that was all that mattered. I thought I had shit figured out. I was wrong.

A brunette takes the stage at the start of the new song. Her cherry pumps add seven inches to her already long legs. Her black bikini consists of three triangular scraps, and with the flashing lights and backlight, for a second, I swear she's Paulina, back from the dead.

An apparition of everything that went wrong when I let myself believe the life I chose wasn't bad for everyone around me.

The girl spins, and her hair fans around her shoulders. Her bangs fall to her eyebrows, and she smiles as the vision fades. She's older than Paulina was. Curvier. Happier.

My heart races as panic surges through me. I close my eyes and take a deep breath through my nose while clenching my fists.

Then, I let it out.

I count to ten while the girl in my memories runs down the street with her dark hair in pigtails. I watch her grow up—change. Until she's no longer my best friend. She's the mangled corpse they left outside the gate to the Twisted Kings property.

Then, I let her go.

Again.

Opening my eyes, I scan the room, not able to shake the tingling on the back of my neck. And when my gaze lands on a figure walking into the club, it's like I'm manifesting all the reasons I'm so on edge today.

Luna walks into Sapphire Rise with Venom at her side, and I swear the girl bleeds innocence. While all the strippers in the club are dressed up with fake eyelashes and layers of lipstick, Luna's face is clean. Her hair is still fuzzy from being freshly washed, and she practically floats like an angel toward me.

Her jeans and baggy T-shirt are understated. Yet that sliver of stomach where she's knotted her shirt is sexier than anything going on around us.

No one in my life has stolen my attention like Luna Cassidy. Still, when her pretty, blue gaze meets mine across the club, I know I should have left her where I found her because if I'm not careful, she'll share Paulina's fate.

Venom reaches me first, with Luna trailing a few steps behind him.

"Why the fuck did you bring her here?" I snap at Venom.

I try to remind myself he's damn good at hiding a body because I really want to kick him out of the club for putting her in danger right now. His flirtations with Luna are one thing, but taking her out of the compound when the man who hired her is trying to get her back has me itching to reach for my gun.

"Prez said you needed a disc with a software update. She asked me for a ride to bring it to you."

"I need the disc, not her. Are you trying to get her fucking killed?"

I take a step toward Venom, but Luna slips between us, planting her hand on my chest. The heat of her palm and her delicate fingers ground my feet to the earth.

"He didn't know." She looks up at me. "I offered to come, and I'm fine."

Under the club lights, her hair is a deeper purple, and it turns her blue eyes the faintest shade of violet.

Luna presses her lips together. "You promised to show me the new system in action, remember? I figured now was as good of a time as ever."

"That was before all this shit happened."

She hitches an eyebrow. "I'm not living my life in fear, Ghost. And I'm sure as hell not hiding at the clubhouse. So here I am, either show me or don't, but I'm not leaving."

Luna crosses her arms over her chest, acting so strong when she's all skin and bone. Fragile, whether she likes it or not.

"What do you need from me?" Venom asks. "Want me to take her back?"

"Just put the disc in the office." I resist the urge to shove a screwdriver through his temple. "Then go see if Chaos needs help with anything. I'll let you know when she's ready to head home."

Luna's eyes narrow as Venom stalks off, but she doesn't break my stare. "You could be nicer to him for bringing me here."

"He only brought you here because he wants to fuck you, and it's an easy way to get you alone."

"Is it a crime for a man to want to fuck me now?"

She's testing me again. Thinking if she pushes hard enough, I'll snap. This time, I don't take the bait. I step back.

"I'll show you what we're doing in the VIP rooms, but then you're leaving."

"Yes, sir." She rolls her shoulders back, and even if she's trying to be sarcastic to piss me off, all her words do is make me want to put her on her knees.

We're standing in the middle of a strip club, with tits and ass all around us, but I can't tear my eyes off this girl. She tugs her lower lip between her teeth, and I mentally make note of exactly how long it's been since I've let myself touch someone the way I want to touch her.

I think about how long it's been since I've let anyone touch *me*.

It aches knowing I don't deserve whatever heaven exists between her legs, but I sure as shit wish I did.

Turning, I don't wait for her to follow me as I head toward the back of the strip club to the VIP hallway.

I could have turned her away with Venom the second she walked in the door, but fuck if I'm letting him have any more time with her before I get a sense of where her head is at. She can't be mine, but she is. And if he so much as looks at her again, I'm going to take a razorblade to his eyelids so he's forced to watch me pull his intestines out of his stomach.

Stopping at the end of the hall, I hold the door open for Luna and watch as she walks into the private VIP room ahead of me. The lights are low in here, and the music is quieter. A couch sits against one wall, and there's a private stage directly across from it.

When the door clicks shut, all I smell is Luna's honeysuckle shampoo.

"I thought we were checking out the new security system." Luna's eyebrows pinch when she looks at me. "What are we doing in here?"

"I can't run the software update until tomorrow." I pull out my phone, stepping to the far wall. "The updates will take a while, and Steel doesn't want the cameras down while the club is open."

She nods, watching me move around the room. I walk slowly along the wall, making note of any blind spots as I monitor the feed on my phone.

"What are you doing?" Luna paces, stopping at the stripper pole and running her fingers down it.

"These are new cameras. I'm just confirming we have full coverage and no blind spots." From the corner of my eye, I watch her skim her hand down the silver pole. "People like to fuck with the cameras in these rooms, so I set tampering sensors that will alert us if that happens."

"Wouldn't want anyone getting away with something under your watch, huh?" Luna turns her back to the pole, slowly starting to sway to the music. "Is that camera recording already?"

"Yeah." I glance down at the feed, where I can see Luna on my phone, gripping the pole behind her.

"So, you can see this?" She lifts her arms slowly, grazing them over the sides of her breasts and into her hair until she's gripping the pole overhead.

"What are you doing, Luna?"

"Helping you work." She bites her lower lip.

The girl who is trying to break me is coming out to play again. She's inching under my skin, and my defenses are weakening.

"How is what you're doing going to help?" I ask, trying to ignore her as I start walking the length of the room again to make sure nothing mirrors.

Luna grips the pole, spinning her body around so she can slowly walk around it. She's teasing the line between playing and dancing. Her weight is in her hand as she spins, but she doesn't do much more than that.

"I'm making sure you don't have any blind spots. You said that's what you were looking for, right?"

"The stage is clear," I tell her, seeing the full view of her on my screen.

"All of it?" Luna spins again, flipping her hair this time. "Wouldn't want you to miss anything."

She pauses to toe off one of her sneakers, kicking one across the room so it lands in the corner. On my screen, I see her shoe lying sideways on the floor.

"How about that spot?"

"It's good." I swallow hard.

Luna kicks off her other shoe. "What about over there?"

"You already saw me check both those spots." I try to hold firm, but she's making it damn impossible.

"It doesn't hurt to double-check, right? You're the one who taught me to be thorough, Ghost."

"Luna—"

"What about the couch?" she cuts me off, spinning around the pole again.

I can't fucking think.

Luna is still fully dressed, but blood pumps to all the wrong places with what she's doing.

She tempts me into wondering why the fuck I've been abstinent for so long. Some people assume it's because I don't like to fuck, but that couldn't be farther from the truth. Especially considering what I'd like to do to Luna right now.

It was just safer to keep my distance. After what happened with Paulina, I didn't want to risk letting anyone close again.

"The couch is fine." I grind my teeth.

"How do you know? You didn't check the couch yet, and from what I can tell, you're walking every inch of the room, aren't you?" She eyes the couch. "People do all sorts of things on those couches. You should double-check."

I should unlock the door and call for Venom right now. He could take Luna back to the clubhouse, and I could work in peace. Instead, I humor her by walking over to the couch and sinking down onto the cushions.

"So?" she asks, pausing with her back to the pole again, gripping it behind her.

I glance down at my phone, switching the camera angle to the couch, and see myself sitting on it. "All good."

"Good." She hums, her body swaying to the music. "Because now that you're sitting, I think we should talk."

"About what?"

"You went against your club for me, Ghost." Her hands move from the pole to her hips; she trails her fingers under the line of her shirt, teasing the smooth skin of her stomach. "You went against *your president* for me. That's something big. But you pretend you still don't care. Why?"

I stretch my arms across the back of the couch, watching her. "I care."

"Then why not do anything about it?"

"I already told you we can't."

"Because you don't fuck patch bunnies?" She slowly undoes the knot in her T-shirt, playing with the fabric.

"You're not a patch bunny."

She shrugs. "Fine. Then because you don't fuck *anyone*. Why is that?"

"It's just better that way."

"Hmm." She twists her hips as the music kicks up, tipping her head back. "Are you worried you're going to hurt me, Ghost? Because trust me, you can't."

"You'd like to think that." My shoulders tense. "But you're wrong."

"Then why get me into this mess in the first place?"

Because you're everything to me, and the idea of leaving you behind made me want to finish what I started on the cliff in Arizona.

I manage to swallow that sentence. She doesn't need to hear it. It will only make her realize how fucked up I am. Or worse, she'll start believing in things that aren't possible.

When I'm silent for a moment, she frowns. "The least you can do is stop lying to me."

"I've never lied to you."

"Omitting the truth is a form of lying."

I shrug, not arguing because she's technically right.

"Tell me something. No lies." She starts teasing her fingers at the hem of her T-shirt again, and the movement of her fingers has me hypnotized.

"What do you want to know?" I'm stepping on a land mine, but I can't help it.

Luna smirks, slowly peeling her T-shirt up and overhead. Her silky skin is unmarked perfection, unlike the inked mess of memories I've made of mine. Her nipples peek through her blue lace bra. It's bright and matches her eyes. And when she pulls the shirt fully overhead, and her lavender hair brushes her skin, it takes everything in me to stay put.

A devious little grin curls in the corner of her mouth, and she tosses her shirt to another corner of the room. It puddles against the wall.

"How about that spot? Is it good?" She smiles at me with pure wickedness in her eyes. "Wouldn't want you to miss anything."

13

Luna

STRIPPING FOR GHOST WASN'T how I planned to approach him tonight, but at least it's working. He hasn't stopped staring at me since my shirt came off.

I knew he'd be angry I left the compound and that he'd be even more upset that it was with Venom. But I only did it to provoke a reaction. To see just how far I could push him before he would finally show me how he really feels.

I planned to confront him about how he's been ignoring me. But after the door to the VIP room shut behind us, I had a better idea. Talking hasn't gotten us anywhere up until this point, so I figured I'd try something different.

Ghost showed me his hand. He vouched for me to his club because he can't deny the pull between us just like I can't. I just need him to admit it.

His cool gaze falls to my chest, and even if it's warm in this room, my nipples pebble at his attention. My T-shirt sits in a puddle across the room, and his stare has my skin burning up.

Ghost grips the back of the couch so hard his tattooed knuckles are white, and his thick arms ripple with tension. But he doesn't move. He stays seated with his knees spread as he watches me. Not bothering to hide the bulge fighting against his jeans.

"Do you want me to stop?" I take a step forward, slowly walking off the stage toward him. "Are you worried someone can see us?"

I glance up at a camera in one corner of the room, then back at him, pulling my hair off my shoulders.

"No one can see us."

"Except you." I skim my fingers down my sides. "You can watch this back if you want, right? While you're pretending you don't see me—pretending you don't care about me even if you brought me into this—you can play this back. You can watch what I'm doing as many times as you like."

Ghost leans forward, planting his elbows on his knees. "We're not doing this right now, Luna."

"Are you sure about that?" I pop the button on my jeans. "Shouldn't we at least benefit in some way before this all goes bad?"

"Nothing's going to go bad for you. I promise."

"We both know you can't promise that." I slowly unzip my pants, sliding them down my legs and kicking them off until I'm standing in front of him in nothing but a bra and underwear. "So, if this is all we have, shouldn't we at least stop lying to ourselves and do something about it?

Or are you really going to let me stand in front of you like this and pretend you aren't affected? That you're just protecting me like you do everyone else."

"You're not *everyone else*."

I can't help smiling. "Then what am I to you, Marcus?"

He swallows hard when I use his legal name.

It's why I did it.

I want that reaction. I want his eyes on me as he swallows hard. I don't just want Ghost; I want Marcus Jasper. If I'm going all in, then so is he.

"You think you can handle what you're bringing on yourself, Luna? But you have no idea what it means to get involved with a man like me."

"Try me."

Ghost thinks I'll break. He thinks I'll back down. I won't. We've been playing this game for over a year, and I'm ready to see what's at the end of it. Especially now that I know tomorrow is no longer promised.

The Twisted Kings could decide I'm not worth the trouble.

The man who hired me a year ago could finally catch up.

Right now is all I have left.

"Well?" I hitch an eyebrow.

Ghost leans back, jutting his chin. "Come here, Luna."

Relief floods my chest as I walk up to him.

I'm the one who started this. I pushed him to see if I could make him break, but now that he's caving, the control is starting to shift. The gleam in his pale eyes calls out to me, and even if I'm the one stripped of my clothes, he has all the power.

I walk until I'm standing between his legs, and only then does he lean forward. He snakes his arm around my waist and pulls me onto his lap so I'm straddling him.

We tease the same line we did the other night at the party. I sink down, and my core settles over the hard length bulging behind his jeans. Digging my fingers into his shoulders, I'm met with the unrelenting tension he always holds inside him.

I think about what Tempe said. These men are hardheaded and stubborn, but I'm determined.

Ghost has been watching me for a year. Keeping this distance like it can keep me safe. But whatever forces are out to get me found their way in anyway. He might think he's dangerous, but so is everything else in this world.

Leaning forward, I brush my lips against his. But instead of claiming the kiss, he wraps a tattooed hand around the front of my throat and holds me a breath away.

"What's wrong, Ghost?" I rock in his lap, basking in the low growl rumbling in his chest. "Scared if you kiss me, you won't be able to stop?"

He brushes his lips over mine. "What you're asking for is gonna get you hurt, beautiful."

"I can get hurt either way."

"Not if I have anything to say about it." With his free hand, he grazes my thigh, trailing inward until he's brushing his knuckles over my pussy.

"Why are you always trying to keep me safe?"

"Because you're the kind of girl who deserves a hell of a lot more than you get from life, Luna. You deserve to feel good. To be worshipped. To be treated right."

"You're the first person to think that." My voice cracks, and it's nearly a whisper.

The moment the words are out, I wish I could take them back.

"I'm not." Ghost peels my panties to the side, rubbing his thumb over my slick core. "But it's a shame if I'm the first person to say that to you. You, Luna, are so pure you're unholy. So beautiful it should be a sin. And your smile..."

He dips his hand down and drives two fingers inside me, stealing my breath.

"Pure fucking sunshine."

"Marcus." I moan as he rolls his thumb over my clit, driving his fingers deeper.

His hand holding my throat tugs me in so he can lick my lower lip. A graze of his teeth turns into a trail of kisses that pepper my jaw and throat. Everywhere except where I need him.

His fingers pump in, but I need more. I need everything.

"Please, Marcus. I want to feel you." I roll my hips in his lap.

"I want to feel you too. More than you know." He kisses the side of my neck, gripping my throat tighter as I start to ride his hand. "But I'll settle for this."

His fingers sink deeper as I rock in his lap. I'm desperate to feel him in every way, but I accept this is what he's offering. It's all he's capable of in this moment.

Maybe someday we can become more. Or maybe we'll never get the chance.

"This is all I can give you." He hums against my neck, rocking his thumb back and forth over my clit. "Fuck my fingers. Show me how you'd ride me if I let you."

"Marcus."

"Mm-hmm." He tightens his grip on my throat. "Say my name again, Luna. Let me hear you."

My nails rake the back of his neck as I pull him closer, chasing the pressure that's starting to build. I scratch at his skin, desperate to rip us open so we can connect. But the walls are so thick I can't scale past them.

"Please, Marcus." I bury my face in the side of his neck, gripping the front of his cut as I ride his hand. "Please don't stop touching me."

One hand grabs my hip as he grinds me against him. His fingers sink deeper, and when he curls them, my vision darkens.

"Fuck, you're perfect." Ghost takes control of my body, forcing me to accept him deeper.

"Right there," I moan.

It's like he can read exactly what I need—exactly what I like. We've never been intimate, but somehow, he just knows.

His hard cock rubs against me as I ride his hand, but he refuses to break. He submits himself to this torture as he pleasures me.

"Take what you need from me. Let me feel that perfect pussy work for it."

I wrap my arms around Ghost's shoulders and grind against his hand, chasing my release. I ignore the distance and hug my body to him, imagining he's giving me more than this. His thumb rocks over my clit, and my body buzzes as I come harder than I have in my life.

My soul hovers and Ghost claims it.

I'm floating outside my body as I shake, and he forces me to ride out every pulse of my climax.

Planting my hands on his chest, I pull back to look at him. I'm sure I'm a mess with how unapologetically I just used him, but he doesn't seem to mind.

His pale eyes burn up as he slips his fingers out. But when I try to lean in and steal a kiss, he grabs me by the throat again.

Slicking his fingers down my neck, he leans in to lick my throat. To get a taste of what he won't let himself have.

So close.

Yet, always so far.

"You're beautiful, Luna." His lips brush my collarbone, teasing me. "But I can't have you any more than this."

I meet his eyes, and I can't help but tell him the truth. "Too bad you already do."

14

Ghost

Mistakes have been made.

Ones that have been easy to resist up to this point because enjoying a woman isn't worth what I'll cause them if they stick around too long.

But then in walked Luna Cassidy.

A girl who is every wet dream come to life. Brilliant. Beautiful.

She's a ray of light, and I'm the black hole drinking her down like she can cast sunshine into the darkness.

What I wouldn't give to get one taste of her. One kiss. If it wasn't just my soul on the line, nothing could have stopped me from giving in.

But when Luna blinked, looking up into my eyes, she reminded me why I can't be selfish. Just because she's an angel from heaven doesn't change the fact that I'm the chains from hell. I can't let her be my salvation just to damn her soul in return.

The line is drawn.

Or so I thought.

Everything is getting really fucking blurry lately. The sight of Luna stripped down to her lacy bra and panties gave me a stronger hit than a bottle of whiskey.

She sunk onto my lap, and I almost believed I deserved to hold her. Her nails bit into my shoulders, and she rocked over me as I slipped my fingers into paradise.

My hand decorating her throat is the only necklace I want her to wear for the rest of her life.

I snapped.

Her slick pussy gripped me, and I tried not to think about how tight she'd feel wrapped around my cock. I resisted every urge to flip her over and break my abstinence streak.

Five years ago, when I decided I do more bad than good, it was simple giving up sex. Fucking a girl isn't worth the consequence of letting them get close. Before I met Luna, I thought a lifetime of celibacy might not be the death of me.

All it took was one look in her ocean-blue eyes to doubt every decision I'd ever made. It wasn't easy at all. I just hadn't met a girl who made me want to break my promise to myself.

But what happens if I give in?

What happens if I'm selfish?

I might already know the answer, but my body is starting to physically resist it.

The hallway is quiet when I step out of the VIP room. I give Luna her space to get dressed and come to terms with what happened. We can't have more, no matter how much I want to.

I wait at the end of the hall until Luna steps out next. She shuts the door, pausing to adjust the knot at the bottom of her T-shirt, and I watch her from a distance. She's showing off more skin than she was when she first walked into the club, and I'm not the only one who notices.

"Damn." Venom stops beside me, grinning.

"What the fuck are you looking at?"

His eyebrows pinch at my tone. "Nothing, boss."

My teeth grit as I watch Luna pull her hair into a knot on the top of her head. "Good."

I feel Venom's attention moving from me to her. If I'm lucky, Chaos won't think anything of us disappearing because Luna and I regularly work together. But Venom sees it. The wheels in his head are already turning. He might spend more time pissing me off than impressing me lately, but he's not an idiot.

Luna glances up at me, and her cheeks brighten. Her lower lip is puffy from biting at it, but the tension she walked into the club with has dissipated.

She stands staring at me from the other end of the hall, and I know we're in trouble because her gaze lights a match to the dark caverns of my heart. She adds kindling to this fire that's catching, and we're both going to burn if we aren't careful.

I'm tempted to drag her back into the VIP room and follow the blush on her neck, down her chest, and over her whole body. I'd like to strip her bare and figure out what makes her skin prickle. What makes her pussy drip. What makes her scream.

"Oh shit." Venom looks from Luna to me. "I swear I didn't know that Luna was your girl, Ghost, or I wouldn't have tried anything with her."

I look over at him and consider saying she's not mine. But I don't owe a prospect an explanation, and I don't mind him thinking she is.

"Did you ride here on your bike?"

I might not be willing to claim Luna, but there's no way she's getting on the back of another man's bike after she just came on my fucking hand.

"No." Venom shakes his head. "I drove her here in one of the club's vans."

Good. At least he's smart enough not to have a death wish.

"Are you good to get her home, or has Chaos been feeding you shots?"

"I'm good."

I nod, crossing my arms over my chest. The last thing I want to do is send her home with Venom, but I need to finish up what I was working on before she got here, and if I don't get her out of my periphery, I'm not going to be able to keep resisting her.

Luna stops at my side, looking up at me. I swear she's smaller now. More fragile. She might be strong as hell, but I can't see past her mortality.

Skin. Blood. Bone.

People are so fucking breakable, and that's never bothered me until her.

"Venom's taking you back to the clubhouse."

Luna frowns. "You're not coming?"

"Can't yet. I still have shit to get done tonight."

Plus, if I put her on the back of my bike later, I might never let her go.

Luna wets her lips, looking around the strip club. It's rowdier now than when she arrived because it's getting later, and I wonder what she's thinking.

Sapphire Rise is supposed to be topless only, but after a certain point in the night, Chaos doesn't stop the girls from doing what they want for extra tips. And tonight, it's madness.

Luna is watching a girl do the splits on a pole, and then her gaze darts to me, but I don't sense she's jealous that I'm spending time at the club working. She's seen worse back at the clubhouse, and sometimes, she'll sit around and watch.

Luna knows what she has to offer, and I have no interest in anything going on around me. Nothing here appeals to me except for the purple-haired splash of brightness staring into my eyes.

"Venom, give us a second."

He nods, walking to wait by the exit.

Luna steps closer with him gone, but there's still a gap. I want to close it, but I can't, and it has my skin crawling.

"Why are you sending me back? I can just wait while you finish up what you need to do." Her eyebrows pinch. "I can just go home with you."

Those words have never sounded so good.

Her on my bike.

Her in my bed.

I want it all, and that's the problem.

"It might be five minutes, or it might be five hours." I tuck my hands in my pockets to stop them from reaching for her. "You should get some sleep."

"I don't mind—"

"Go with Venom," I cut her off, averting my gaze because if I keep staring her in the eyes, she's going to see the truth in them. "I've got shit to do, Luna, and I can't be worrying about you while I do it. What we did didn't change anything. It's not like you're my old lady."

She flinches like my words are a physical punch to the gut, and I hate it. When she steps back a step, I don't blame her.

"I'm not asking you for your fucking property patch, Ghost." She narrows her eyes. "But the least you could do is be a decent human being."

"Luna—"

"Don't worry about it." She holds up her hands. "I get it. You're just like the rest of them."

Her hard expression cracks as she turns away, revealing the hurt behind her anger. I almost reach out and stop her.

I almost risk it.

But I don't.

I watch her from the corner of my eye as she brushes past Venom and out the exit. And the pinch of confusion on his face tells me everything I need to know about her expression.

Venom disappears out of the club after Luna, and I disappear down the VIP hall, continuing until I reach the office this time.

I'm here to work tonight, but Luna fucked that up. Now, she's messing with my head.

By the time we come out the other side of this, she's going to hate me, and maybe that's for the best. Then she'll stop asking me for things that will hurt her.

Sitting down at the computer, I tip my head back and drag my fingers through my hair. All I see are Luna's eyes in the darkness. I can still smell her perfume lingering on my clothes. I can feel her heat wrapped around my fingers.

I'm losing my fucking mind over this girl.

Tonight, I was supposed to be getting the system ready for the software updates tomorrow, but Luna makes it impossible to think.

I'm not sure how long I've been staring at the wall when my phone rings, cutting through the silence.

"What?" I answer, expecting to hear Soul on the other end of the line, giving me crap about missing the party at the clubhouse tonight.

"We're being followed." Venom's voice cuts through, and I'm immediately out of my chair.

"How many?"

"Two bikes..." There's a pause. "Maybe three. Or four. There's too much traffic in this part of the city to tell."

At least they're still in the city. Even if they are being followed, our rivals know better than to start shit this close to the Strip. It would draw the attention of law enforcement.

"All right. I'm getting Chaos. Keep as much distance as you can, and don't stop moving. I've got a tracker on the van, so we'll find you. And Venom, you keep her safe, or I'll fucking gut you. Do you understand?"

"I understand, boss."

Right as I'm about to hang up, I hear metal crunch, and it has my entire body tensing as the line goes dead.

"Fuck." I walk down the VIP hall and into the bar, knocking Chaos on the shoulder when I get there. "We've gotta go. Now."

Chaos doesn't ask questions. He barely acknowledges the stripper in his lap before setting her on the stool beside him and following me. "What's up?"

"Venom's got a tail. And I think whoever is chasing them hit the van before the line went dead."

"What would the Iron Sinners want with one prospect?"

I swallow hard, barely able to breathe past the lump in my throat. "Luna's with him."

"Shit." Chaos pulls his helmet on as I hop on my bike. "This isn't about him then."

"No."

Pulling out my phone, I'm glad I'm paranoid enough to have tracking devices on all club vehicles and phones so I know where the members are at all times.

Venom and Luna are still moving, which means what I heard wasn't a crash. But when I see they're getting farther outside the city, panic swells in my chest. He's heading back to the clubhouse, but there's nothing out there to stop their tail from making a move on them.

"In the mood to spill some Iron Sinner blood?" I start my bike and look over at Chaos.

He chuckles. "Like you even have to ask."

15

Ghost

CHAOS FOLLOWS ME AS we weave through traffic, and I curse myself for not sending Luna back to the clubhouse the second she walked through the doors of Sapphire Rise. Worse, I curse myself for not being the one to take her there myself.

At least then, I'd know she's safe with me.

Venom might do everything he can, but he's still proving himself to the club. He's not patched, and after Reyes worked behind our backs as a double agent, I don't trust anyone who hasn't pledged their undying loyalty.

Besides, even if Venom is one of us, he won't risk absolutely everything. She's not a member, and she's not my old lady.

I'd be her shield. Her safety. I'd do what I swore when I dragged her into this. I'd protect her.

My tires hum against the pavement, and I focus on the vibrations running through my hands. I push aside my doubt and focus on what I can control at this moment. I cut through traffic with ease because being on my bike is the one place where the world makes sense, and I let the city lights blur as I fly by.

I focus on the cool air tickling the back of my neck as we make our way out of the heart of the city, and my only thought is closing the distance between me and Luna.

Part of me wishes Venom had stayed in a more populated area until we could catch up with him, but the other side of me is grateful there's nothing holding me back.

Taillights come into view ahead, and if this goes down, nothing will stop me from putting a bullet in their heads.

Out here, we answer to nothing but dirt and sagebrush. No judgment. No witnesses.

The roar of engines gets louder as we eat up the distance between us and the three motorcycles ahead. Chaos pulls to my side, and we fan out, taking up both sides of the road. No one's coming, and no one will. It's late, and the only people on this stretch of pavement are those with the Twisted Kings.

The van is still in the right lane, with two motorcycles on its tail, while one slowly inches to the driver's side.

I glance over at Chaos, and he points to the one on the left. He'll take care of that one while I figure out the other two.

Reaching behind me, I pull my gun out of my holster and take aim at one of the two men following behind the van. If Legacy were here, he'd aim for the tires and send them rolling in the dirt, but I don't have as good of a shot as he does, so I aim for center body mass.

No survivors.

No mercy.

The second before I pull the trigger, the Iron Sinner looks back, changing the angle so I clip him in the shoulder. The hit makes him swerve, but it doesn't take him down.

He reaches for his gun, and I pull the trigger again, getting him in the back this time. It sends him rolling. He flips so many times there's no way he'll survive it.

One down.

Two to go.

Venom weaves the van, forcing the Iron Sinner, who is trying to creep up to his side, to pull back. Chaos seizes the opportunity, getting on his tail. He comes up beside the Iron Sinner and aims his gun, but right before he pulls the trigger, the Iron Sinner slows, and Chaos's bullet hits the back of the van.

Venom slams on the brakes, and the van comes to a stop, while Chaos continues to follow the Iron Sinner trying to escape.

I stick with the last biker tailing Venom and Luna. He pulls to a stop and aims his gun at me.

If I were smart, I'd get behind the cover of the van. But then a bullet might hit Luna, and I can't risk it. So I recklessly drive straight at him, hoping he has shit aim and calls chicken before we collide.

At the last second, he steps to the side to avoid getting hit by my bike.

He tumbles to the ground, and I slam on the brakes, hopping off. Before he can find his bearings or reload, I storm over to him and kick his helmet so hard it cracks.

His gun falls to his side as I grab the bottom of his helmet, shoving him to his knees. I force him to look up at me, but when his body sags, I notice a pool of red forming beneath his cut.

He's been hit.

I pull off his helmet, but his body slumps to the ground, and empty eyes stare up at me. Another dead Iron Sinner is always a good thing, but the dead can't talk, and right now, I need answers.

"Fuck." I dig his phone out of his pocket so I can hack it later.

Chaos is circling back down the road as I head to the van, so he must have taken out the final biker who was following Venom and Luna.

The Iron Sinner phone in my pocket beeps, and I pull it out to see an app flagging a location.

Our location.

And when I open the app, I'm met with a mirror of the program I use to monitor the locations of everyone in the club.

This new hacker is giving me a run for my money, and I'm getting tired of it. I need to get back to the clubhouse to shut this down before they make a move on someone else.

Pulling out my phone, I dial Steel, watching Venom help Luna out of the van.

"What's wrong?"

"Three Iron Sinners just tried to take out Venom when he was getting Luna back to the clubhouse."

"Where are they now?"

"Dead." I glance at the body of the one I left on the road. "Gonna need a clean-up crew five miles out from the clubhouse."

"Send me your location."

"That's the other issue. They're tracking us. Whoever hired Luna is good, and I think they've taken over for Richter. They're in our grid, watching all our locations. I need to get back to the clubhouse to shut them out."

"All right. Is it just you and Venom?"

"Chaos is here."

"Have him wait with Venom for me and Soul. You get back here and shut that shit down. Tempe has a tracker in her purse, and I swear to fuck if—"

"They won't. I'll take care of it, Prez."

"How the fuck do they keep getting in?"

My hands clench because I know I should have better answers by now, but I don't. "I'll figure it out."

"All right." The sound of his bike starting cuts through the line. "Get it done."

Steel hangs up, and I tuck my phone in my pocket, watching as Luna circles the van, visibly shaking. I want to walk over to her—to comfort her.

I want to make sure she's okay, but my feet are cemented in place.

She's mine, but she's not.

I'm helping her, but I'm hurting her.

My temples throb as I pinch the bridge of my nose.

"What's the word?" Chaos stops beside me.

"Steel wants you and Venom to wait here for him and Soul. I need to get back to the clubhouse and stop them from tracking us."

Luna stops beside me with her gaze cast down. Her arms are wrapped around her body as she shivers.

"You okay?" Venom asks, reaching out but pausing at the last second before touching her.

I should be the one asking that question.

I should be the one pulling her in to warm her up and offering her comfort.

What the fuck is wrong with me?

"I'm fine," she says, but her tone doesn't match her words.

Her eyes dart to me, and they might as well be razors slicing my chest open.

"Come on." I offer her my helmet. "You're coming with me."

I turn back toward my bike before she can argue or agree. Before she can think I'm doing this out of care. Before she can think anything more than the fact that I'm trying to keep her safe.

It's better this way.

Luna disappears into her room the moment we get back to the clubhouse, and I lock myself in my office, not saying a word to her because I'm an asshole, and there's no good explanation for how I'm treating her.

This is why I don't entertain relationships anymore. And it's why I've refused to show her an ounce of attention.

After what we did at the club, she's expecting something I can't live up to. Something that will end with her six feet under. Someday, I'll have to sit her down and explain it, but not now. There's no time.

Once I'm locked in my office, I can finally think.

I locate the weak point in our system and figure out exactly how the Iron Sinners used it to gain backdoor access to my tracking software. I set up another layer of firewalls and disappear into my work.

Once I'm confident I've solved one problem, I spend another hour downloading the data off the Iron Sinner's phone before destroying it so they can't trace it back here. There's not much on it, which means their new tech specialist is probably as smart and paranoid as I am.

Still, I spend a few hours digging through every text, tracing every phone number, and searching the browser history—public and private—to learn everything I can.

I manage to ignore thoughts of Luna until there's nothing else to think about but the loading bar on a software patch at four in the morning.

This is when I should shut it down and go to sleep. The updates will happen in the background, and I can reset this shit day.

Instead, I find myself flipping through the clubhouse cameras like I don't already know where I'm going. Like

I won't inevitably end up on the ones I shouldn't be accessing. I flip over to Luna's laptop camera, cursing her for leaving it open like she always does.

It takes a moment for the picture to focus, and when it does, I see her lying in bed sleeping. Her blanket is at her waist, and I watch the rise and fall of her chest with every breath. She tosses and turns a few times, like she senses me watching her, before she settles again.

On my other screen, I pull up the footage from Sapphire Rise. At first, I tell myself I'm just double-checking my work from today, making sure I didn't miss anything. But as I move back one hour to the next, I know what I'm after.

You can watch this back if you want to, right?

Luna's question from earlier echoes in my head. She knows I'm sick without me having to admit it, and it didn't even seem to bother her.

Pulling the footage from the VIP suite, I move it to a private server and delete it from the club's records. Then I press play and sit back, watching her sway her hips on the stage.

Watching her peel off her shirt.

Her pants.

Walking over to me.

That's the moment I should have made a different decision than pulling her into my lap.

I can still feel her wet pussy gripping my fingers. I can still smell her pleasure in the air.

Reaching down, I pull my cock out and submit to my sickness. My need for her eats me up inside. On one screen, she's sleeping. And on the other, she's riding my hand.

I stroke my cock, but it's not enough because I don't really have her.

I play back the sounds of her moaning while my fingers disappeared inside her, and I imagine my name escaping her lips as she came. I pretend it's her pussy slicking down on me, tightening and begging for my cum.

My spine tingles, and my body burns as I watch her tip her head back. And when her lips part on the screen, I imagine standing over her and coming down her throat.

Ropes of cum shoot into my hand, and I consider walking into her room and shoving it on her tongue to give her the answers she's been looking for.

Yes, I want her.

Yes, I need her.

I can't live without her.

She's mine, and it's getting harder to deny it.

16

Luna

SCROLLING THROUGH MY TEXTS, I open the one I received in the middle of the night from Ghost. He messaged me the video recording of us in the VIP room at the strip club, confirming what I hoped when I teased him that he could watch it back.

It might be twisted, but I like the idea of him remembering me like this. It's proof he wants me, no matter how much he tries to resist.

I found myself watching it on repeat while I fingered myself this morning, but my hand couldn't do what his did. I came twice before giving up on the idea that anything could come close to the feel of Ghost inside me.

Frustrated and still on edge, I climbed out of bed and got dressed.

It's embarrassing I let him affect me like this. Especially when Ghost was an asshole after what happened. He sent me home with Venom, and even when he came to our rescue, he didn't bother asking how I was doing. Somehow, us getting closer drove us farther apart.

I should hate him.

So why can't I?

I'm obsessed with this man, and the more he resists, the more determined I am to break him.

I secure my ponytail and roll my shoulders back. The lavender is growing out, leaving more blonde at the roots, but the tips are still solid purple. Smoothing my hair, I stare in the mirror and try to find my confidence beneath the blanket of doubt that's been weighing heavily on me.

Tonight is a big deal for the club. They're throwing a chapter mixer to celebrate Chaos getting out of prison. It was originally scheduled for right after he was released, but after the Iron Sinners took Tempe, celebrations were postponed.

But now it's finally happening, and it's going to be wild. If there's one time the club goes completely off the rails, it's when Twisted Kings from different chapters converge in one place. I can't wait. I'm counting on the madness.

Ghost has been shutting me out for over a year, and I'm done accepting it. I'm going to use this opportunity to show him what he's missing out on, and just like at the strip club, I'm going to make it impossible for him to deny me.

I smooth my hands over my T-shirt, brushing my fingers over the logo in the center—a black skull wearing a gamer headset. My shirt shows off a sliver of my stomach, which is just enough to tease the man I've got my sights on this evening.

I considered dressing up but decided against it. It doesn't take a short dress to tempt this man, and that's one of the things I like about him. My jeans hug my ass and legs, so if anything, this shows off my figure as much as any skirt.

Wren walks into the bedroom wearing a towel, and she pauses in the doorway, looking at me. "You look hot tonight. Understated... but hot."

"Thanks." I glance over at her. "I thought you were already out there with Reina. But you're not even close to ready for the party."

"I got a little distracted halfway through doing my makeup." She walks over to her closet, dropping the towel when she finds the dress she's looking for. "Chaos came to ask me a question, and then one thing led to another..."

"And you started over?" I smirk. "I thought you were over Chaos because of his stripper obsession?"

"I thought I was. But good lord, that man can do incredible things with his hands." She flutters her eyelashes. "Not to mention his cock."

"I'm pretty sure the Lord wants nothing to do with any of that."

"I wouldn't be so sure. That man can make a girl see heaven." Wren laughs. "What about you? Why are you all dressed up?"

"I'm in jeans and a T-shirt."

Wren's eyebrow hitches. "An itty-bitty T-shirt and very tight, very sexy jeans. Don't think I don't see you, Luna. Let me guess... you're trying to get the attention of one very tall, very tatted biker who is also pretending not to notice a certain purple-haired vixen."

"Fine. So what if I am?" I turn back to the mirror, smoothing my fingers down my shirt. "Wish me luck."

"Like you need it." Wren slips her dress on. "That man can't take his eyes off you. Tonight won't be any different."

I'm counting on it.

Tightening my ponytail a final time, I spin to face Wren. "See you out there."

I leave her to finish up as I step out of our room. The entire clubhouse is thundering with music. Twisted Kings from a number of different chapters are here tonight, so there's barely any room to move around.

The club from Seattle was first to arrive, followed by a group from LA. More must have filtered in since I disappeared to get ready because I can barely move through the clubhouse with all the bodies crammed into it.

The back doors to the clubhouse are open, and Twisted Kings fill every corner, spilling out onto the back patio.

No locals or outsiders are welcome tonight, so the guys are relaxed, cutting loose completely. Some are already wasted, while others talk and catch up.

Patch bunnies from all different chapters circle the room while prospects serve drinks.

The few old ladies who came with their men have their jackets on, showing off their property patches and making it clear they're taken.

Steel is sitting on his usual barstool, with Tempe standing between his legs.

While some old ladies avoid these kinds of parties because they don't want to witness what their men will do in the name of celebration, others show up proudly. Not many of the guys are known for being loyal, but the few who are want to show off their women. Steel is one of them, holding Tempe at his side. I get the impression he would never do anything to break her trust, and neither would she.

Beside Steel, Chaos is downing shots with Reaper, the president of the Reno chapter. I've met him a few times as he's taken trips through Vegas, and his antics make Soul seem tame. When he spots me walking up, he winks. He's got the whole tall-dark-and-handsome thing going for him, but he'll flirt with anything in a skirt, so I've never bothered taking him up on his many offers to celebrate one-on-one.

When I finally get to Tempe, she reaches out to squeeze my hand. Steel isn't going to let her go with everything going on around us, so I don't bother going in for a hug.

"Luna, you're here." Tempe smiles; her voice is pitchy because she's clearly buzzed. "I was just telling Lyla about you."

Tempe motions to a girl standing in front of her, who has the most purple eyes I've ever seen. Her dark hair makes them stand out even more, and they're as bright as her smile. A biker from the LA chapter has his tattooed arm wrapped around her shoulders.

"I like your hair." Lyla smiles, pointing at my purple ponytail.

"Thanks. I like your eyes."

"Purple hair, purple eyes." Tempe laughs. "What a coincidence, right? Lyla, Luna. You guys are practically twins."

We're not even close, but I smile, appreciating seeing Tempe letting loose for once.

"You guys are from LA?"

"Yep." Lyla nods. "Steel's done so much to help the club rebuild after everything that went down there. Blaze wanted to be here himself, but with Candy nine months pregnant, he couldn't risk it. So Sage and I made sure we came to represent."

I'm guessing Blaze is the president, but I've never met him.

Lyla tucks herself closer to Sage's side, and he kisses the top of her head.

I've never wanted to be anyone's old lady because I don't need validation from a man, but as I watch Sage with Lyla and Steel with Tempe, there's a pang of jealousy in my chest.

What's it like to have that kind of companionship?

Someone who cares about you enough to want to tell the world you belong to them—that they'd do anything to keep you.

Sage tips Lyla's chin up, pulling her attention. "I promised Chaos we'd do shots. Ready, butterfly?"

"Of course." She smiles before turning back to me and Tempe. "I'll catch up with you later."

Sage and Lyla disappear, and I slip onto an empty stool as I watch them walk over to Chaos, who is taking another shot.

"I give him an hour before he's too drunk to walk."

Steel laughs. "I doubt he'll last that long. He started drinking at one, and his tolerance is shit since he got out of prison. Speaking of, I better join them while Chaos is still responsive."

"You coming, Luna?" Tempe asks as Steel snags her hand.

"I'm good. I'm going to get a drink, but I'll find you later."

She smiles, disappearing into the crowd, and I know that's probably the last I'll talk to her tonight.

I've made my appearance.

I've put on my show.

Soon, everyone here will be too wasted to know what's up and what's down, and they won't be worried about what I'm doing.

I'm on a mission, and nothing is distracting me from that tonight.

Ghost steps into the room, and for a man who stays in the shadows, his presence is deafening. He stands in the doorway between the main bar and the hallway that leads to the ranked members' rooms. His height has him towering over almost everyone here, giving me a clear view of him above everyone else.

As if he senses me, his eyes find mine across the room, and a shiver runs the length of my spine.

He holds my gaze for a moment, and I wonder if I'm imagining the silent challenge in them. But the second I blink, he looks away, moving through the crowd to meet up with the rest of the Vegas Twisted Kings, who are taking a shot and cheering to Chaos's freedom.

Ghost doesn't usually drink, but given the circumstances, he downs one. The room erupts, and it's so loud that they drown out whatever speech Steel is giving.

It's parties like this that scare most people away from club life, but to me, it's home.

My life has never been quiet or comforting. Between the revolving door of foster families and the constant uncertainty that brought, I've experienced more loneliness than stability in my life. And I've seen more bad than good.

But here, in the eye of this Twisted Kings storm, I belong. I've found people who don't judge me. People who make me feel like I can be whoever I want.

Unapologetically.

Spinning around on my barstool, I face the bar, and Venom is already sliding a drink across it for me. It's a gin and tonic—my favorite.

Usually, this is when he would flirt or ask me to meet up with him later, but instead, he continues down the bar. He must have noticed something between me and Ghost at Sapphire Rise because he's been quieter since then.

Glancing over my shoulder, I find Ghost through the crowd. His back is to me, and even that is breathtaking. His broad shoulders are strong, and his tattooed arms are on display in his tight T-shirt and Twisted Kings cut.

I think about how Tempe and Lyla are walking around with their men's names on their backs tonight. I never wanted that, so why do I feel bare all of a sudden?

"Hiding from me?"

I look over to see Reaper walking up with a smile. He stops between me and Ghost, and I spin on the barstool to face him.

"If I am, I didn't do that great of a job, did I?"

"Guess not." He plants his hand on the bar, caging me in.

Last time he was in town, I made the mistake of kissing him, and when he looks me over, I'm pretty sure this time he's after more.

"You're looking lovely as always." Reaper's blue eyes scan my outfit. "Are you gonna finally let me get you that drink this time?"

"Already got one, sorry." I tip my glass up.

"Something else, maybe?"

I could say yes.

If Ghost refuses to claim me, I'm free to do whatever I want. But as I look past Reaper and see Ghost staring at me over his shoulder, I know there's no point pretending. There's only one man who has my attention, and I'm going all in, even if all he does is break my heart.

"Not this time, sorry." I fake a frown.

"Oh shit." Reaper follows my gaze to Ghost. "It's always the quiet ones. Guess I missed my chance."

The truth is, he never had one. If I'm honest with myself, I've been Ghost's from the beginning.

17

Ghost

"I don't think Steel would appreciate you starting a war with one of our brothers over her." Legacy grabs my shoulder, giving it a shake.

He looks at my hand, and I follow his gaze, realizing I pulled a switchblade out of my pocket at some point, and I'm messing with it.

My fingers itch to shove the point through Reaper's temple for touching Luna's arm, but I know Legacy is right.

Flipping it closed, I tuck it back in my pocket. "I'm good."

Legacy hands me another shot, and we clink glasses before draining them. The whiskey slides down my throat, and I try to relax.

I don't usually drink at parties like this, but with everything going on with Luna, I need to get out of my head. At least the clubhouse is locked down for anyone who isn't a

Twisted King. The perimeter is crawling with prospects, and there's nothing that will get past a sensor without setting off all our alarms.

Legacy takes my empty glass, handing it to one of the prospects walking by. He hasn't been partying with us as frequently since his nanny's been in and out of the hospital with health issues, but Steel's grandma, Pearl, is watching Bea and Austin tonight because he can't miss a mixer.

It's important the entire club is here in a show of support for one of our brothers. Chaos was willing to sacrifice the rest of his life for us. We owe him our thanks, and after he helped me last night, I owe him my life for helping protect Luna.

"I heard you and Luna had some alone time at the club last night." Legacy takes a sip of his drink. "Care to elaborate?"

I look over to see Chaos and Soul taking another shot. "When are the two of them not running their fucking mouths?"

Legacy laughs. "Never."

I should have known better than to think a stripper was enough to distract Chaos from noticing what I was up to last night. He might party harder than most of the guys here, but he doesn't miss a thing.

"Luna was just helping me check for blind spots in the VIP hall," I lie. "I finally figured out how the Iron Sinners got the drop on us in our own club. They were sending prospects in without their cuts and adjusting the cameras to mirror so we couldn't see anything."

"They're fucking with our shit in our own damn club? I swear I'm going to enjoy watching the life drain from their eyes the second we get our hands on them." Legacy shakes his head. "But also, don't think I'm falling for your diversion tactics. Cameras, Ghost, really? Just go talk to her, brother. I don't need a lecture on all your tech shit. Just admit you like the girl already. Unless..."

He looks up, and I follow his gaze to where Reaper is still talking to Luna. He's taken a step back, but I still don't like how he's smiling at her.

"I'm sure the girl won't be lonely if you decide to chicken out."

"Shut the fuck up." I drag my hand through my hair.

"I'm just fucking with you." He grabs my shoulder. "But I'm serious. I've watched you let life pass by for five years without doing shit about it. You deserve something good."

"You're one to talk."

"This isn't about me, and it's not the same. I've got Bea, and that's all the good I need right now. I'm gonna give that little girl the life you and I both deserved growing up. And I'm not bringing anyone else in that could fuck that up for her."

"I know." I sigh, feeling guilty about even bringing it up when I know my brother does everything he can to give his daughter the world. "But I've got the two of you. Maybe I don't need shit else either."

"You do." Legacy looks over at Luna. "And we both know what that is. It's okay to let someone in, Ghost."

"So she can end up dead?" I grit my teeth. "I'm not risking that with her."

"She's in danger with or without you. You know that."

"She doesn't need me to make it worse. Them taking her is one thing, but her ending up—" I cut myself off.

I can't say it. I can't even think it.

"Her ending up like Paulina?" Legacy finishes my sentence anyway. "I know that's what this is about, and I can tell you a hundred more times that wasn't your fault if you need to hear it, but you're not going to believe it until you see that for yourself."

"They were sending me a message. It *is* my fault."

"They were sending all of us a message. Because that's what they fucking do. You tried to warn her, and she didn't listen. She was too busy with that asshole boyfriend and not seeing past his shit."

"It's not her fault."

Legacy frowns, dipping his thumbs in his pockets. "You're right, just like it's not yours. This is on the Iron Sinners, no one else. Paulina paid for things we were too young and naïve to know how to deal with at the time. But things have changed. *We've* changed. That shit's not happening again. You know I'm right, Marcus."

It's rare we call each other by our legal names, especially in the clubhouse. But that's how I know he's serious.

Legacy cares. If anyone's a brother to me, it's him.

"Maybe." I look over at him. "But I can't unlearn that lesson after what they did to her. Paulina might have been fucking the wrong guy, but it was me being her friend that made them do what they did. And I can't risk that happening with Luna."

"Whether you like it or not, she's already in that kind of trouble." He squeezes my shoulder. "People aren't as oblivious as you seem to think. If we know how you feel about her, you better believe the Iron Sinners do too. Why else would they send *you* that text? The second you brought her back from Albuquerque, you showed your hand. She's tied to you whether you want her to be or not. There's no point trying to fight it now."

"I don't deserve that girl."

"Maybe she doesn't deserve you. Have you ever thought about it like that?"

I hitch an eyebrow, and Legacy laughs.

"Just saying, at this point, you don't have much else to lose."

"Legacy," Chaos shouts from across the bar, nearly falling off his barstool.

Two young club girls stand on either side, and I don't recognize them, so they must be from one of the other clubs. He points to the blonde, knowing she's Legacy's type.

"Go. Have fun."

Legacy grins, starting toward the bar and yelling at me over his shoulder, "You too, brother."

He disappears, and I head over to Luna, even though I shouldn't. She hasn't taken her eyes off me since I stepped into the room, and I'm consumed by her attention.

Reaper spots me coming and dips away to have a drink with Havoc, telling me he's still pissed at me for giving him a black eye the last time he was in town. I never told him it was because he put his lips on Luna, but if he wasn't one of Steel's closest friends, I would have done much worse.

"Making friends?" I stop in front of her.

"You know me." She smiles, but there's a challenge behind it.

She wants me to notice.

She wants me to do something about it.

Luna is a magnet for attention. And it's not just because she's beautiful. She's a force like the sun. It's impossible not to gravitate around her. She makes a damned man feel like his soul is worth saving, and in a club full of bikers who sacrificed theirs for their patch, we're drawn to that kind of purity.

"I got the video you sent me." She tries to maintain a stoic expression as she says it, but a blush crawls her cheeks.

"Figured I might not be the only one who wanted to remember it."

"You were right."

I know. Because I know her.

She's dirty and perfect, and if I was the man I was five years ago, I'd be tempted to show her just how much I love that about her.

"Speaking of..." She drains the rest of her drink, setting the empty glass on the bar. "I could use a repeat performance."

"We ca—"

"I know." She rolls her eyes. "We can't. It's dangerous. You don't want me."

"Never said that last part."

A smirk ticks in the corner of her mouth. "No, you didn't, did you?"

"Luna..."

"It's fine, really." She slides off the barstool, stepping close. "If you're going to be a jerk, maybe I'll just find other company tonight."

I stop her before she gets the chance to slip away, snaking a hand around her waist and pulling her back to my chest. My other hand tangles in her ponytail as I tip her head back to force her to look up at me.

"You're not doing that," I warn her.

Just because I can't claim her doesn't mean her body isn't mine now. I've waited over a year to touch her, and now that I have, I'll be damned if anyone else gets to.

"Want to bet?" Luna wets her lips, tempting me. "I know you want me, Marcus, no matter how much you try to fight it. If it makes you feel better to lie to yourself and say you don't, that's fine. You can try to keep your distance. The question is, how long are you going to be able to sit back and watch before you just can't help yourself?"

"What are you talking about?"

"You'll see." Luna smiles, but it's not sweet.

It's wicked.

Pure sin.

And I have no choice but to let her go, watching her disappear through the crowd before I'm tempted to bend her over and fuck the defiance out of her right here.

I'm still staring off into space, thinking about what she said, when my phone pings. I pull it out of my pocket, expecting movement on the perimeter. But instead, it's a text.

When I open it, I'm met with a picture of Luna lying back on the bed. She's still wearing her skintight white gamer T-shirt, but she's ditched the jeans, and her knees are tipped open with just her hand covering her perfect pussy.

Luna: Since you like to watch…

And that's when I realize it's not her bed she's lying on. It's mine.

18

Luna

Ghost wouldn't take his eyes off me the whole time Reaper was talking to me, and it was the confirmation I needed that I was doing the right thing tonight. He might have been trying to resist, but the second Reaper touched my arm, Ghost pulled out his knife and held it at his side.

He knows I'm his; he just needs the okay to act on it.

After all, his mind might resist, but his body wants me. I felt the proof when he stopped me from storming away. His thick muscles tensed, and his hard cock pressed against my ass as I taunted him. He's aching to put me in my place, and I want him to do it.

Which is why, the moment he let me go, I knew what needed to be done.

I cut through the clubhouse, beelining to Ghost's bedroom. Once inside, I stripped off my jeans and lay on his bed. He might have been able to deny me at the strip club, but it will take more than patience to refuse me here.

Setting up my phone on the nightstand, I spread my knees and sent him a photo that was just enough of a tease to lure him in.

The trap is set. The only question is, what beast am I begging to the surface?

Just because Ghost is reclusive doesn't mean I haven't sensed his dominance. If let off his leash, there's a monster waiting to come out.

I'm begging for it.

Desperate for it.

I want to feel those claws ripping me open.

My fingers graze over the comforter while I wait. It's soft and freshly cleaned. His pillows are like clouds, and his room is spotless. It's exactly what I'd expect from a man who is precise and controlling over every little detail.

While the rest of the clubhouse reeks of stale cigarette smoke, Ghost's room smells like leather and wood polish. And when I bury my nose in his pillows, they smell like him.

After I send the text, it doesn't take more than a minute for Ghost to step into the room.

His jaw clenches at the sight of me on his bed, but instead of kicking me out, he shuts the door behind him, resting his back against the wood as he locks it.

His tattooed forearms flex when his hand tightens on the handle.

"You got my text?" I scoot back, stretching out my bare legs to tease him.

"How did you get in here, Luna?"

"You mean because the door was locked?" I bite my lower lip. "Tempe's been teaching me a few things."

"Like breaking and entering?"

"Maybe."

Ghost narrows his gaze, finally lifting off the doorframe. Every step he takes toward the bed makes my body throb as a weight settles in my core with my anticipation.

When he finally reaches the bed, he grabs my calves with his large hands and pulls me down to the bottom. He leans over me and grips my jaw, tipping my face to his. Any gentleness is gone, and I'm faced with the beast he hides in his silence.

My legs rest on either side of his, and I hold the comforter, trying to stay strong.

"Why do you keep pushing this?" His fingers dig into my cheeks. "Why can't you let this go?"

"Because you don't scare me, Ghost."

"I should."

"Well, you don't. What are you so afraid of?"

"People around me end up hurt."

"Like whoever the girl was before me?"

His expression cools. "Something like that."

I figured. The only reason Ghost would have sworn off women is because one broke his heart or got hurt because of him. He's a biker. That's how this world is.

Swallowing my jealousy at the thought of him loving anyone else, I refuse to break his stare. "Then don't let that happen."

His cool eyes ignite like the pit of the hottest fire. Blue to the core and burning me from the inside out. His jaw clenches as a smirk cracks his cold expression, and the faintest glimmer of amusement paints his face.

"You're such a fucking brat, Luna. Striking matches and not thinking about what you might end up burning down."

"What are you going to do about it?"

His lips brush mine—a breath away. I wait for him to pull back and disappoint me again. My heart races to try and catch up before he does. But right as he shifts back, I grab his wrist, and it shatters his resistance.

Ghost's lips meet mine in a brutal kiss. The full force of his irritation floods out. Anger that I won't let this go. Frustration that he can't hold back. He punishes me with his kiss as the stubble on his jaw roughly rubs my skin.

But I don't pull away. I grab his face and kiss him deeper.

He tips my head back, holding my jaw and claiming me. His fingers pinch my cheeks, forcing my mouth open, and his tongue tastes like whiskey. His kiss deepens, and it turns into something more intimate.

"Fuck, Luna," he mumbles against my mouth as he pulls back, brushing his lips over mine. "What are you doing to me?"

I drag my hands down the sides of his neck, sliding my fingers over his cut as I trail lower. But just as my palm grazes the large bulge growing behind his zipper, he snatches my wrist and stops me.

I wait for him to pull my hand away, but he doesn't. He holds my palm over him, pressing it to his thickening cock.

"How long has it been, Marcus?" I rub my palm over his length.

A growl vibrates in his chest. "Five years. Give or take."

"Are you really going to keep that countdown ticking forever?" I tighten my hold over him, aching to feel him inside me. "Or am I worth breaking that streak for?"

His gaze softens as he looks down at me. "Worth it?"

"Or, you know—" I stutter, suddenly nervous that was the wrong choice of words because what if I'm not?

Up until now, everyone in my life has considered me disposable. Using me for my worth and then throwing me out. I don't know if I can handle Ghost feeling that way about me.

He dips down for a kiss. It's gentler this time, even if it's somehow even more intense. And when he pulls back, he stares deep into my eyes.

"You're worth more than you can comprehend, Luna. More than a man like me is owed in twenty lifetimes. You're worth bargaining my own damn soul."

Warmth floods my chest with his words. Tears sting my eyes, but I manage to hold them back. I think I've loved this man as long as I've known him, but to hear him say that makes everything swell to the surface.

"Then stop holding back, Marcus. I need you." I try to reach for a kiss, but he resists me. "I know you've kept your distance, and I respect your reasons for it. But I can't keep doing this. My whole life, things have been fleeting. I can't be just another person's temporary landing place."

Pressing my lips together, I wish I'd kept that to myself. But Ghost brings out every insecurity. He reveals every truth. Which is what that is—if he can't give me more, I can't keep trying forever.

"Fuck me." It's nearly a whisper. "Don't you want to?"

"Want to?" He releases my jaw, dragging his hand to my throat and pinning my back to the bed. "You don't understand, Luna, and that's the whole fucking problem. Wanting to fuck you doesn't even begin to describe what I want from you."

Ghost keeps one hand on my throat, using the other to reach between my legs. He pulls my panties to the side, slowly dragging his knuckles over my pussy. His touch is barely a whisper when I'm desperate for the pressure that will bring me my release. He skates his thumb up and down my wet core, teasing a moan from my lips, and only then does he sink two fingers in.

"Want you?" He brushes his mouth over mine with the gentlest graze that has my nerves prickling. "I want you so bad there's no getting enough of you. If you give me one taste, I'll swallow you whole. I have control over most things in my life, but needing you—craving you—isn't one of them. You like to run, but if you give yourself to me, I can't let you. I'll hold you so tight you can't fucking breathe. *That's* what you make me want. You hand yourself over, there's no going back."

His confession should terrify me because it's a threat as much as it's a promise. And he probably expects it to scare me away, but instead, I tip my knees open, hoping he means what he said.

"If you want me, then do something about it."

"Fuck." Ghost releases my neck and grabs my thighs, widening them as he dives between them.

His tongue skates in a circle over my clit, teasing me before he fucks me with it. I grip the comforter overhead, trying to hold on. But his warmth, paired with the rough scratch of the stubble on his jaw, makes my hips buck. For a man who's spent five years refusing to touch a woman, he kisses me between the legs like he's after a reward.

Ghost hums against my pussy as he drives two fingers in, and when he sucks on my clit, my fingers fly into his hair. He moves from sweet to rough. From slow to intense. Ghost watches me as he drags his tongue up my pussy, and I ache with the need for him to give me something to grip.

"Take off your shirt," he commands.

I do as he says, stripping off my shirt and bra while he rips my underwear down my legs.

I'm completely exposed. And while I've imagined this, nothing compares to him standing over me, stripping his cut off his thick shoulders. He drapes it on the back of a chair before grabbing the back of his T-shirt and tugging it off in one swoop. The planes of his tattooed chest ripple with the moonlight shining through the window, and every inked inch of muscle is bare to me. His tattooed fingers slip to his jeans, and he strokes his cock, watching me wiggle in desperation.

His eyes are like cameras taking me in and recording every second.

Hearing every breath.

Memorializing this moment.

"You're beautiful." He strokes up his cock as he shoves his jeans down. "Scoot back. I want your cum on my sheets and your sweat soaking my pillow by the time I'm done with you."

I plant my hands at my sides and scoot backward, watching Ghost stalk me with his gaze as he strips off his pants. His body is a towering statue that I can't take my eyes off of, but when my gaze drops to his thick cock, I swallow, absorbing his size.

It's going to be a lot more to take than his large fingers.

"Worried about what you see?" He strokes his cock slowly, catching me staring.

"No." It comes out pitched as I shake my head.

"You are." He climbs onto the bed and lowers his mouth by my ear. "But you're going to take every inch, aren't you, Luna?"

Ghost drags his cock over my pussy, and I squirm at the feel of him. He toys with my clit, but when I lift my hips and seek him out, he pulls his cock away and moves down to fuck me with his tongue.

"Just because you have a greedy little cunt"—he licks my pussy—"doesn't mean you're ready to take me yet. We need to warm you up first. Don't you agree?"

He shoves three fingers inside me this time, and I tilt my head back as a scream escapes. His tongue flicks back and forth over my clit, and my vision darkens. The waves inside me are cresting, but he doesn't relent. He thrashes his tongue, dragging my climax out like he's setting off a bomb. My ears ring as I come, and a tear slips down my cheek.

The intensity is almost more than I can handle.

"Fuck you taste so good." Ghost kneels between my legs, stroking his cock as he continues to toy with my pussy.

He drags his thumb through my excitement, then lifts it to his lips and sucks it into his mouth.

"So good." He strokes his cock. "You might as well be my greatest sin."

"Then take me to hell with you."

Ghost smirks, grabbing my hips and flipping my body around so I'm face down on the bed. He tugs my ass in the air, lining himself up.

"Remember what I said, Luna. You brought this on yourself. Now show me why this pussy is where every inch of me belongs."

Ghost grabs my ass, positioning his cock at my center, and when he thrusts forward, the room darkens. The stretch is so intense that I open my mouth, but what comes out is silence. His thick cock brings me to my limits.

"Good girl." He caresses down the backs of my thighs, slowly rocking. "Halfway there."

19

Ghost

Luna's head jerks as she looks over her shoulder at me. "Halfway?"

Those wide blue eyes make me wish I hadn't turned her around. I'd like to see just how big they can get when she finally takes all of me.

"Mm-hmm." I rock again, looking down at her body wrapped around my cock.

I really should have brought a camera so I could take a picture, but I'll have to save that for next time.

I'll record it.

Memorialize it.

She stretches to take more of me, and it's the most beautiful thing I've ever seen. Her determination. Her body accepting me.

She drips as I start to back out, and her excitement glistens on my length. Rocking my hips forward, I go an inch deeper this time.

"Holy shit." She grabs the blanket, burying her face into it.

I'm a lot to take, and she's so fucking tight I might blow my load before I'm fully seated. But I resist the urge because I need to feel her come on my cock first.

Grabbing the globes of her ass, I slowly work in and out, shifting deeper with each thrust and appreciating how she starts to move with me. Until my hips meet her body. My balls slap against her pussy, and I bottom out.

Fuck, she's stunning.

She glances over her shoulder with hazy eyes and a sheen of sweat on her forehead. Her body rocks with pain and pleasure. I warned her not to let me do this, but she didn't listen. She didn't believe me when I said that if she handed herself to me, I'd take it all.

Now she's mine.

I've spent years becoming desensitized, numb, and withdrawn.

Luna crashed through every barrier.

An angel like her doesn't belong in hell, but if that's where I'm headed, I just might have to take her with me now.

Luna rocks her hips when I pause deep inside her, and I let go of her ass to watch her chase her pleasure.

"That's it, beautiful. Fuck my cock. Let me see you work for my cum."

She moans, resting forward on her elbows as she slides off my cock almost all the way to the head before she sinks back again, taking me. Each time, she takes me deeper. Her moans get louder, and her pace quickens. She's chasing her release and using me to do it.

I steady my breath and try not to think about it because she feels so fucking warm and wet and good. And it's been so long that the sight of her is enough to get me off, but the feel of her nearly vaporizes me.

Reaching around, I toy with her clit as she continues to rock. I need her to come again before I do. And with how she's moaning from her hands and knees, I'm not going to make it long.

Wrapping one hand around her ponytail, I reclaim control, fucking her with hard, deep thrusts. I can't help it. I need to make this girl see stars until she realizes I'm the only one who can open her mind to that part of the universe.

"Marcus," she screams when I strike her deep and fast.

I don't let up. I can't anymore. Her body is my land to stake—to claim. She asked for this, and she needs to know why she shouldn't have done that.

We'll either heal each other or destroy each other. I'd be fine with either at this point.

Tugging her ponytail, I force her back to arch. It tilts her hips so I can fuck her at a different angle. Her slick pussy tightens, gripping my cock so hard I'm grunting through the pain. I can barely handle her pleasure.

Luna screams as she comes. Her body convulses, and I feel every squeeze.

Pulling out, I flip her over and sink back in because I need to see her wide eyes filling with pleasure and fear as

I drive as deep as I can. Her tits bounce with every hard thrust.

She pants against my mouth when I kiss her lips, and I wrap my hand around her throat, where it belongs.

Balancing on one forearm, I fuck her with everything I've needed since I laid eyes on her. She chokes for air between kisses, taking me perfectly. Her body is slick with sweat, and her eyes are hazy as I bottom out inside her again and again, but she takes it all.

This girl was meant to be mine. I knew it the first time I looked into her eyes.

Her legs wrap around my hips, and her nails claw at my chest.

It's been too long, and she feels too good to last right now. She reaches one hand down and cups my balls, and I come so hard my insides feel like they're caving in. I piston my hips and empty myself into her, not bothering to pull out.

I'll deal with the consequences later.

She might be on birth control, or she might not. I'm not sure I care.

Resting on my forearms, I settle between her thighs, catching my breath. Maybe I can just live like this. Feeling her wet cunt on my cock. Stretching her until she's molded to take me and only me ever again.

"That was..." Her blue eyes blink up at me, and a tear slips down her cheek. "Sorry, I'm not sad."

"You don't have to be sorry." I wipe the tear away, licking it from the pad of my thumb because I need to know what every part of her tastes like.

Her pain.

Her pleasure.

Luna Cassidy.

"That was intense." She lets out a sigh. "You're larger than I expected."

"I'll take that as a compliment."

She smiles. "It was."

"You take me so well." I brush the side of her cheek. "You're perfect."

Her pussy clamps my cock with the compliment, and blood starts rushing downward again. I love that my words draw that reaction out of her, but if I don't pull out, I'll start fucking her, and she's probably already too sore for that.

Flipping off her, I land with my back on the bed beside her, staring up at the ceiling.

She's quiet for a moment, and I wonder what she's thinking. The longer she goes without saying anything, I get this sinking feeling that what we did is wrong, even if I can't find it in myself to regret it.

"Should I go now?" she says finally, looking over at me.

I roll onto my side, facing her. "Why would you go?"

Her gaze moves to the door. "To give you space. Or to shower."

"You want to shower?"

She shrugs. "I know how the guys are—"

"I swear, Luna, if you're about to compare this to how those assholes are with patch bunnies, I don't want to hear it."

Her lips purse, and I can see her trying to bury a smile. "Why?"

"You know why." I hop off the bed, grabbing her legs and pulling her down it.

Lifting her up, I toss her over my shoulder and smack her on the ass.

"Ghost!" she shrieks, and it's adorable.

"You want a shower; you can have one in my bathroom." I carry her into the bathroom and set her back on her feet to turn on the water. "But I'm joining you."

When the water warms, we step into the shower. The stall doors are foggy, and Luna steps under the water first. It runs rivers over her body, dripping from the peaks of her nipples.

"You're staring." She smiles up at me.

"I am." I grab her by the waist and pull her in for a kiss because I can't help needing to taste her. "I might have to install cameras in my room just so I can stare at you from every angle while I fuck you next time."

I probably shouldn't have said that out loud. It's a bit twisted. But when her eyes light as she smiles up at me, I love that she's excited by the prospect of it.

"Only if you let me watch it with you."

"Deal." I kiss her on her forehead, and we rotate so I can stand in the water.

She grabs the bar of soap and starts washing her body, but it doesn't take me long before I'm stealing it and taking over.

I'm going to memorize every inch of her skin now that she's given me access. I draw my rough hands over every curve and see how beautiful she is when suds cover them.

Her hair is a darker shade of purple when it's wet, and I wonder what she looks like when it's her natural blonde. I want to see every version of her. I want to get to know them all.

When I'm done washing her body, I move to my own, taking my time.

I'm in no rush when I have a view of Luna, wet in my shower.

Turning to rinse myself off, I wince when the stream of water strikes the still-healing skin where the club branded me for lying to them.

"What is that?" Luna steps back to get a look.

She didn't see it in my room because it was dark, and she was distracted. But there's no hiding the wound from her under the harsh fluorescent lights in the bathroom.

"Nothing you need to worry about." I grab her hand as she reaches for it, kissing the back of it.

Her pinched eyebrows tell me she doesn't believe me, but she drops it either way. Luna has been around the clubhouse long enough to know how it works, and even if I don't like lying to her, there are things I won't be able to tell her, no matter what she is to me.

"Come here." I spin her around and grab the shampoo.

I work it over her scalp until it's bubbly, burying my fingers in the strands and washing it for her. Her shoulders relax as I work her scalp, and I notice a small scar on the back of her shoulder blade. I thought over this past year,

I'd learned everything there was to know, but clearly, I've missed things.

"It smells like you," she says, tipping her head back as I dig the suds into her scalp.

"Sorry, I don't have any flowery shit in here."

"Or conditioner," she points out.

I hum because she's right. I don't need conditioner or body wash when a bottle of shampoo and a bar of soap does the trick. It's been so long since I've even been with a woman; I forgot they prefer all that.

"I can get some."

She looks up over her shoulder. "For me?"

"Obviously." I chuckle, rinsing her hair. "Who else would I be fucking in the shower?"

"And here I thought this was innocent." She teases her bare ass against my cock, which is rock hard because the sight of her is all it takes to get my blood pumping.

"Careful, beautiful. If you keep that up, you're really going to be hurting tomorrow." I grab her hips as she pushes her wet ass against me. "A man only has so much patience."

"And here I thought you were unbreakable." She bites her lower lip, smiling. "But you're right, I am sore."

"Here." I turn her around and move her to sit on the little ledge in the shower.

Kneeling down, I spread her knees and groan at the sight of her puffy pussy. She's definitely going to hurt tomorrow, and I love it. But for now, I just want to make her feel good.

"What are you doing?" she asks as I slowly start to kiss from her knee up the inside of her thigh.

"Kissing you better."

Her mouth opens like she's about to argue, but I cut her off with my tongue on her clit. I kiss her nice and slow. I take my time until she's coming on my tongue. Because all I want to do for the rest of my life is make this girl feel good while protecting her from the inevitable.

20

Ghost

BEA RUNS FOR THE soccer ball in pink cowgirl boots and a tutu over leggings. Her outfit isn't made for playing soccer, but she doesn't care. She runs around the yard, kicking the ball. And when she loses control and her little legs don't get her there fast enough, she has to dive for it.

If the grass were real and not turf, her clothes would be covered in stains. It's lucky for Legacy we live in the Vegas desert, where water is scarce and the heat is blistering, because it saves him from having to buy her new clothes every week.

When she finally gets the soccer ball into the net, she spins around and smiles. "I got it, Uncle Marcus."

"Good job, Honey Bea."

She's as sweet as her nickname and always buzzing around.

Being an uncle suits me. We watch princess movies, put puzzles together, and build things. I get to spend time with her without having to worry about balancing the responsibility of being a parent with being a member of an MC. I don't know how Legacy does it. Most of the time, he makes it look easy, but since Margaret, his nanny, started getting sick, I can tell it's weighing on him.

Legacy steps through the glass sliding door at the back of his house, waving a water bottle in the air. "Beatrice, come drink some water. It's hot out here, and you're going to get dehydrated."

I can't help but chuckle at him, even though he's just looking out for his daughter. Compared to the cocky playboy he is at the clubhouse, he's the opposite at home. Sometimes, it still catches me off guard when he's domestic.

Bea runs across the yard, jumping into his arms and giving him a big hug. He kisses the top of her head as he sets her down, and she takes the water bottle.

"Tempe will be here in just a few minutes."

"Will you be back before bedtime?" Bea digs her toe into the turf.

"If I can."

She frowns, knowing that unless he says he will, it's probably a no. Legacy would rather disappoint her now than give her false hope like his dad always did.

King, Legacy's father, was revered by the club. He's remembered for his loyalty, from his patching-in ceremony to the day he took three bullets to the chest protecting one of his brothers. But he was a better Twisted King than he ever was a father. He didn't spend much time with his family, and he was more focused on forcing Legacy to follow in his footsteps than raising him. It's a wrong Legacy is determined to right with his daughter.

"You okay watching her for a few more minutes?" Legacy asks me as Bea runs to meet me at the lawn chairs.

She drops into the one at my side.

"We're good. Finish what you need to."

He's been on the phone with the hospital half the morning, getting everything situated for Margaret to return home. She'll need a nurse to stop by daily, and there are special instructions for her medications.

Still, Legacy's going through all the trouble of taking care of her, just like she's helped take care of Bea. When Legacy unexpectedly became a father, he didn't know what he was doing. And as a member of the Twisted Kings, he didn't trust anyone to help him.

The only reason he finally caved and let Margaret help was because she was good friends with Jameson's grandma, Pearl.

Margaret moved in with Legacy when Bea was two months old, and she's here whenever he can't be. She cares for both of them and, amidst her medical struggles, I'm starting to see just how close Legacy is with her.

He's paying all her medical bills, and he moved her into a room downstairs to make it easier for her. If she doesn't get better, I don't know what my brother is going to do. He doesn't trust people, especially with his daughter.

Legacy disappears back into the house while Bea takes a drink of her water. She taps the toes of her pink cowgirl boots together, never sitting still.

It's a warm day, but we're in the shade of the house, so it's bearable.

Bea swishes her feet back and forth, watching the gate to the side yard.

"Waiting for Austin?"

She nods, smiling big. "We're playing super spies. He's got a new spy tracker, and he said I can use it if I'm careful."

"That so?" I chuckle, knowing she's probably talking about the broken old phone I gave Austin.

He was convinced it could be used to track bad guys, and I figured there was no harm in letting him have fun since it doesn't work anymore.

I'm not sure why kids gravitate toward me when most adults avoid me, but since Austin moved onto the compound, I've noticed it is becoming a trend. Bea and Austin constantly follow me around, and whenever they're at the clubhouse, they sneak into my office because they want to mess with all the buttons.

They don't know it yet, but I've been working on a laptop for them. I'm writing a fake crime-fighting program that they can mess around with. I figure the kids can put it to good use when they play in their new mini clubhouse.

The kids.

I remember when that's what we were.

Punk teenagers getting into trouble and pissing off our parents because we had nothing better to do. We thought we understood the club back then, but all we really saw was the abundance, drugs, guns, and women. We didn't understand the responsibility we'd eventually be faced with when we took those seats in church.

We didn't see the real danger of people relying on us when we operate outside the law.

Glancing down at Bea, I remember looking up to Legacy's dad and his friends like she looks at us now. Like we're good. Like we're protecting something.

I suppose we are, even if it doesn't make us heroes.

The sins I'd commit to protect Beatrice King would send me straight to hell. And the same thing goes for Luna.

"Do you think my daddy's ever gonna fall in love again, Uncle Marcus?" Bea stares at the glass sliding door.

Legacy is standing on the other side on his phone. He pinches the bridge of his nose, clearly stressed.

"I'm pretty sure he has all the love he needs right here." I tickle her side, and she giggles.

"I mean, like he loved Mommy." Her laugh fades.

She's too young to understand Legacy never loved her mom. They barely even knew each other before Sera got knocked up and disappeared. When she came back, it was long enough to let Legacy know he had a kid and that she wanted nothing to do with either of them.

That was that.

He didn't love Sera, and Sera didn't love anything but pills and booze.

If anyone finds happiness and love, I hope it's my brother. He's a good guy beneath the cut, and he deserves it.

I lean back in my chair, watching Legacy disappear deeper into the house. "Someday, probably."

Bea turns to me. "Are you lying, Uncle Marcus? Daddy says it's always better to tell the truth, even if someone isn't going to like it."

"He told you that, huh?"

Bea nods sharply, crossing her arms over her chest. "Except he didn't like when I said I was the one who got the paints on the carpet, and I didn't lie."

"Well, paint can be tough to get out."

"Yeah." She frowns.

"In that case, I don't know. Maybe your dad will love someone, and maybe he won't. But do you want to know a secret?"

Bea nods, and I lean closer to whisper.

"No matter what happens, you're the only love he needs in the world. I mean it."

A smile lights her face, and she grabs my arm, hugging it. "I love you, Uncle Marcus."

"Love you too, Honey Bea." I kiss the top of her head, brushing my hand over the back of her blonde hair.

"Just in case Daddy doesn't love anyone, can I throw the flowers when you and Auntie Luna get married?"

"Who said I'm getting married?"

"Daddy." She nods sharply. "He said you two are silly but that you love Luna a whole lot."

"He did, huh?"

"Yes."

I shake my head because, of course, he did. "Sorry to break it to you, sweetheart, but your daddy doesn't know everything."

"Daddy's the smartest. He knows. If Daddy says you're going to marry her, he means it. And I can tell you crush her, Uncle Marcus."

"I crush her?"

"That's what it means when you like someone. You crush them." She tips her chin up proudly. "You crush Auntie Luna."

As if she's been summoned, the back gate swings open, and Austin runs through it, with Tempe and Luna following behind him. Luckily, it's a good distraction, and Bea bails the second she sees Austin to go play with him.

But I sit back, watching Luna and Tempe walk across the yard, hearing Bea's words like they're on repeat in my head.

You crush Auntie Luna.

I do.

It's a fucking problem, and there's no fixing it.

Tempe leans closer to Luna to whisper something that they both giggle at. Their eyes are set on me, and I'm pretty sure it's only a matter of time before the whole clubhouse finds out what we did.

"Hey, Ghost." Tempe gives me a devious smile as she stops at the chairs. "Where's Legacy?"

"Inside on the phone."

She nods, turning to Luna. "I'm gonna let him know I'm here, then we can grab the kids and go."

Tempe disappears into the house, and Luna drops into the chair Bea was sitting in.

"Are you leaving with Legacy tonight?" she asks, her gaze fixed on the kids running around the yard.

"Yep."

"Be safe."

"Always am."

Except tonight feels different. Usually, when I'm out on a run, all I'm worried about are the men at my side. Protecting them is my sole focus and all that matters. Now, when I look at Luna, knowing she'll be here without me, I can't help wishing I could split myself in two. If anything happens at the club while I'm gone, I won't be there.

"You and Tempe were awfully giddy a few minutes ago. Anything I should know?"

Luna bites her lip, glancing at me. Her purple hair is down and curled at her shoulders, and her tank top shows off her perfect skin.

"We were just talking." Worry flashes in her eyes. "I swear she won't tell anyone about us."

I reach out, grabbing Luna's hand and pulling it onto my lap. "I'm not asking because I'm ashamed, Luna. Just curious."

"Oh. Okay." Her eyebrows pinch.

"What?"

"It's just, I know you don't date people. Or... do anything like what we did."

I can't help but chuckle at her innocence when I know just how dirty and straightforward she can be in other situations.

"So?"

"So, I guess I thought that would mean you'd rather keep this quiet so the guys don't bug you."

"They're dicks. They'll bug me either way." I kiss the back of her hand. "They're also my brothers. They'll say what they want, but they mean well. Their judgment isn't what keeps me single."

She hums, looking out at the yard, and I sense a question on the tip of her tongue. If I was smart, I'd stand up and start kicking the soccer ball with Austin and Bea to avoid it, but I don't.

"Why then?" she asks.

"Why what?"

"Why are you single?"

I rest my head back against the chair, close my eyes, and take a deep breath. I could lie to her, but like Bea said, lying hurts worse than the truth sometimes. And this is a truth I can't take back.

"Because of Paulina."

Five years later, and I still hate saying her name out loud. It stirs up every regret that lives inside me.

"You loved her?" Luna's voice pitches with her question, and I sense a hint of jealousy from a girl I didn't think capable of it.

Turning to look at her, I graze the back of her hand with my thumb. "Not like you're thinking. She was like a sister to me. We grew up together, and after my family died, she was there for me. She knew me outside of the club, and after a while, there weren't many people like that anymore. You would have liked her."

"Why do you think that?"

"Because she was sweet but always looking for trouble. Just like you." I squeeze Luna's hand. "And just like you, I should have kept her away from all this."

I rake my hair back, and Luna turns in her seat to face me.

"What happened?"

"It started small. She came to my patching-in party and then another. And another. She started falling for the wrong kind of guy—"

"Bikers?"

"Iron Sinners." I click my tongue, trying to harness my anger. "She thought she was in love. She dropped out of school and started dancing at one of their clubs. Her whole life was about him and then came the drugs. Everything changed."

"I'm sorry."

"She tried to get out when she caught him fucking one of the other girls at the clubhouse, and she came to me for help. I told her I'd fix it."

"Did you?"

I shake my head. "Didn't get the chance. He found out she came back to the Twisted Kings, and the Iron Sinners decided to send a message that nothing that was ours was untouchable. The things they did..."

I swallow hard, and Luna leans forward, listening.

"I should have never sent her home that night. I'll never be able to erase the image of her the next morning, lying outside the property line."

My mind flashes to the dark memory of Paulina's naked body dumped at the Twisted Kings gate. She'd been beaten and raped—tortured. Patch didn't go into details for my sake, but I know whatever they did had to have lasted for hours.

"It was all because she was close to me. If I had kept her away from the beginning, things could have been different. She was supposed to keep going to school. She was going to do something. And now with you—"

"I'm not her, Marcus."

I want to believe that more than anything. "If anything happens to you…"

"It won't." She forces a smile, and I wish it was reassuring. "Thank you for telling me."

She probably sees it as me opening up, but it should be a warning. If I ever found Luna like I did Paulina, I'd never survive it.

"So that's why you kept your distance all those years?"

I nod. "There's enough blood spilled on this land without adding people I care about to it. It was easier to just not get close to anyone again."

Until you.

I don't say that, but I look into her blue eyes, knowing it's the truth.

21

Luna

It doesn't matter that it's a Wednesday night. The guys will find any reason to party. From what I've heard between drinks and cheering, Ghost, Havoc, and Legacy's run went well, and they're celebrating.

The guys aren't back from the run yet, but the rest of the club has already started drinking without them. Mixed drinks and beer quickly turned into shots, and now, most of the room is drunk.

Reina drops onto the couch beside me, splashing my leg with her beer. Unlike her and the other girls, I didn't get dressed up tonight. I wasn't planning on partying at all, but they were so loud that I couldn't sleep. So I joined the madness in an oversized T-shirt, flimsy sleep shorts, and slippers.

Maybe I should care how I look, but it's their fault I'm awake, so this is what they get. Besides, this is how I look seventy-five percent of the time, and clearly, Ghost doesn't mind.

I still haven't said anything to the patch bunnies about what happened between me and Ghost. I confided in Tempe because I knew she wouldn't judge me for it, but my friendship with Reina and Wren is more fragile.

Right now, they don't see me as a threat. I focus on school, and they chase the guys' property patches. It makes it easy to coexist with one foot in their world and one foot out.

But old ladies and patch bunnies don't mix. The second they think Ghost and I are becoming something more, I have a feeling it will impact my friendships.

I'm still navigating what Ghost and I are to each other. Just because we fucked doesn't mean he's ready for more. What if once he fucks me a few times, he decides he was using his abstinence as a crutch, and he's now ready to indulge in all the perks of being a Twisted King again?

What if he breaks my heart?

The thought alone has me spiraling, which is why I can't admit what we are until I know for sure.

Reina takes a sip of her beer, following my gaze to the show happening on the pool table in front of us, where Mayhem is fucking Kristen's throat. "When did this pool game turn into a live-action deep-throat performance?"

"Somewhere around them forgetting who was stripes and who was solids." I tilt my head to the side as Mayhem grabs Kristen by the throat, shoving his cock deeper. "I've seen way too many of their dicks."

"Is there such a thing?" Reina giggles, taking another sip of her beer.

Kristen is lying with her back on the pool table and her head hanging off. It can't be a comfortable way to give head, but I can't stop staring at them either. If they cared, they'd go find a more private place to do it, so I don't bother being discreet about it.

I'm not actually thinking about Mayhem and Kristen as I watch his cock slide in and out of her mouth. I'm wondering how I'll ever give Ghost head when he's as thick as he is, and my jaw has limits.

"You look like you're in pain." Reina nudges my arm.

"I'm fine." I take a sip of my drink and hope my cheeks aren't as red as they feel. "I was just thinking about something."

"Blow jobs?" She laughs.

And I can't help laughing with her. "Yeah, basically."

Looking around, I wonder what it says about me that this scene isn't out of the ordinary. It doesn't even phase me anymore. In the last five minutes, I've watched Kristen give Mayhem head in three different positions, and I didn't so much as flinch. It's to the point where I don't know how the patch bunnies are interested in fucking any of them.

If I was around five years ago when Ghost was this promiscuous, would I still want him?

I try to picture it, but the idea of him with another woman makes my temples throb.

Lifting my glass to my lips, I finish what's left of the melted ice. "I need another drink."

Plus, I should probably stop watching Mayhem get his dick sucked, given I don't know how Ghost would feel about that.

"Me too." Reina hops up, holding onto my arm for support as we walk over to the bar.

Venom is busy pouring shots for a couple of the guys at the other end, so we slide onto the barstools, waiting. Reina messes with her white-blonde hair, checking her lipstick in the mirror behind the bar.

"You look so nervous tonight." Reina frowns, flipping her hair off her shoulders. "When's the last time you got laid?"

"I don't know," I lie.

Reina rolls her eyes. "It's not good for you to hold onto all that pent-up tension. You need some dick. Trust me, you'll feel better."

She's not wrong, given I feel much better after Ghost fucked me sideways, but I can't tell her that.

Venom finally stops in front of us, and Reina immediately starts batting her eyelashes at him.

"Shots?" She nudges my arm.

"Just a gin and tonic."

"Lame." Reina rolls her eyes, turning her attention back to Venom as someone taps me on the shoulder.

I turn to see Soul and Stevie standing next to me.

"Luna, settle a bet for us." Soul grins.

Venom is still deep in conversation with Reina and is in no rush to get me a drink, so I decide I can use the distraction.

"All right." I turn on my barstool, and Soul's gaze immediately falls to my bare legs.

"Nice outfit."

"You woke me up. So this is what you get. Pajamas."

"Didn't say I was complaining." He winks. "But it's only two-thirty in the morning. Why the fuck are you sleeping?"

"Most people go to bed before the next day rolls around."

Soul glances around. "Not here."

"Hence why you fit in so well."

"You're getting off track." Stevie knocks Soul on the chest.

"Right. Right." Soul brushes his dark-blond hair off his forehead, straightening his spine. "Stevie doesn't think I could fuck a girl while I ride."

"On your motorcycle?"

"Obviously."

"While moving?" I hitch an eyebrow.

"See." Stevie laughs. "Told you it's fucking stupid."

"You do realize if you crash, you're breaking a hell of a lot more than just your dick, right?" My eyebrows knit.

"I won't crash then." Soul grins.

Stevie shakes his head, crossing his arms over his chest. "I swear something is wrong with you, brother. Sex doesn't need to be an Olympic sport. What happened to just getting laid?"

"Who says it *doesn't* have to be an Olympic sport?" Soul argues. "It's not a crime to enjoy fucking."

"Here. Here." Mayhem cheers, stopping between them and smiling, clearly done with his little performance with Kristen.

I roll my eyes. "It's not a crime to survive your sexcapades though. It's one thing to have fun, but it's another to lose all your skin fucking someone."

Soul digs his phone out again. "Watch this. Trust me, it's possible."

He pulls up something on his phone, and Mayhem and Stevie tilt their heads as they watch whatever is on the screen. When Soul spins his phone around, it's a video of some couple fucking on a bike while he drives down the road.

"See. Possible." Soul puts his phone away.

"I never said it wasn't possible. But smart... no way. I'm with Stevie on this one. Sorry."

"I thought you were more fun than that." Soul tips his head back and groans. "Come on. Live a little. It looks fun, doesn't it?"

"I guess if you're just trying to check it off your bucket list."

"See." He points at me like I've just proved his point, even though I don't understand the appeal. "I've got my bike out front right now; we could test it out if you want?"

Soul winks, and I roll my eyes. He knows I have zero interest in him, and I know he sees me like his little sister. Still, it doesn't stop him from always trying to get a reaction from anyone and everyone.

But right before I have a chance to answer Soul's question, an arm wraps my stomach, and the smell of Ghost's shampoo floods my senses. Ghost tugs my back flush to his chest and, in one move, claims me right in front of his brothers.

Soul's eyes widen, and I feel Reina staring at me from the corner of my eye. But he doesn't let me go.

Ghost holds me tight, and I can't help sinking into his arms.

"Not with my girl, brother."

22

Luna

Soul smirks, like even though Ghost is shutting him down and claiming me, he's the one who somehow won.

"Understood." Soul takes a sip of his beer.

"Can I get you a drink?" Venom asks Ghost, and I look over to see he cut his conversation with Reina short the second Ghost walked up.

Prospects look to ranked members like they're gods. Which is probably another reason Venom stopped flirting with me since that night Ghost put me on the back of his bike after the incident with the van.

"Whiskey," Ghost orders, still not letting me go.

Venom nods, and I look up over my shoulder at Ghost.

"You're back. And you're…" I pat the back of his hand, where it's resting over my stomach.

"Touching you."

"Touching me." I smile. "Here. In front of everyone."

"Does that bother you?"

"Definitely not."

Spinning on the stool, I wait to see if he'll pull back. He doesn't. He widens his stance and moves my legs between his. With him standing and me sitting down, he's even taller.

Havoc walks up behind him, and his eyebrows pinch as he looks to where Ghost has me caged. When his gaze meets mine, he smirks, winking.

It feels like a secret getting out. One that wasn't well kept, given how the guys are looking at us.

I scoot closer to Ghost, letting the warmth of his body be my comfort. I've been chasing him like he's a figment of my imagination. I wasn't even sure if he actually liked me or if I just liked him so much that I was imagining it.

Now, I'm drinking up every bit of his reciprocation. It's giving me life. Validation. Purpose.

Havoc stops beside Ghost, and Venom hands him a beer at the same time as he hands Ghost his whiskey.

"Clean run tonight." Havoc taps his bottle against Ghost's glass. "Nice work."

Ghost nods at him, taking a sip of whiskey and then resting the glass on the bar. I wet my lips, remembering how whiskey tastes on him, but holding myself back from doing anything about it as I look up at him from my barstool.

Ghost looks down at me, rubbing circles on my back, and I wonder if he can read my mind. Or maybe my warm cheeks are giving me away.

"Hi, baby." Reina slides next to Havoc, clinging to his arm.

He ignores her, but she doesn't get the hint. Her hand rubs up and down his forearm before she starts tracing a tattoo on the back of his hand with her finger.

I don't know Havoc's full history, just that he was in the military before he patched into the club and that as long as I've known him, he's been closed off to love.

None of that stops Reina from trying.

"I'm gonna shower and pass the fuck out." Havoc steps back, tapping Ghost's glass with his beer bottle one more time before disappearing down the hall.

"You two have fun." Reina winks at me, chasing after Havoc.

She needs to stop tying herself to emotionally unavailable men. If Steel was any indication, she's setting herself up for another heartbreak. I look up at Ghost and wonder if I'm one to talk since he shut me out for so long. But this is different—I think. How he's acting doesn't feel like he's holding me on a string.

I run my fingers down his cut and trace the letters of his name on the patch, hoping he's not going to break my heart.

"You want another drink?" he asks.

I glance at my gin and tonic, noticing Venom still hasn't refilled it and deciding that's for the best. "No, I'm good."

"Let's go sit." He laces his fingers through mine and tugs my hand, pulling me from the barstool to follow him.

Eyes are on us as we weave through the room. Patch bunnies whisper, and club members grin at Ghost.

He leads me to the couch I was sitting on before I moved to the bar, and when I try to sit on the cushion next to him, he pulls me onto his lap instead so I'm straddling him.

My thin pajama shorts ride up, but my T-shirt is long enough to hide my ass.

"Get good." Ghost reads my T-shirt, smirking.

I shrug. "It's an important message. More people should do it."

"Couldn't agree more, beautiful." He pulls me in for a kiss.

It's overwhelming in the best way. His teeth tease my lip, and it sends shivers through my body. I'm breathless when he pulls back, and there's no use trying to hide the blush creeping up my neck and cheeks.

Someone yells from the bar, and I look over my shoulder to see Soul taking a body shot off one of the new girls.

"At least there's never a shortage of entertainment in the clubhouse." I shake my head, turning back to Ghost.

His gaze moves to the pool table. "I noticed."

My eyes widen. "You saw that? You weren't even here."

"I see everything that happens at the clubhouse, Luna." He tucks my hair behind my ear, glancing up at one of the cameras in the corner.

"And here I thought I was special."

"You are special. Why do you think I spent the entire ride back with my eyes on you? It sure as fuck wasn't to watch Mayhem get his dick sucked."

He smirks, and I drag my teeth over my lower lip.

"Does it bother you that I've seen all the guys practically naked?" I scrunch my nose.

Ghost grabs me by the front of the throat and pulls my face to his, nipping at my lower lip. "Does it bother you that *I've* seen all of them practically naked?"

He grins, and I can't hold back the laugh that bursts out of me. "I was serious."

"So am I, beautiful. I don't care what you look at. So long as you don't touch."

"Touch them?" My face sours just thinking about it. "I definitely don't want any of them."

The club members are like brothers to me, and I've never thought of them as anything but family, apart from Ghost.

"I only want you." I wrap my arms around his shoulders.

"How bad do you want me?" Ghost still hasn't released my throat, but his free hand moves down to my hips, pulling me to rock my core over him.

I mirror the movement. "So bad."

Ghost skates his hand over my thigh, between my legs. He reaches under my baggy T-shirt and slides my flimsy pajama shorts to the side. No one can see me since I'm facing him, but we're not being discreet either.

"Then I want you to show them who you belong to, Luna." He sinks a finger into my pussy, and I bite back my moan. "I want you to fuck me so we can watch it back later, just like you've watched everyone else. Can you be a good girl and do that for me?"

"Here?" My eyes flutter as he drives a second finger in. "Are you sure?"

He leans forward, pulling my head to the side so he can kiss my collarbone. "They still think you're fair game to flirt with—to consider. But you're not. You're mine."

"I'm yours, Ghost."

He hums against my neck. And even if I usually call him by his real name when we're intimate, this feels different. This is more than just us connecting or admitting what we are to each other.

This is him making a statement to his club—his brothers.

And I've never been this turned on as he toys with my clit, and I ride his hand in front of anyone who wants to look over and watch us. It doesn't matter who sees; the only person I care about is the one who won't take his eyes off me.

I tip my forehead to Ghost's. "I want you to fuck me. Right here."

"Then take me out." He laces one hand into my hair, guiding my hips back with his other one to reveal his zipper.

I trail my hands down, unzipping him. Reaching into his jeans, I stroke his cock, relishing in the rumble in his chest as I grip him harder. But before I pull him out, I shift to shield him from the room with my body.

"Are you worried someone's going to see my cock, beautiful?"

I narrow my eyes at him for calling me out. "It's *my* cock."

"That's right." He lifts my hips and positions me over him. "So, claim it."

I'm thankful I'm in a T-shirt that's five sizes too big for me because it acts like a dress. And even as I hover over Ghost's giant cock, no one can see it.

But they know. I feel them watching as I start to sink down over him.

People fuck in this room all the time, and I've watched them with disinterest or curiosity. Sometimes, it's the only way to pass the time. But none of it is what Ghost does to me as he lowers me down onto him. As his cock impales the deepest parts of my soul.

"You're a lot to take." I moan as he pulls me in for a kiss, shifting my hips so I can ride him.

He tilts my hips, and I lose my breath at the angle.

"You like that?"

"Mm-hmm." I can't form words.

Ghost wraps his hands around my thighs and controls my movements. And when I tip my face up to the ceiling and spot the camera, I think about Ghost watching this back later. I think about seeing myself ride him in the middle of the clubhouse.

A man who's been untouchable, but he caved for me. I might not think much of myself, but when Ghost looks into my eyes, he makes me feel seen.

"You're so beautiful when you're taking me." He grabs the sides of my face, watching my expression change.

I grab his shoulders and continue to rock in his lap, chasing the building fire in my belly. I'm not wearing a bra, so when he pulls us chest to chest, my nipples pebble at the sensation of his hard chest rubbing against me.

"Ghost." I sigh, and he pulls me in for a kiss.

Our tongues tangle, and it doesn't matter who else is in the room. It's just me and him.

Maybe we were always meant to be this. It was an inevitable pull that tugged us down this road until we had no option but to give in.

"You feel too good, Luna." He drops his hand so he can sneak it under my T-shirt to roll his thumb over my clit. "I need you to come for me before I disappoint you."

Something about that confession is what sends me over the edge. That he's desperate for me. That he can't resist how I make him feel. It's been so long since he's given in that every touch has him on the brink.

I love having that power over him.

I shake in his arms, and he drives up into me as he holds me against him, coming deep and making me whole.

"You're perfect." He kisses my shoulder, moving to the center of my throat. "You're beautiful."

We pause, looking each other in the eyes, and I believe him, even if it terrifies me.

He could change his mind.

They always do.

This moment might be all I get. But instead of letting it terrify me, I hold onto it.

From the corner of my eye, I see movement, and I'm still catching my breath as Soul walks up to us. There's a sway to his step and a drink in his hand.

"Ghost, brother—"

"I swear if you touch me when I'm still inside my girl, I'm gonna fucking kill you," Ghost cuts him off.

"Oh shit." Soul grins, throwing his hands up as he steps back. "Sorry, find me later."

Burying my face in the side of Ghost's neck, I shake my head. "Your girl, huh?"

"*My* girl." He kisses my shoulder. "No going back."

No going back.

If only his rivals and my past would let that happen.

23

Ghost

IT TAKES LUNA SEVENTEEN minutes after she wakes up before she comes to find me.

It's possible she thought I was joking when I told her I was going to install cameras in my bedroom so I could watch her from every angle, but I wasn't. And I don't regret that decision when I have work to do in my office, but I don't want to leave her alone.

So while she sleeps, I keep her up on one of my screens while I work on the other. Her nightmares have been getting worse lately, but she doesn't talk about them, and I wonder if it has anything to do with the person who is after her.

She's buried something in her beautiful mind, and I want to know what it is so I can make it right.

After Luna moved to Vegas with the club, I looked into her. I unsealed her juvenile records and dug into every foster family she lived with. She was put in the system at three years old, and from then to the age of eighteen, she lived with six different foster families.

Between eighteen and twenty, there's no record of her. All I know is I met her a couple weeks before she turned twenty-one, and it was a few weeks later she moved to Vegas when we returned home.

Since then, I've studied everything there is to know about her. And now that she's mine, I'm determined to make sure I haven't missed anything.

When Luna used to wake up in her bed, she'd spend a long time scrolling through her phone. In my bed, she sleeps a little longer, and when her eyes finally flutter open, the first thing she does is reach for me.

It makes me wish I'd grabbed a laptop and worked from there. But I know I wouldn't get as much done.

When she finds my side of the bed empty, she buries her nose in my pillow, and I wonder how that makes her feel. Because ever since that first night I fucked her, I don't want my room to smell like anything but her.

Vanilla hand lotion.

Honeysuckle shampoo.

I made sure to move hers into my bathroom so she could get ready in there while filling my space with her scent.

Luna curls into the blanket and stares up at the ceiling, but I can't read her face. She chews the inside of her cheek, and I wonder if this morning she woke up with the memories from her dreams.

After seven and a half minutes, she pulls back the sheets and makes her way into the bathroom. She piles her hair on top of her head, washes her face, and puts her glasses on. I like that she doesn't feel the need to cake her face in makeup for me. She looks pretty with or without it, but it says something that she knows I don't care either way. I'd rather she be comfortable.

Luna rubs her fingers under her lashes and tugs at the dark circles, but they don't go away.

Her past is haunting her, and it's showing in her eyes.

I'm getting close to fixing it, but there are still pieces missing from the puzzle. I know the new Iron Sinner tech specialist is the one who hired Luna a year ago, and I know they're the same person who used a flash drive to hack our payroll records and find her. But I still have no idea who they are.

They're skilled.

They ping their location off satellites so I can't nail down their location or hack their server remotely, and it's irritating the hell out of me.

I watch Luna on the screen. She leaves the bathroom, wandering around my room naked. She walks over to the T-shirt she was wearing last night, brushing her fingers over that and her pajama shorts. I can tell she's considering putting them back on, but she moves to my dresser instead. She opens the top drawer and slips into a pair of my briefs. They're baggy on her small frame. And when she slips one of my T-shirts overhead, she's swimming in it.

I was wrong if I thought she couldn't be sexier than when she's wearing nothing because there's something about her wearing my clothes that has me gripping the bulge in my jeans. If I wasn't almost done with this trace, I'd storm into my room just to fuck her in that outfit.

She's let the beast out of the cage, and now there's no putting him back.

Luna leaves my room wearing her favorite fuzzy pink slippers, and she makes her way to my office first. I kill the feed before she opens the door, turning to face my other screen.

She cracks the door and peeks her head in. "Good morning."

Her blue eyes shine when she blinks at me, and there's no lens that can capture her unfiltered beauty.

"Mornin'." I lean back in my desk chair and spin to face the door when she's yet to step inside. "Come here."

I can't help it.

I need her near me.

Luna smiles, slipping inside my office and shutting the door. The moment she's within reach, I snatch her hand and pull her onto my lap. She sits sideways, and I wrap my arms around her waist, pulling her in for a kiss. She tastes like spearmint toothpaste and heaven.

Her fingers tangle in my hair as she brushes it off my forehead, and when she pulls back, she trails her fingertips over my temple. "Do you ever sleep?"

"Only when my body gives out on me."

"That can't be good for your health."

"I'm fine. There are things to do. People to look out for."

Including her.

Luna scans the room. "Need any help?"

As much as I could use it, I'm the one who made this mess, so I need to clean it up. And the more she knows, the more trouble she'll be in.

I shake my head. "I've got it covered. Most of the guys are still sleeping or at the shop today, so it's quiet. Do you have any tests you need to study for?"

"I just turned in my programming final. But it's okay; I'll see what the girls are up to and keep busy."

"Or you can hang out with me in here while I work." I eye the chair no one ever sits in at the side of the room.

"In the Ghost cave?" She quirks an eyebrow, and I can't help but laugh.

"Sure. If that's what you're calling it."

"That's what it is." She smiles. "You rarely leave, and it's not very well lit."

"You can turn on another light if you want to."

"Or I could just open the curtains... unless you're suddenly allergic to sunlight."

"Whatever makes you happy, beautiful."

Her cheeks pinken when I use that word, and I love that I draw out that reaction.

She glances around the room. "I guess I can bring my laptop and game here if it won't bother you."

"You never bother me."

"Even when you're trying to focus?" She skates her fingers down my cut, aiming for my belt.

"Even then." I catch her wrists before she dips her fingers beneath the band of my pants. "But unfortunately, that's going to have to wait until I get this data to Steel. He's been waiting on it since yesterday."

"Wouldn't want to piss off the president."

"I promise I'll make it up to you later." I kiss the back of her hand. "Go get your computer."

"And coffee." She yawns. "I'm barely functioning after last night."

Good. If she was, I'd be worried I hadn't done my job of properly fucking her.

"Want a cup?" she asks.

"I'm good."

I limit caffeine like I limit alcohol. It's easier for me to focus when I'm not wired or foggy. The work I do is meticulous, and if my head isn't clear, I get sloppy.

"I'll be back." She smiles, dipping out of the office.

"I'll be here."

The second she's gone, I flick on the feed to watch her make her way down the hall. If she knew I was always watching, she might think I was stalking her.

Maybe I am.

Doesn't mean I'll stop.

I'll just keep it to myself. After all, it's for her own good.

Luna sits with her feet kicked up on the desk and her laptop balancing on her lap. Her fuzzy pink slippers shift back and forth as her feet tip side to side. She has a coffee mug and a bottle of water on the table, and a collection of phone chargers, textbooks, and nail polish bottles slowly taking over my desk.

While I've spent the day working, she's alternated between studying, gaming, and painting her nails.

Looking up, I catch her eyebrows scrunching as she frowns.

"Everything okay?"

"Fine. Just a little annoyed. Rider was supposed to help me with this raid today, and he's been M.I.A." She glances up at me when I don't say anything. "He's just a friend, nothing more. I've never even met him. It's a raiding thing. We dungeon together; he heals me. Never mind. I should stop talking."

"I like when you talk." I lean back in my chair, watching her.

"Even when it's about nothing?"

"Especially then."

When she talks about her game, she lights up, and I can't help but absorb that energy. There's only one other place she gets this excited, and it's in my bed. Someday, I'm going to mix the two together and see what happens.

"So you like gaming, huh?"

"It's a nice escape from the real world." Her game makes a sound, pulling her attention back to the screen. "And it was a good distraction growing up."

"In what way?"

Her eyes flick back and forth from her game to me, and she bites her lip, likely debating how she wants to answer. Official records never paint the full picture, and from her nerves, I can tell there are probably stories that never made it into her case worker's files.

"Not all of the houses I lived in growing up were good ones." Luna shrugs. "Some were fine. Some were amazing even. But the one I moved into when I was fifteen wasn't. Lots of yelling. Sometimes worse. It depended on the day, so gaming made for a nice escape."

"They hurt you?"

Her fingers pause on the keys, and I swear the oxygen leaves the room while I wait for her answer.

"Not on purpose."

She says it like I'm not going to have to kill someone for *accidentally* laying a hand on her. Intentional or not, no one touches this girl. Past or present. But I manage to swallow that down for her sake.

"Explain."

Luna leans back, nervously biting the inside of her cheek. "No one was *trying* to hurt me because they knew my case worker would check in regularly, and they couldn't risk losing the checks I came with. But my foster dad was an asshole, and everyone else in the house wasn't as lucky as I was."

My fingernails dig into my palms, and I make a mental note to go back and figure out what foster home she lived in when she was fifteen.

"My foster brothers got the worst of it. Steven was older, so he'd take the brunt of it for Brandon, but if their dad got drunk enough, there was no stopping him."

"He beat them?"

She nods, and her eyes gloss over. "The worst I got was when he accidentally hit me with a book he was throwing at Steven from across the room. It nicked me on the shoulder and left a little scar. But that was nothing compared to witnessing what he did to them and not being able to do anything about it. He told me if I said anything to my case worker, he'd make them pay for it, and I couldn't risk that."

Of course she tried to protect them. That's who Luna is. Her heart is good to the very center.

"What happened to them?"

She blinks, like my question snapped her back to this moment.

"I don't know. I never looked back after I left, and I'm guessing they didn't either. Sometimes bad things draw people together; other times, the people you experience it with are too much of a reminder, and it pushes you away."

"I get it." I scoot my chair back. "Come here."

She slaps her laptop shut and stands, walking over to sit on my lap.

"What about you? How did you grow up?" she asks. "You lived with Legacy's family, right?"

"Most of my childhood, yes. I moved in with his family when I was ten." I wrap my arms around her waist, holding her against me.

"What about before that?"

"My parents were still around."

"I didn't realize you knew them." She frowns. "You never talk about your parents."

"There's not much to talk about. My father was an alcoholic, and my mom wasn't much better. But at least she pretended to give a shit." My throat burns thinking about them. "Even when they were around, I spent more time at Legacy's house than mine. So, after they died in the car crash, his family took me in."

"A car crash?"

I nod. "Dad was wasted. He and my mom started arguing, and she swung at him, then he lost control of the car."

"You seem to know a lot about it."

"I was in the car with them."

Luna's eyes widen. "I'm sorry, Marcus. I didn't know."

"You couldn't have." I brush her cheek with my thumb. "I only remember it in bits and pieces. I remember the before, and I remember the after. The actual accident is really fucking blurry."

"Now I understand a little more about why you and Legacy are so close."

"He's the closest thing to family I've got left."

And the last person I planned to let in until Luna stormed into my life and changed everything.

"Well, you have me now." She smiles tentatively. "If you want me around, that is."

"Want you around..." I dig my fingers into the back of her hair. "More like I need you around."

"You mean it?"

"More than you can process, Luna Cassidy."

She smiles, and I pull her in for a kiss. I sink into the illusion that her good balances out my evil. Maybe it does—even if just for this moment.

24

Ghost

AROUND LUNCHTIME, LUNA DISAPPEARS to eat with some of the girls while I continue to work. She brings me a sandwich at one point, and it's the kind of domestic thing I see Tempe doing for Steel when he's stuck at the club late, but it's not something anyone has ever done for me.

I've always been responsible for myself—even when my parents were still around.

They were always too busy getting drunk or high to remember they had a kid. Then they were gone. Sometimes, I forget that should probably affect me. But as I told Luna about them, I realized I don't feel that loss anymore.

They exist now as a hole in my chest that I assumed couldn't be filled.

Until Luna brought me a sandwich, and it colored in this blank spot inside me. She slips into gaps I didn't realize existed.

Leaning back in my chair, I wait for a final security update to download. I close my eyes and try to think about anything but Luna because then I'll just start missing her too damn much, and she just dropped in to give me a kiss fifteen minutes ago.

I imagine the Vegas grid and try to decide where the man who hired Luna is hiding. I've narrowed it down to a few locations, but hitting every one will spread us too thin and wear on our already limited resources.

Steel needs answers.

Havoc needs a plan of attack.

I'm chasing my tail while Legacy follows the money, and even if we've come so close to figuring this out, we aren't there yet.

At least Luna was able to confirm what accounts she was hired to look for. It was a shell account that we no longer use, but at the time, it was where we were holding the funds we stripped from the Merciless Skulls when we took them down. It's possible they were aiming to take back the funds we stole, but with their hacker's skill level, we shouldn't have been able to get it in the first place.

None of the dots connect.

At some point, I must drift off to sleep because my entire body gets heavy. My mind goes dark when the whirl of the fan creates the peaceful hum of white noise.

But in the silence, something pulls me back.

Pressure on my thighs intensifies, and heat glides up my cock.

My body jerks, and my eyes fly open as my attention snaps to the floor between my legs.

Luna's lips pop off the head of my cock with a devious smile. "Hi."

I almost come all over her face at that. Pieces of blonde hair frame her cheeks, and her bright eyes are so sweet and innocent. Her delicate fingers grip the base of my cock, sending all the blood in my body coursing through me.

My mind is still waking up, but my cock is rock hard and aching for her.

"Fuck, Luna." I thread my hand into her silky strands as she drags her tongue up the underside of my length. "You feel so good."

I'm frustrated she was able to sneak up on me while I was sleeping, and equally desperate to worship her for waking me up like this. She teases my shaft, and it tingles down to my fucking toes.

Luna kneels between my legs, still wearing my T-shirt, but she's added leggings underneath. Her nipples peak against the thin fabric, and it's the perfect little tease. She strokes my cock with both her hands, wetting her lips.

"Sorry if I surprised you." She strokes from the base to the tip.

"I'm not."

She smiles. "I wanted to try something."

"It looks like you're doing more than trying, beautiful." I grab the top of her head and dig my fingers into her hair.

"Mm-hmm." She sinks her mouth over me, forming a perfect circle with her lips as she flicks her tongue on the tip.

"Fuck." I rest my head back in the chair, not taking my eyes off her. "You're perfect."

She takes me deeper at my praise, wrapping her fingers around my thick length and stroking what she can't take. With every bob of her head, she works to take me deeper, and when I hit the back of her throat, she groans in frustration.

"You've got it." I grab the top of her head, and her blue eyes snap into focus. "Next time, I want you to swallow. Let me see you take another inch."

There's no way Luna can take my entire length. Her jaw is already stretched to its limits. But she tries anyway. Tears spring to her eyes as she sinks her mouth over me. This time, when I reach the back of her throat, she swallows, and I almost come at the feel of her mouth working around me.

Her throat tightens as she pulls back. She inhales sharply, and spit coats my cock. But she doesn't give up, and she doesn't take her eyes off me.

This girl is absolute perfection.

She wants to please me.

To be vulnerable with me.

She swallows me deep, and she gets another half inch down her beautiful throat before she gags and has to pull back. Her throat resists what her mind wants, and I love watching her work for it.

As she lowers again, I press the top of her head to guide her. I've never seen such beauty as tears spill from her eyes.

"You feel like heaven." I brush her cheek with my knuckles when she pulls back.

Her fingers stroke me, and her lips pop off the head in a sound that's going to play on repeat in my mind until the end of time.

"I can't take it all. I tried."

"Is that what this was about?"

"Maybe." She bites her lower lip.

Hooking my thumb into her mouth and over her bottom teeth, I peel it open. "Not in your pretty mouth, you can't."

I lift her off the floor and spin her around, pinning her chest down onto my desk and holding her by the back of the neck against it. Reaching my free hand down over her round ass, I shove the T-shirt up and peel her leggings down to her thighs.

I slide my hands between her legs, finding her dripping. "Did sucking my cock get you this excited?"

"Yes." She tries to nod, but she struggles because of the way I'm holding her.

Her fingers scratch at my desk, and her skin flushes as I drive two fingers into her heat.

"You still want every inch of me inside you, beautiful?"

"Please, Marcus."

Last night, she called me Ghost because I fucked her in a room full of my brothers. I appreciate that she knows who she belongs to in there. But here, my cock pulses with her calling me Marcus. Because she's the only woman allowed to claim me like that.

My grip on the back of her neck holds her in place as I line myself up with her slick pussy. It takes all my patience not to drive into her in one thrust because the sight of her body taking me has me close to blacking out. I hold her down, watching her cunt swallow me inch by inch.

Grabbing one of her legs, I hitch it up on the desk so I can get even deeper.

Luna's lips part as she loses her breath. She can't pull away with how I have her hips pinned to the desk, so she's forced to take all of me.

"Such a good girl taking every inch." I thrust forward, pausing when I bottom out. "That's it. Squeeze me with that greedy cunt."

Her nails scratch the desk as she pulses her core. Maybe I asked for too much because it has my head swimming and my balls pulling tight. Luna drips down the inside of her thighs, and I sense she's already right on the edge.

But I hold her there, forcing both of us to hang in this limbo between pleasure and desperation.

"Marcus."

"Yes, Luna?" I pull out slowly, all the way to the tip, admiring my glistening shaft as I thrust back in.

"Please. I—"

She can barely speak when I don't relent. I start fucking her with everything I've wanted to give her since the first time her blue eyes met mine through the computer screen.

"What do you need from me?" I release her neck to grab her ass.

It jiggles as I fuck her harder.

"I—" She gasps. "I need to come."

"How bad?" I drag my hand down and collect her excitement, sliding my wet finger up to her ass and pushing a finger in.

"Oh—" I drive in deeper, and it cuts her off again. "I'm—"

She can barely talk. She turns her face to the desk and presses her forehead against it.

"You full yet?" I ask her, toying with her ass while I fuck her deep over and over.

"Yes?"

"Is that a question or an answer?" I thrust hard, and she gasps. "Who do you belong to, Luna?"

"You." Her words are mumbled between screams.

"That's right." I thrust deep. "And that's what you're going to get. All. Of. Me."

With each pump, her pussy gets slicker.

"Come on my cock, and show me how much you want it." I fuck her against the desk.

Her deep breaths turn to screams, and anyone walking past the office will know what we're doing. But, like last night, I don't care.

I've never felt the need to claim someone before Luna, but with her, I'm desperate. They need to know. *She* needs to know.

She's mine.

Luna's body shakes as her pussy grips me like a vice, and her climax pulls mine out of me. I bury myself deep and fill her up. The pulse around my cock squeezes out every last drop, and I give her everything her body asks for.

Pulling back, I release her so she can lower her other leg to the ground, and when my cum drips down her leg, I shove it back in.

"I need to meet with my president." I drive my fingers deeper, plugging my cum inside her. "But you're going to sit with me inside you while you wait. And when I get back, I want you to spread your knees so I can fill you up again."

Luna looks over her shoulder at me, biting her lip as I draw her leggings back up her legs.

"Understood?"

"Yes, sir."

It's official. This girl was made for me.

25

Luna

I'VE NEVER MISSED ANYONE before, so I don't know what to make of this stinging sensation in my chest. But Ghost has been on a run with some of the club for the past three days, and I can only assume that's why I have this pit in my stomach.

I *miss him*.

Waking up in his bed isn't the same without him here. It's empty and cold.

I've considered going back to my room, but then I wouldn't have a piece of him at all, so I don't.

Besides, he told me to make his room my own while he's gone, so I don't think he's bothered by the fact that I am. A chair in the corner is filling with a pile of my clothes, and my makeup, shampoo, and moisturizers are slowly taking over the bathroom. My possessions bleed into every corner.

I'm not as neat as Ghost is, with clothes tossed everywhere, so he might take one look when he returns and kick me out. But I hope that's not the case.

When he's here, I need to be around him. When he's away, I need to be surrounded by things that remind me of him. If he knew my level of obsession, he'd probably cut things off, and I wouldn't blame him. I fell for him, barely knowing anything about him, and now that I do, these feelings are growing more intense.

I make the bed when I'm done showering and getting ready for the day. It's not something I care about in my own room, but Ghost keeps his space spotless, and with my things already taking over, it's the least I can do.

Tempe wanted to have coffee this morning, so it's still early when I walk into the clubhouse kitchen. With Steel gone and his grandma on a trip with friends for a few days, Tempe and Austin have been staying in their room at the clubhouse. Anytime that happens, there are strict orders in place regarding parties, and the guys keep to it with the threat of dealing with their president if they don't.

Even if they weren't under orders, I get the feeling they still wouldn't be partying as hard lately.

The guys are on edge again. Even Soul, who tends to be the most carefree of the group. With Steel, Havoc, and Ghost gone, he's been working nonstop. And I haven't heard him complain once about the fact that he needs to behave with a kid wandering the clubhouse.

I've barely seen the ranked members these past few days, and prospects are rotating patrols. Something bad is on the horizon, but I don't know what's coming.

I pull my phone out of my back pocket as I walk down the hallway and look at the last text I received from Ghost. It came in just over twenty-four hours ago. A little too long to feel comfortable, even if it's sweet.

Ghost: Morning, beautiful. Thinking of you.

I'm not sure how Tempe does it. It's one thing to live this lifestyle temporarily, but I'm learning that being involved with one of them is different. Ghost may trust me, but there are certain things he'll never be able to share with me. I'll never know where he is at all times or if he's in danger.

Club business.

Part of me wants answers, but I know they keep it between the club members for a reason.

I scroll back through our texts over the last few days and pause on the video clip he sent me.

It's a recording of him fucking me at the club party. The angle of the camera gets a clear view of my face as I ride him in front of everyone. I watched it at least ten times last night, but after coming twice, I knew nothing was going to take the edge off like he could.

Shoving my phone back in my pocket, I step out into the den.

Reina and Wren are walking outside in bikini tops to soak up the sun, and when I wave, they're hesitant to wave back.

Things are already changing between me and them. I can't tell whether it's because I'm having sex with Ghost or because I'm no longer sleeping in the room the three of us share, but they've been slowly cutting me out.

"Hey." I drop onto the cushion beside Tempe.

Austin is kneeling on the floor, coloring and playing with his cars.

The floor is polished, and the clubhouse is spotless, which means Steel must have put the guys under strict cleaning orders for his family to be crashing here.

"Don't let those girls get to you." Tempe frowns, watching Reina and Wren sit outside with Kristen.

"They're not." I pretend I'm unaffected. "We're friends… or we were. I don't know what we are now, but I'll be okay."

"It's the old-lady effect." Tempe offers a sympathetic smile.

"But I'm not an old lady."

"From what I've heard, you might as well be. Where did you come from just now, Luna?"

I lace my fingers in my lap. "Ghost's room. He said I could use it if I wanted space to myself with him gone."

"Exactly." She nudges my arm, leaning close to whisper so Austin can't hear us. "And I heard a little rumor you two had some fun at a party a few nights ago. Very *public* fun."

I bite the inside of my cheek. "I'm not the first one to do that."

"I'm not judging." Tempe smirks, and it makes me wonder what sneaky things she and Steel do without anyone knowing about it.

"Anyway, I'm allowed to have fun. And it's not like I've offended any of them. He's never shown any interest in any of them, so it's not like I took away one of their options."

Tempe folds her legs under her on the couch, turning to face me. "It's not your fault, Luna; it's just the dynamic. You're either one of them, or you're a threat; there's no in-between. It doesn't matter if Ghost was interested in them or not; the status has changed. It's their insecurity. There's nothing you can do about it."

"What if they're not the only ones feeling insecure?" I'm probably pathetic for even asking. "What if I'm just like they are to him, and now that he's broken his abstinence streak, he'll get over it and move on? What if this is all just temporary, and I'm being naïve and blind to it?"

"Something tells me that's not going to happen." She squeezes my hand. "Ghost sees you, Luna. He likes you. It's been obvious since the first time I saw you two in the same room together. Let yourself have this. Let yourself be happy."

Happy.

My heart rejects the idea immediately. Happiness is what gets people into trouble. It's what makes you feel secure right before the rug is ripped out from under you. Everyone in my life has discarded me, and I can't survive Ghost being one of them.

"It will be okay." She takes a sip of her coffee. "Trust me."

Venom walks into the room with his sights set on me like he's on a mission.

I'm used to him being relaxed and flirty with me, so I don't know how to feel about this other side of him. Venom might be a fuckboy like most of the guys here, but he has a sweet and caring side, and I hate that he's no longer showing me hints of it, just like Reina and Wren are acting like we aren't friends anymore.

He stops at the couch. "Ghost needs the coordinates of the confirmed Iron Sinners safe houses. He said you know where those are, and you can get those to him?"

A tinge of irritation surfaces because Ghost could have asked me himself. There's probably a chain of command, but I miss hearing from him.

"Yeah, I know where he keeps that information." I turn to Tempe. "Catch up later?"

"Of course." She drops to the floor to help Austin color, and I follow Venom out of the den to Ghost's office.

"All he needs are the coordinates?"

Venom nods. "That's what he asked for."

"I'll send it to him."

Venom disappears while I step into Ghost's office. It doesn't feel like him when he's not here. Desert dust has settled, and there's no hint of Ghost's soapy scent—just wood cleaner and a cinnamon plug-in.

Circling his desk, I try not to think about the last thing we did on top of it. He fucked me so hard I was sore for two days.

Almost immediately after, Steel gave the order that they had to leave, and I saw him long enough for him to pack some things and say goodbye, but we never got a chance for him to make good on the promises he left me with in here.

Sitting in Ghost's chair, I start up his computer and wait for the screens to come to life. Once it does, I open our shared drive and type in the password for the surveillance archive. Ghost stores everything in clearly labeled folders, so it's easy to locate. I find the one with the most recent Iron Sinners locations and drag them into a shared folder so he can access them from wherever he is.

Glancing at the blank spot on his desk where my laptop sat the last time I was in here, I realize I haven't played my game since Ghost left. And I haven't heard back from Rider either.

Pulling out my phone, I open my gaming app and find Rider's name. It's unusual for him to be silent this long. I glance up at the files and see them still transferring, so I shoot off a quick message to see when he wants to tackle the next raid.

But the second I hit send, a chime rings out from Ghost's desk.

It's a strange coincidence. And it makes me think about what Legacy said.

Are there ever really coincidences?

I send another message to be sure, and when I hit send, I hear the chime again.

Something is wrong, and my mind is rejecting the thought settling in.

The first time Rider messaged me was shortly after I moved into the clubhouse. It was nothing but friendly conversation at first. We would game together and talk about our day. Slowly, it evolved into a friendship, even if I was always careful and spoke generally or with code names in place of actual people.

I told him about Ghost. Confided in him about my crush.

Which is why my hand shakes as I pull open the top drawer to the desk and see a phone staring back at me. I tap the screen to wake it up, and a message with a little owl sits on the screen. The same message I just sent.

Ghost is Rider?

It doesn't make sense.

I've never seen Ghost waste time with video games, and I've talked to Rider with Ghost in the room.

Except, Ghost is always looking at his phone. Could it really have been him all along, and I didn't know it?

Picking up the phone, I unlock the screen and see our messages staring back at me. Confessions, concerns. I see the proof that Ghost has been keeping massive secrets. And as if that isn't bad enough, there's a blinking symbol in the corner of the screen that catches my attention.

I shouldn't keep digging. I shouldn't open the app that's staring at me. But I ignore the red flags and click the blinking icon anyway.

An app opens, showing me a series of clubhouse feeds.

Most of them mirror the same rooms on the screens in Ghost's office. The den, the bars, the hallways. But then, the feeds keep going, and the surveillance moves into areas of the clubhouse I didn't know Ghost was monitoring.

I click on one labeled *Owl* and see my bed in my room staring back at me. There's only one place it could be coming from—my computer.

Locking the phone, I shove it back in the desk, slamming the drawer shut.

Ghost has been watching me every moment of the day. In the clubhouse. In bed.

On top of that, he's been pretending to be someone else to have entire conversations with me.

I've been worried about my level of obsession, but Ghost has been stalking me.

The computer beeps as the file finishes, and I stand up so fast my head spins.

Rubbing my fingers on my temples, I try to process everything he knows and everything he must have seen. I'm still thinking through it all when a scream rips through the clubhouse, snapping me out of my thoughts.

I look at the door, and something loud pops from the other side, followed by yelling and a series of gunshots.

Tempe is out there.

Austin is out there.

I rush for the door, but the second I swing it open, a large body dressed in all black barrels toward me. His face is masked, and he's too quick and fast to slip from his grip. He grabs me at the waist when I try to run, but he snatches my arm, and my head hits the doorframe as I fall.

"Let her go." Venom's voice sounds strange as my temples throb, and the hands holding me loosen their grip.

Venom steps between me and the man in black, and I watch as he takes a punch.

"Run," Venom grunts.

I want to help him, but I can't. I need a weapon. I need to find Tempe and Austin. I need to get us out of here.

But the moment I turn the corner, I'm stopped in my tracks by the barrel of a gun.

"Freeze."

26

Ghost

THE SECOND WE CROSS the city border back into Vegas, my hands itch to get back to the clubhouse. It's been three days since I've seen Luna, and I feel like I'm going through withdrawals.

Keeping an eye on her through a camera isn't the same as holding her in my arms. Now I understand why Steel is in such a shit mood when the club goes on long runs that take him away from Tempe and Austin.

As a club, we have things that need to be taken care of on a daily basis, but my body isn't currently in agreement. My heart's aching for her and her big smile, her blue eyes, and her purple hair. I need that girl like I need oxygen, and I'm suffocating without her.

But we can't go back to the clubhouse yet.

Steel, Havoc, and I take the turn in the opposite direction of the clubhouse, making our way toward the Strip. It's a weekend, so it's packed with cars and people. We're forced to slow to a roll as the sun beats down on us. Our cuts draw the attention of people passing by, and I don't miss them keeping their distance.

All I need is to check off this final thing, and I can get back to Luna.

Chaos is meeting us at Sapphire Rise, and when we finally reach the parking lot, I pull next to his bike. As the road captain, he'd normally be out of town with us. But given his parole officer will throw him back in prison if he crosses state lines, he's stuck in Nevada.

While Chaos is anxious to hit the road, I prefer sticking to the clubhouse. Our motel was worse than sleeping in the bunkhouse back at the club, and I'm in desperate need of a shower and a nap. We did the entire eight-hour ride back from New Mexico in one day so we wouldn't have to spend another day on the road, and I'm exhausted.

"I'll find Chaos." Havoc walks into Sapphire Rise first, tying his dark hair in a knot on the back of his head.

Steel beelines for the bar, and I follow him.

"Do you think he'll show?" I slide onto the barstool next to Steel.

"I think he doesn't have any other choice but to meet with us, so yes." Steel flags down the bartender, and she hurries over when she recognizes him. "Water."

"Make that two." I hold up my hand.

Her eyebrow quirks at our orders. I doubt many bikers ask for water when they come here, but we still have to make it back to the clubhouse, and I'm beat.

The bartender slides two glasses across the bar. "Let me know if you need anything else."

Steel takes a long drink, and I turn around, leaning my back against the bar and scanning the room. Everything reminds me of Luna lately, and when I glance at the VIP hall, I can't help picturing the last time we were here.

Pulling out my phone, I check the cameras at the clubhouse. Luna is sitting in the main den, talking to Tempe and smiling. It calms my nerves that she's fine with me gone.

Steel stands, and I look over to see Rick Zane walking straight toward us. He owns half the casinos on the Strip, so I'm not surprised to see security on either side of him. But when a couple of bikers wearing Iron Sinners cuts come into view, I slide off my stool. We're well aware he's been funding our rivals for some time now, but bringing them into our club is blatant disrespect.

Steel points at the bikers. "If they don't get the fuck out of my club, this meeting is over."

Zane smirks. He had to have expected it. But, given his arrogance, I'm sure he wanted to see how far he could push it.

"Leave us." He glances over at one of the piece-of-shit Iron Sinners before looking back to Steel. "But my security stays."

"Fine by me." Steel crosses his arms over his chest as Havoc and Chaos make their way back to the front of the club. "This way."

Havoc waits for the Iron Sinners to leave the club before leading everyone to the conference room upstairs.

Chaos trails the back of the group to keep his eyes on Zane's men.

They're smart enough not to do or say anything as we take seats at the table.

Steel and Zane sit across from each other, both waiting for the other to speak. It's a long silence before Zane can't handle it anymore.

"Hope you didn't ask me here just so you can stare deeply into my eyes, Steel."

"I'd rather put a bullet between them." He smirks.

Zane shakes his head, adjusting his cufflinks. He's wearing a suit that costs more than any of the girls downstairs make in a month, so I'm not surprised that he's unaffected by Steel's threat. No one gets that much money and power and manages to keep their hands clean.

"Let's talk then." Zane smiles like the cocky asshole he is. "How was New Mexico?"

Steel leans forward, lacing his hands together. "Funny you should mention our trip, seeing as no one should have known we were gone."

"I have my sources."

"I'm sure you do. The question is, why do you care about old territory, Zane? That's Road Rebels land now."

"It's not the territory I'm interested in."

"Don't tell me you're baiting my allies to switch sides. They're smarter than the Merciless Skulls were. They wouldn't be stupid enough to accept your help thinking it wouldn't bite 'em in the ass."

"Don't know what you're implying."

"Yes, you do." Steel narrows his eyes. "The Iron Sinners were on your books when they pretended to help out the Merciless Skulls last year. Tell me, why did you care about a club operating out of New Mexico? We both know you're expanding West, not East."

"Let's just say I was protecting my interests."

"You mean the interests of the Iron Sinners. They're the ones who picked up trafficking routes and resources after the Merciless Skulls fell. They even got themselves a new tech specialist to try and level the playing field between our clubs."

"I wouldn't know," Zane says. "Maybe you should check with Titan if you're so interested in day-to-day biker operations. I've got more important things to worry about."

"See, that's the problem, Zane. Titan is on your payroll. So, while you sit in your casino and pretend to have your hands out of this, we both know you don't. It's your money, and you're not stupid enough to give him unilateral control over that. He might think he's still in charge. But we both know you're the one calling the shots. You keep the Iron Sinners funded, and they help protect your dirty interests."

"My businesses are above board. Ask the city."

"I'm not interested in the politicians you pay to let you get away with shit. I'm more curious why you'd waste so much money funding a losing battle. Until I realized something."

"Enlighten me." Zane smirks.

"You and your Iron Sinners didn't fund the Merciless Skulls to help them win against the Road Rebels. If you did, your inside man wouldn't have made it so easy for us to hack their servers and drain their bank account. You wanted them to lose it. You wanted the club to fall. Did they know that?"

Rick Zane taps the table, not answering.

"I think that's a no," Havoc answers for him.

Steel hums. "If the Iron Sinners were always going to let the Merciless Skulls lose to the Road Rebels, why send them there? To draw us out?"

"Always thinking it's about you..." Zane's eyes gleam. "Do you want to know the difference between real business and your little club, Steel? I can see the big picture—the future—while you're still focusing on the past. I see possibility, while you're staring at a loss. I grow, and you shrink. Eventually, that will be how I crush you."

"So that was the plan—to grow. You did all this to absorb the Merciless Skulls? There are easier ways to do that."

Zane's eyes gleam as he sits silent.

"Unless..." Steel shakes his head. "Titan didn't want to look like a traitor to his allies by overtaking a friendly club. You helped them start a war they'd lose so we would show up and take them down for you."

"When someone falls, someone wins, Steel. You should know that. And you should be thanking me. From what I heard, you picked up a pretty little hacker for all your trouble. Has she been getting along with your men?"

At the mention of Luna, I reach for my gun, slapping it on the table and aiming it at Zane. His security guards immediately make a move, and two barrels are aimed at me. My finger itches to pull the trigger, but Steel holds up a hand.

"Not here, Ghost."

I know he's right. Killing Zane in a Twisted Kings strip club will bring nothing but heat. He's too rich and connected. Still, it takes everything in me not to pull the trigger.

"Interesting that you're fond of her. Titan has a friend who wants her back." Zane taps the table, and my finger tenses on the trigger. "I couldn't care less what happens to the little hacker. Pussy isn't worth this much trouble. But for the sake of your club, it might be easier if you hand the cunt over in a show of good faith."

My teeth clench. "You can tell your friend she's where she belongs now, so he can fuck off with that request."

Zane crosses his arms over his chest. "And here I thought we were at this table to negotiate."

"I never said this was a negotiation." Steel stands up, planting his hands on the table. "I'm here to make you a one-time offer."

"This should be interesting." Zane smirks.

"Cut off your funding to the Iron Sinners, and once we burn those pieces of shit to the ground, we might actually let you walk away from this."

We won't, but Steel has to let him think it.

Zane stands up, facing off with Steel. "It's good to see you've got a backbone. At least more than your father ever did. He was too afraid of war because he knew better than to go after me or my interests."

"You're going to burn with the Iron Sinners if you don't walk away from this. And that's if they don't turn on you first. Titan isn't loyal to anyone but himself, no matter how much money you throw at him to clean up your messes."

"Titan is a puppet. Just like you're going to be. The Iron Sinners are one link in a very long chain. I don't need them to get to you. You're going to stop fucking with my plans one way or another."

Zane's phone chimes, and he glances down. His eyes gleam when he reads the message.

"Speaking of, consider this a warning." He tucks it back in his pocket. "It's always good meeting a formidable champion on the battlefield, Steel. But Vegas is mine. Not yours. And not Titan's. Remember that."

Zane turns and leaves with his bodyguards trailing him, but his threats loom heavy in the room.

"I don't like the sound of that." I cross my arms over my chest.

Havoc shakes his head. "Me either."

My phone dings, and I pull it out, hoping it's Luna. Instead, I'm met with a notification from one of my perimeter sensors. I open the app, and every single one on the East side is going off.

"What the—"

Steel's phone rings, and I meet his gaze as he answers it.

"Who?" he asks the person on the other end of the line.

I flip my phone around, showing him the feed. "The ATF."

27

Ghost

IN THE THREE MINUTES it takes me to walk from the conference room to my bike, I pull footage from inside the clubhouse and find Luna.

She was coming out of my office when the ATF raided. And even though Venom tried to stop them, an agent grabbed her and slammed her head into the doorframe. Her eyes swam with hazy surprise as she found her footing. Eyes as clear as a blue sky, and he made them dim.

He's a dead man walking. And so is Zane, who I'm certain is behind this.

He's making a statement that he doesn't need the Iron Sinners to fuck with us. And right now, I hate that he's right.

Zane is lucky he's gone by the time I step out of the club, or nothing would have stopped me from putting a bullet in his head.

I shove my phone in my pocket and climb on my bike. Havoc, Chaos, and I fall into formation behind Steel, weaving in and out of traffic.

If I'd thought I had snapped when Zane was talking about Luna, it's nothing compared to the rage coursing through me now. I'm a live wire. And clearly, Steel feels the same.

In a situation where the ATF raids the clubhouse, Steel should stay as far away as possible so they can't tie him to anything they find. He's lucky he wasn't there in the first place. But with Tempe and Austin both on the property, nothing is keeping him away from his family—even the threat of prison.

The final stretch of road leading to the clubhouse feels endless. The desert has never been as dry, hot, and infinite.

Before I met Luna, I felt like I was wandering in that desert. I roamed empty land with no hope of finding an oasis. I sipped just enough water to keep me from wishing for things I couldn't have.

Luna crossed my scorched path and offered me hope. She made me believe I can be a better man.

Zane is going to burn for her.

The Iron Sinners will beg.

The ATF will wish they never fucked with us.

I vowed to protect her with my life when I brought her here, and I meant it.

When the clubhouse is within view, the first thing I see is the lights. Feds surround the front of the compound, and they line a path all the way to the front door of the clubhouse. At a distance, there are a few cars in the section of land where the neighborhood sits.

An agent tries to wave us down as we approach, but Steel blows past them. One is reaching for his gun when Havoc rolls to a stop to talk him down. I follow Steel while Chaos pulls over to help Havoc.

The front porch is filled with staff and patch bunnies. One girl is vomiting over the railing, and a few others are coughing. They must have used a smoke bomb when they first came in.

Anyone wearing a cut is lined up in the dirt, on their knees, with zip ties securing their hands behind their backs. Our attorney, Tanner Monroe, beat us here, and he's arguing with the agent who appears to be in charge.

I search the scene for purple hair, but I don't see her.

Rolling past an ambulance, I spot Tempe and Austin inside. They're both awake and talking, but Austin has an oxygen mask over his nose and mouth. Gripping my handlebars tighter, I watch Steel storm up to them and wrap them both in his arms.

I cut the engine and climb off as Steel kisses Tempe on the top of her head and says something before peeling away.

I've seen Steel work an enemy with a pair of pliers and a crowbar in the Shack. I've watched him choke a man to death with his bare hands. I've seen him do things that would keep most people up at night. But when he sets his sights on the agents crawling the property, I know I've never seen this particular look in his eyes.

"Prez."

He starts to rush past me, but I hold out my arm, stopping him.

"I will shoot you where you fucking stand if you try to stop me, Ghost."

"Not before they do." I move in front of him. "Your family needs you right now, Steel. We all need you. And if you walk over there and do what I think you're going to, this isn't going to go how you think it is. You'll get one at most before they turn fire on you. There are too many of them, and that's exactly what Zane wanted when he sent them here. Don't take the bait. Be pissed later. Wait out the battle so we can win this fucking war."

Steel tips his head back, dragging his hands into his hair.

"We'll make him pay," I promise. "And the first step is getting these pigs off our fucking land."

Steel's jaw ticks, and he grabs onto my shoulder. "You're right. Thanks, brother."

This time, when he starts walking toward Monroe, I don't try to stop him, even if I still see the tension in every step. He'll reign it in for his family because he knows, like I do, that taking anyone down right now will either send him to prison or land him six feet under. And then, we may never get the chance to make Zane and the Iron Sinners pay for fucking with us.

Soul meets Steel at Monroe, talking through whatever deal is being made. Agents start cutting the zip ties off the wrists of our brothers, setting them free. And once again, I start searching for Luna, finally spotting a flash of purple hair through the kicked-up desert dust.

Luna is sitting on the porch with her hand on her head, and Patch is kneeling in front of her, dabbing at a cut on her forehead. I'm tempted to take back everything I just said to Steel because the sight of her hurt turns the world around me to white noise. But when her blue gaze connects with mine, fear and hope swim together.

The only time I've seen Luna cry was when she was taking my cock so deep in her throat she couldn't breathe. Except right now, she blinks, and something inside her cracks as she looks at me.

After Paulina died, I believed I'd never let anyone close again. All I bring is pain, and all the club brings is trouble.

I broke that vow, and now I need to clean up the pieces. Luna is the only light left in my world, and I refuse to let them put that out.

My feet finally unfreeze, and I head toward Luna.

She jumps up and runs into my arms. "Marcus."

I hug her so hard I lift her off the ground. One arm holds her at the waist and the other wraps around the back of her head. I kiss the side of her face, and she's so fucking fragile I can't stand it.

"I've got you, beautiful. I should have been here." Setting her down on her feet, I tip her chin up to me.

My thumb brushes over the apple of her cheek up to the angry bruise that's already forming.

"I missed you." She grips my cut.

"I missed you too." Leaning down, I give her a kiss, but it might as well be my heart.

I've missed kissing her. Holding her. Touching her.

I want to tell her I'll never be gone that long again, but it's a lie. One time, I was gone for three weeks when the club took a trip to Maryland. Wearing this patch will always put a space between what I want and who I am, and she'll have to accept that.

"I should have been here for you," I mumble against her mouth, kissing her again.

"Don't do that." She shakes her head. "This isn't your fault. I don't hold it against you."

Maybe she should. Us going to New Mexico to investigate Zane and the Iron Sinners might be what started this in the first place.

"Don't do that," she says again, gripping my cut as she buries her forehead against my chest. "Don't start pulling away because you feel guilty about this. It's not your fault. I'm okay. I promise."

She's scared.

And not because of what's going on around us. She's worried I'll see this as a reason to shut myself off from her—that we'll go back to how things were for the past year.

Tipping her chin up, I force her to look me in the eyes. "I'm not pulling away, Luna. And I'm not letting you go, remember? You're all that matters to me. I'll keep you safe. Always."

"I believe you." The words are nearly a whisper, but there's something behind them that I can't quite pinpoint as she looks up into my eyes.

As quickly as it flashes, it fades. And I hope she sees that I'm telling her the truth. I'll do whatever it takes to make sure she doesn't hurt again.

She trusted me with her body and her heart, and they're my most prized possessions.

Cupping her cheeks in my hands, I lean down to kiss her. I take whatever scraps of good the universe thinks I'm owed, and I worship at the altar. Luna's fingers dig into my shirt, and I absorb all she has to give.

She breathes life into these cold, empty bones. And when she breaks the kiss, resting back on her heels, we're both breathing like we're running out of air.

"I missed you so much." A tear rolls down her cheek.

I wipe it away with my thumb. "I missed you more. All I want right now is a shower, a burger, and to crawl into bed with you and show you just how much I've missed you these past three days. But I need to help deal with this shit. And it pisses me off that I'm finally home, and there are still things coming between us."

"Me too." She frowns. "But I understand."

Patch walks up beside us, and I look over at him.

"Does she need to go to the hospital?"

He shakes his head. "Her head's gonna hurt like hell for at least a day, but she doesn't have a concussion. I'll report it to Monroe so he can make sure it's added to the list of grievances."

"Good." I glance up as Wren starts throwing up over the railing. "Go deal with that. I've got Luna."

He nods, starting up the steps of the porch as Luna curls against me. Across the yard, Legacy is handing Bea to Margaret while he yells something at an ATF agent. Margaret pats his arm, saying something that calms him down, but the tension doesn't release from his shoulders as he watches Margaret get his daughter into the car.

With Bea gone, Legacy heads in my direction.

"Try not to get locked up, brother," I tell him when he stops in front of me. "If for no other reason than that little girl."

"They stormed her fucking room."

"And we'll make them pay for that."

Luna looks up at me. I'm sure she knows the bad shit I do for the club, but hopefully, she understands.

Legacy nods, and her gaze moves between us.

"I'll give you a minute," Luna says. "I'm going to check on the girls. Find me when you're done."

Lifting on her toes, she kisses me and walks away. I watch her go, appreciating that she's understanding when none of this can be easy on her.

"How'd they even get in?" I turn back to Legacy. "They can't just storm this place without a warrant."

"Said they were operating on a tip."

I laugh, but there's no amusement in it. "Yeah, and I know where it came from. Just got out of the fucking meeting."

Legacy dips his hands in his pockets, nodding his understanding. "Please tell me you've got some good news from your trip."

I pull my phone out of my back pocket and shoot a text off to Legacy. "Better than good. We found the account we've been looking for. Drain it."

"Steel's sure? It's gonna start a war."

I look around at the agents still crawling around the property and at Tempe carrying Austin toward Steel with that little boy wrapped around her. "We're already in one, brother."

And right now, war sounds good.

28

Luna

When I wake up in the middle of the night, I'm curled against Ghost's side, so I know he came to bed at some point. But by morning, the room is empty again. My arm stretches to his side of the bed, and the sheets are cold, telling me he must have climbed out of bed a while ago.

After the ATF cleared out, Steel held church, and all the guys disappeared for a while. Anyone not in that room worked on cleaning up the mess the ATF left behind. Every so often, Ghost would pop out to check on me.

Once church ended, Ghost locked himself in his office. I'm surprised he came to bed at all, given he doesn't usually sleep when something goes down at the clubhouse. Which means he must have done it for me.

I stare up at the ceiling, watching the sunbeams dance through the window. The clouds cast shadows on the popcorn ceiling as the room lights and dims with each one that passes. I imagine faces in the bumps on the ceiling as I stare up at them and try to process the past twenty-four hours.

Yesterday afternoon, when I discovered all the secrets Ghost has been keeping, I was in shock. Teetering on a ledge between confusion and hurt that there were things he was still keeping from me. I was still reeling when the club was raided, so I haven't had time to fully process everything I discovered.

It all happened so fast, and I'm overwhelmed with information.

Now, in the light of morning, I work through the truth.

Ghost has been watching me. More than that, he's been pretending to be someone else to get close to me. All this time, I thought he was keeping me at a distance, but he's been right there.

I should be upset that he's still not telling me everything when he promised to be honest. I should feel violated that he's been watching me in my bedroom and keeping a secret identity to learn all my secrets.

But after what happened with the ATF, when I saw Ghost returning home and walking to me through the crowd, none of that mattered.

I missed him.

He was back.

He was mine.

Ghost is the only person who makes sense in this madness, and when he held me, I knew I was safe, no matter what twisted lengths he's willing to go to in order to make that happen.

Climbing out of bed, I shower and get dressed. The bruise on the side of my forehead is worse than it was last night. It's slowly turning from red to purple, and the gash from the corner of the doorframe is raw and ugly. I clean it up and hide it as much as I can with my hair before walking out of the bedroom.

When I open the door, I can already hear people stirring. There's still so much to clean, but we decided it would be best to do the rest in the morning. I slip my phone in my back pocket and tie a knot in my T-shirt as I head down the hallway, ready to help.

But when I step into the den, no one is cleaning. Instead, every ranked member of the club is standing around. It's only eight in the morning, and it's rare to see them all up this early. But from their worn expressions, I sense they didn't sleep much, if at all.

Ghost catches sight of me walking into the room, and he immediately walks over to me, cupping my jaw in his hand.

"You're awake." He leans down to kiss me. "How's your head?"

"The medicine is starting to kick in. Thank you for leaving that on the nightstand."

"Of course." He brushes his thumb underneath the bruise.

"Did you get any sleep?"

"An hour. Two, maybe." Ghost looks down at me. "I had work to do."

"This is bad, isn't it?"

Ghost wraps his hands around my waist, pulling me to him. "No one attacks our club and expects to walk away from it, Luna. But more than that, no one touches you but me."

I should be terrified of that response. But I live here; I've accepted it. These men aren't good, but they protect their own. And as I look up into Ghost's pale-blue eyes, I don't fear what he might do for his club—for me. I fell for a man who will make those who hurt the ones he cares about suffer, and I accept that truth.

"Everyone is awake early." I look around the room. "What's going on? Don't you all usually meet in church?"

"This isn't a meeting. We're going on a ride."

"The whole club?"

He nods. "The whole club."

I look around and take in the scene differently. The clubhouse is still messy, but the mood in the room is different than it was last night. Hints of defeat have faded, and the men are starting to rally.

It's a show of force. They're making a statement after the ATF raid, reminding their rivals they're still standing.

Skimming my fingers over Ghost's cut, I tug it tighter over his chest. "Will you be back tonight?"

"*We* will." A smirk curls up in the corner of my mouth. "You didn't think I was leaving you behind for this, did you, beautiful?"

"You want me to go with you?"

He nods. "You're my woman, aren't you?"

Ghost stops just shy of calling me his old lady, and I'm an equal mix of relieved and disappointed. There are still things we need to talk about, as well as threats looming. But stupidly, I crave those words from him.

"I want to be. But..." I look over to see Tempe on Steel's arm.

"But what?" Ghost asks.

"Are you sure? Sex is one thing. But I know me getting on the back of your bike is something different."

Especially when riding with the club.

I've been on the back of Ghost's bike once, when he took me back to the clubhouse after Venom and I were run off the road. But this is different. This is the club making a statement. Putting me on the back of his bike in this moment is meaningful.

"Luna, sex isn't nothing to me. When I fuck you, it's something important. Something I haven't done in so long that my stamina is downright embarrassing now." He grins, drawing out my smile. "Sex means something to me with you."

My chest warms with his confession. "It means something to me too."

"Good." He kisses the center of my forehead. "Then you should understand that you on the back of my bike is where you belong. If I'm riding for my club, then I sure as hell want to be riding with my girl."

"I'd like that too."

He smiles, tipping my chin up so he can kiss me. There's comfort in it. Peace in it. It's like he and I were always meant to be like this—with each other—and we're just now finding the confidence to do something about it.

"Tempe said she has an extra leather jacket for you to wear if you need it," Ghost says. "And I already made sure it's not patched."

"Wouldn't want me riding around with the president's name on my back, huh?" I tease him.

Ghost grabs me by the front of the throat and pulls me closer. "There's only one name that belongs on your back, and that's *mine*. Maybe tonight, I'll write it in cum just to remind you."

My core clenches, and there go my panties because I'm instantly needy. I never thought I was the kind of girl who wanted a property patch, but when Ghost sinks his lips to mine, I want him to claim me in every way possible. Including whatever filthy plans he has for us later.

Ghost releases my throat, and I sink back on my heels, looking up at him.

"Should I eat first?"

"We're grabbing breakfast in the city." He snakes his arm around my shoulders, leading us back to the group where Chaos and Steel are planning the route.

And when we leave, I feel Reina watching me walk outside with the group at Ghost's side.

Tempe's right; they no longer see me as one of them, but I didn't expect that to sting as much as it does.

Tempe hands me a leather jacket, and I shrug it on. It's already a warm day, but Ghost won't let me ride without the proper protection. He hands me a helmet, swinging his leg over his purple bike, and for the first time, I take notice of the shade as it shines beneath the sun.

"Can I ask you a question?" I adjust the straps on the helmet, and he reaches to help me.

"Mm-hmm."

"Your bike was black when I met you, right?"

His fingers pause. "Yeah."

"Why did you change it?"

Ghost snaps the helmet strap, lifting a lock of my hair. "I think you already know the answer to that question."

"Really?" I smile.

"Really." Ghost grabs the ridge of my helmet at my chin, tugging me to him. "Any more questions, beautiful?"

I try to shake my head but can't with how he's holding my helmet. "No."

"Then climb on, Luna."

Ghost straddles his bike, and it's practically pornographic. His strong thighs hold it in place, and his thick shoulders tense as he grips the handlebars.

Grabbing his shoulders, I climb on behind him, and the vibration between my legs has excitement humming through me. He reaches for my thighs and pulls my body flush with his, wrapping me around him.

Soul shouts something that makes Havoc laugh, but I can't make it out over the roar of engines. And when the bike rolls forward, my stomach leaps to my throat.

It's not my first time on a motorcycle, but this is something new. Like I'm accepting something I didn't think I wanted.

The club rolls into formation, and I hug Ghost tightly, accepting the security of his presence and the freedom of this moment. The sun beats down on us as we travel through the desert, and I shed a piece of myself on the road behind us.

I close my eyes and soak in the warm desert day. The chorus of motorcycles hums across the desert, and I think about all that I've lost.

Parents I never knew.

Families who carved out pieces until I thought I was no longer worth it.

Pain and heartbreak and struggle.

But when I open my eyes to look around at the bikes surrounding me, I'm faced with the family I never expected. A club that protects me like I'm their sister. A man who guards me with his life.

They found out I was working against them and trusted me anyway. They stood up for me when they could have let me take the fall for my mistakes.

Everything Ghost and his club have done has been to keep me safe.

I wrap my arms tighter around Ghost's waist, and one of his hands rests over mine. The bike coasts, and he laces our fingers together. We say everything we need to without any words, which makes sense since that's how we started.

He saw me and couldn't let me go. I saw him and wanted to stay.

Regardless of what either of us has done, I sense it would have always ended like this. He's my destiny, and I'm his obsession.

He's mine, and I'm his.

29

Ghost

WE SPEND THE MAJORITY of the day making noise in the heart of Vegas. From breakfast on the Strip to circling Zane's hotels and the Iron Sinners clubhouse, we make sure they know that their attempt at taking us down failed.

I'm sure Rick Zane thought he was smart calling in a favor with his buddies at the ATF, but the Twisted Kings aren't dumb enough to store anything that can get us in trouble at the clubhouse. Every gun on the property is registered, and every computer has a tamper feature to wipe the system if anyone but those with a code tries to break in.

Most of what we do might be illegal, but we keep it away from where we live—from the brothers' families.

After spending the morning in the city, we drive out to the lake and waste time. We wait until the sun is ready to dip below the horizon before heading back. Between Havoc checking in with prospects back at the clubhouse and me keeping an eye on the security systems, the rest of the men relax.

Now, we're back at the clubhouse with beers flowing and burgers grilling.

I glance around the patio, and it sinks in how much has evolved over the years.

When I was a kid, I looked up to the cut—to Legacy's dad and the men who came before us. They were a symbol of everything my father wasn't. The cut represented loyalty and family. It protected the person wearing it. I wondered what it was like for people to have your back, while I was constantly on the other end of my father's drunken aggression.

It's ironic that I didn't have a family until mine died.

Legacy's parents took me in, and I learned what it truly meant to be a Twisted King. I've indulged in every phase of being a biker, from being a reckless prospect to gaining rank and taking on the responsibility of protecting my brothers. I patched in with my brother at my side, and I accepted the weight that comes with wearing the crowned skull on my back.

So many kids are drawn to the club because of sex, drugs, and violence. But those of us who prove ourselves know the burden we carry around weighs more than the perks.

It's why kids looking for fun or an escape burn out before they're patched in. To become a brother, you have to hand your soul over. You give up your life for the good of the club. You don't become a Twisted King; the Twisted Kings become you and everything you represent.

It's lonely and hard, and that's why relationships rarely survive it.

Looking down at Luna, tucked against my side as we sit at one of the picnic tables, I wonder why the universe decided I should be so lucky to get something more. Someone who understands this world and doesn't ask me to choose between my cut and her. I already got my second chance in life with Legacy's family, so I don't deserve another.

Why does this girl who outshines the sun want to be mine?

I shouldn't think too much about it, or the world might take this away.

"Who wants to play a game?" Soul drops into one of the empty seats across the table next to Legacy.

"Can't you just chill?" Legacy sips his beer.

"Speaking of chilling..." Soul reaches into his pocket and pulls out a joint, lighting it up and taking a drag. "Come on, you could use it."

He hands the joint to Legacy, who takes a hit. On nights when Legacy has Bea, he barely finishes a beer, but she's with Pearl and Austin tonight, so his eyes are already a little hazy.

"What should we play?" Soul rubs his temples. "Truth or dare? Never have I ever?"

"You're serious?" Legacy chuckles.

"Are you surprised?" Luna smirks. "Soul can't resist a bet, game, or challenge. Even if we all know he'll lose..."

"I never lose."

"The blackjack table says otherwise."

"Buzzkill." Soul grabs the joint and takes a hit.

"She's saving you from yourself, brother." I shake my head. "If not your wallet, then liver failure. Never have I ever? Really? What haven't you done?"

"Things." Soul grins.

Luna's eyebrow hitches. "Really? Never have I ever fucked three girls at the same time."

He chuckles, lifting his beer to his lips. "Point taken."

"You're disgusting."

His smile widens at her grimace, and I'm sure he sees that as a compliment. "You think I'm bad because you're seeing your man's good side. Ghost was worse than me once."

"Stop being an asshole." Legacy knocks Soul on the arm, stealing the joint back.

"It's fine." Luna shrugs. "We all have a past, and Ghost knows I don't judge him for his. If anything, I benefit from his experience."

I look down at Luna sitting next to me, and her hand grips inside my thigh. She's so fucking confident and secure. She has no reason not to be, but still, it knocks me on my ass sometimes.

"You're right." Soul takes a drink. "If I had a chick that cool maybe I'd settle down too."

"On a cold day in hell." Legacy laughs.

Soul leaves the joint with Legacy when he sees Havoc walking by. "I'll be back."

Luna watches him go. "Does he ever sit still?"

"No," Legacy and I both answer at the same time.

"Remember that time in Des Moines?" I ask.

Legacy laughs. "You were still on life number three, and somehow, that asshole had already made it all the way across town to fuck that stripper and come back."

"Life number three?" Luna's eyebrows pinch.

"Oh shit." Legacy takes a hit, standing up. "Sorry, thought your girl knew how you got your road name."

Legacy gives me an apologetic smile as he walks to where Chaos and Venom are standing at the barbeque.

"That sounds ominous." Luna looks up at me. "I always thought they called you Ghost because you keep to yourself, and you're pretty quiet."

"That's probably where it started." I rub the back of her shoulder with my thumb. "But that's not all of it."

She watches me take a sip of my beer, and as much as I want to tell her everything, part of me wants to keep it to myself. She sees me as a safe space, and she knows I'll do anything to protect her. But I'm not sure she's ready to face the extent of what that means yet.

"Will you tell me the rest?" she asks.

I drag my hand down my face, debating if she's ready to hear it. But one look in her eyes and I know there's no lying to this girl.

"The nickname came from King."

"Legacy's dad?"

I nod. "A ghost is what's left of the dead. It's the shit that haunts us. And that's what I was when I moved in with them—haunted."

She frowns.

"It's not as depressing as it sounds." I brush the back of her hand with my thumb. "I was carrying around a lot of shit after my parents died. He said I could let it haunt me, or I could let it be my weapon—where I found my strength. So that's what I did. King reminded me I still had fight left."

"Sounds like you were close with him."

"I was." I tighten my grip on her shoulder, taking another sip of my beer. "But road names are like people; they change over time. Sometimes, I think the name made me, and other times, I think I made it. For a while, I thought it was all I was."

Luna turns her body toward mine, tracing the letters tattooed across my knuckles.

Death.

It's my single truth. What I was born from and what I bring to this world.

"You're more than *Ghost* to me, Marcus." She runs her fingers over the letters. "So much more."

"I appreciate that." Cupping her jaw in my hand, I graze my thumb over the apple of her cheek. "You make me feel like a person again, and I didn't think that was possible."

The smile that peeks from the corners of her mouth is so pure and sweet. Leaning in, I steal a kiss.

A hum radiates through her chest, and my body vibrates at the feel of her in my arms—at her lips on mine. Brushing her cheek, I look down at her and see all the good in the world that I've been missing out on.

"What did Legacy mean about the third life?"

"That"—I release her jaw, sitting back—"is another story."

"One you're going to tell me, or not?"

Luna's one of the least judgmental people I've ever met, but I don't want her to see me differently. Or to think that just because I have a dark side, I could hurt her.

"I promise I can handle it, Marcus." She scoots closer, resting her hand over mine in her lap. "I know more than you think I do."

"Now who's being ominous?"

She bites the inside of her cheek. "I was going to say something when you got back from your run, but then that whole raid with the ATF happened..."

"Talk to me, Luna." I turn to face her, suddenly worried about what could have gone down when I was in New Mexico.

We were on the road two out of the three days, so even if I tried to keep tabs on her, that's impossible on my bike.

"I found the phone in your desk." Her words rush out, and her cheeks blush. "I didn't mean to. But Venom said you needed the coordinates sent, and it was taking a while to upload. So while I was waiting, I messaged Rider to check in. But then the phone in your desk pinged."

Fuck. "That's not quite—"

"I also saw the cameras. The ones around the club. The one in my room..."

She trails off, and I know exactly what camera she's talking about. The laptop she has aimed at her bed. There's no good explanation.

"You've been watching me."

No use denying what she already knows. "I have."

"And you were talking to me as him... as Rider. Did you know I was Snowy Owl, or was it an accident?"

"I knew." And I fully expect her to hate me for it.

Or fear me. After all, she found out the extent to which I've been stalking her for this past year. Which is why I can't figure out why she's still sitting here holding my hand.

"Why did you do it?" Her eyebrows knit.

The lies form a lump in my throat, but I swallow them down. She deserves honesty when she's handed me her faith, regardless of how this conversation ends.

"At first, it was because I needed to be sure I wasn't missing anything when you moved to Vegas. I couldn't find any ties to the Merciless Skulls, but I had to be certain."

I'm treading carefully, gauging her every reaction.

"So you messaged me through my game?"

"It was the easiest way to get to know you without you suspecting anything. You let your guard down for him because we were just talking. I knew you were innocent, but I needed proof for my club's sake."

"So you pretended to be Rider?"

"Technically, I was Rider already." I shrug. "I resurrected an old gamer tag from when I played as a kid. We started talking, and the plan was to stop when I confirmed nothing fishy was going on. But I couldn't."

"Why didn't you just tell me then? Why did you let me think you couldn't care less about me even if you knew I liked you? I admitted that to Rider—to you. But you still ignored me."

"Because I had so many walls up; I'm still working my way around them, Luna. If I let you in, I risked you getting hurt by the secrets I was keeping from the club. At least if we kept it online, there was no risk of that. It was a way to keep you close while keeping you safe. And that's all that mattered."

"What about the cameras?"

If only that explanation was as simple as my reasoning for messaging her.

"I don't have any good answers for that. Nothing you'll like anyway."

"It's crossing so many lines."

"I know."

"It's an invasion of privacy."

"It is."

"I shouldn't like it." Luna's cheeks burn with her blush, and her neck colors with excitement.

"You shouldn't," I agree.

She nods, swallowing hard. "What if I do?"

I take in her expression. I thought her rosy cheeks were anger or irritation, but now, I sense something else.

"Do you?"

Her eyes dart off as her cheeks warm. "I didn't want to. At first, I was embarrassed thinking about what you might have seen and all the things I admitted to you. But you know all of that—you've seen all of that—and you still want me?"

"Of course I fucking want you. You're the only woman on the damn planet worth wanting. I can't take my eyes off you. Literally."

Her cheeks redden.

"That's why I didn't say anything," she says. "Because you weren't the only one watching, Marcus. I saw you too. I've wanted you since the first time I looked up at you, standing in that coffee shop, totally out of place. I want your quiet side, your protective side. I want your light and your dark side. You see me—all of me. And you're still here."

I cup her jaw in my hands, looking down at her. "I promised I wasn't letting you go, remember? I'll always be here for you."

"Then tell me the rest of the story." She angles her chin up. "I already know bad things you've done, and you haven't scared me off yet. Please tell me what Legacy was talking about."

"Because I've hurt people, Luna," I admit. "I've killed people."

"I figured."

"It's not pretty. I drag it out. I make them hurt just like I do inside. And when they're almost gone—on the brink of death—I bring them back and start over. I give them all nine lives just so I can take each one. Just so I can make them suffer."

Her blue eyes stare into mine, and I wait for her to pull away, but she doesn't.

"Does that scare you?" I ask her.

"Would you hurt me?"

"No."

She rubs the back of my hand. "Then no, it doesn't. If anything, I feel like it makes sense now."

"What does?"

"Do you know why my gamer tag is Snowy Owl?"

I shake my head.

"Because they represent a fresh start." She trails her fingers down my cut. "They're a symbol of something new. We don't all do it right the first time, or the second, or the third. But if we're lucky, we get enough chances to fix it. That's what you gave me, Marcus. When I met you in Albuquerque, and you talked about starting over, you gave me another life without realizing it. So everything you do isn't bad or hurtful. Sometimes, you heal, and that's what you did for me. You gave me a second chance."

"You're too sweet if you're trying to see good in me."

"Or you're too stubborn to see it yourself."

She might be right. This might be wrong. But when she doesn't pull away, I draw her in. I plant my mouth on hers, and she gives me more than a new life and a fresh start. She baptizes my tarnished soul.

30

Luna

I SHOULDN'T BE TURNED on by my boyfriend stalking me, but I am.

Ghost ignored me for so long that I was worried he wasn't interested. The truth is, he can't get enough. He needs his eyes on me at all times, and I want that.

We stumble into his bedroom, and he kicks the door shut, watching me back up to his bed. He slowly peels his cut off his shoulders, hanging it on the back of a chair.

"It smells like you in my room." He rips his T-shirt off next.

"Is that a bad thing?"

"Never." Stalking up to me, he dips down, scooping my thighs up and pinning me back down on the bed. "I want to spend all night breathing you in."

He kisses the path down my throat to my chest. Peeling off my shirt, he licks and nips at my skin down between my breasts. He continues until he's burying his face between my legs, inhaling.

"Everything about you smells like heaven." He pops the button on my jeans, dragging them down my legs with my underwear. "Tastes like heaven."

He widens my knees and licks my pussy.

"Marcus."

"Mm-hmm, I've got you, little owl."

Something about him using that nickname feels forbidden. Like a secret that's been revealed. Something dirty I shouldn't want, but I do.

"I need you, Marcus."

"Say my name again."

"Marcus."

"You're the only girl allowed to call me that." His tongue laps at my clit. "The only one allowed to scream my name. Isn't that right?"

"Yes." I dig my fingers in his hair, no longer resisting that I need him with every bone in my body.

His cool blue eyes watch me as he fucks me with his tongue, and I never want them off me.

"Wait." I lift up on my elbows, and he immediately pulls back.

"Are you okay?"

"Oh yes, sorry." I feel bad for worrying him. "It's not that. But I have a question. Do you have cameras in here?"

Ghost's jaw tenses, and I sense he's hesitant to answer, which is probably why he nods just barely in response.

"Where?"

He glances up at the corner of the curtain rod, slowly shifting his gaze around the room and pausing at a couple of other spots. "Everywhere. But I can—"

"Good," I cut him off, smirking. "I want to watch you fuck me."

"Later?"

I glance over at the television. "Right now."

The wicked gleam that flashes in his eyes has my insides fluttering. Ghost climbs off the bed and reaches into his back pocket for his phone. The glow from the screen lights up his strong jawline as he clicks through it. He selects something, and then the television switches on, casting light into the room.

There must be a camera in the center of the framed mirror above his dresser because that's the only angle that makes sense with what I'm seeing. On the television is a clear view of the bed, where I'm stretched out naked.

"Better?" he asks, following my gaze to where I'm watching the live feed of the bedroom.

I tip my knees open, trailing my fingers down my stomach and sliding them over my pussy. "Much better."

The image on the television is so clear I can see my excitement.

I drive a finger in, and Ghost groans, not tearing his attention from the screen. He grips his cock through his pants, watching me play with myself. Slowly, he unbuttons his jeans and kicks them off.

"Is this what you like watching?" I ask as he walks toward the bed with his thick cock heavy in his hand.

"Absolutely." He climbs over me and drips a bead of cum on my pussy.

I drive my fingers deeper as he hovers, pleasuring himself.

"Did you watch me do this in the middle of the night, Ghost? Did you stroke your cock while I lay in my bed pleasuring myself?"

His jaw tenses, and he nods.

"Good." I wet my lips, glancing at the screen and imagining him seeing me doing what I'm doing right now. "I was thinking about you too."

"Don't tease me, Luna."

"I'm not." I look at him, pulling my fingers out and wrapping them around his cock. "I was imagining you sneaking into my room in the middle of the night and flipping me over to fuck me."

"Like this?" He grabs my hips, and the room spins on its axis as he flips me around.

Planting me on all fours, he rotates me so I'm facing the camera. And from this angle, I can see the image of us on the screen as he kneels behind me.

"Yes." I nearly choke on the word. "Like this."

Ghost rubs his cock over my center, wrapping my hair around his fist with the other hand. "Want to know what I imagined?"

"Ye—"

The word doesn't make it out as he drives into me. His tug on my hair forces my back to arch so I can see my face contort with his brutal thrust.

"I pictured this." He pulls almost all the way out, pumping in again and making my tits bounce with the force. "You on your hands and knees, begging for my cock. You taking every inch of me like the good girl you are. And when your fingers picked up the pace, and your mouth parted as you came..."

He pulls back, angling his hips to ease a little deeper on his next thrust.

"I stroked my cock and pictured myself filling your pretty mouth. I imagined my cum dripping from your lips. Painting your tits and streaking your chest. I imagined marking you as mine."

"I am yours."

"Yes, you are." He smirks, thrusting his hips forward and making me lose my breath. "And you're never escaping me now, Luna. I'll always be watching. You're the only thing worth looking at."

Ghost pulls out again, leaving the head of his cock inside me as he angles his chin down and spits. It drips down my ass and pussy as he shoves his thick cock deep. The entire time, he watches me through the screen. And with the camera feed, I can see everything.

The hard, muscled planes of his chest and arms flex with his every movement. The sight of him is intoxicating.

Us together is something I could stare at all night.

Ghost wraps a hand around my body and finds my clit, flicking it back and forth until my eyes are rolling back, and I can't see straight to watch us. Our figures blur on the screen with the pleasure coursing through me.

I think about the things we've done in the clubhouse, the videos Ghost has of us. We'll add this to them and watch it over and over. My man claiming me.

My eyelashes flutter as Ghost works my clit. He widens his knees to strike me at a different angle, and I'm bursting at the seams. My eyes open to watch him on the screen, and he doesn't look away as he fucks me hard and deep, sending my climax ricocheting through every nerve.

My body tenses, and I grip him so hard it makes his jaw tick. With the camera on us, there's no hiding from the truth of what we do to each other.

"You're so fucking beautiful." Ghost pumps his hips. "My greatest sin."

And he's mine.

I accept it.

We watch each other on the screen, and I remember the first time I saw him. I remember every conversation. From the ones where we were us to the ones where we hid behind screen names. We split our souls and share them with each other.

Ghost pulls my hair harder, arching my back even more so he can get deeper, and my chest bounces with each thrust. My neck stretches as I take him. And when his fingers dig into my hip, I know he's close.

I watch Ghost as his thrusts start to deepen to the point where I can barely take him. I'm still so sensitive from my own climax I can't breathe.

He shifts his angle again, and his thrusts get uneven.

But right before he comes, he pulls back, sliding his cock out of me and grabbing it with his palm to stroke it. He grunts as his release shoots all over my ass and back. He covers me with warm ropes of cum, and I watch every second of it.

"You're mine." Ghost lets go of his cock to stroke his fingers through his release, painting it over my skin. "The only name that belongs on your back is mine."

And that's when I realize he's drawing the letters of *Ghost* on my back with his cum.

"Only mine." He crosses the T.

"Only yours."

31

Ghost

WE'VE BEEN ON THE defense too long.

Tonight, it ends.

One of my contacts in the Road Rebels pulled through and got intel on a shipment the Iron Sinners have coming in, and we're shutting it down.

First, we're going for their weapons.

Then, their money.

After that, all bets are off; we're going for the jugular.

"Be safe." Luna lifts to kiss me.

I wrap my hand around the back of her head and deepen it, drowning in her. "Always."

I'm buzzing as I step off the porch and climb onto my bike. Glancing over my shoulder, I catch sight of Luna and Tempe standing with linked arms on the porch, watching us. It stirs something in my chest to know I have someone waiting for me, giving me a reason to return.

Rolling out of the compound on my bike, I think about Luna waiting for me like Tempe waits for Steel. I think about Austin going to bed an hour before that and try to picture what that would look like for us. I never thought of myself as a father when mine was such a shit example, but what if that's what Luna sees for her future?

Could I be someone a kid depends on?

It's one thing to look after Austin or Bea, but having a kid of my own would be different. They'd be my blood. They'd live this life.

Do I want that for them?

Bringing Luna into the world of the Twisted Kings is one thing. She's strong; she can handle it. But I've seen what happens to kids raised here. Legacy, Steel, Havoc, and Soul are all shining examples.

None of them come from well-adjusted family situations. If Luna and I tried, would she think I'm worth the trouble of what this life could bring our kid?

Passing through the gates, I try to leave those thoughts behind before they get me into trouble. Or worse, before my hesitation gets me killed. I'm still not sure Luna's going to stick around, so why the fuck am I thinking about having kids with her?

The moon hangs in the desert sky.

Night hasn't had a chance to cool off the heat of the day, so it's a warm ride. I move as one with my brothers, detouring before we hit the main highway to the Strip.

The Road Rebels let us know the Iron Sinners buy isn't happening for another two hours, but we need to beat them to it if we're going to set up a perimeter and get the jump on them. I wish Titan would show up so we could cut the head off the snake and get this over with already, but he's been underground since his men kidnapped Tempe and Austin.

He knows we have eyes all over the city waiting for him to be vulnerable, and he's being careful.

When we get to the warehouse, we pull around back and hide our bikes so the Iron Sinners won't know we're here. It's quiet, and I do a quick scan for sensors to see if we tripped anything. The Iron Sinners might be upping their security game with their new tech specialist, but the warehouse is unguarded.

Which means they won't see us coming.

I activate a signal blocker to cut off any outside communications. Once the Iron Sinners step into the grid, they won't be able to alert anyone of the attack. It's never my first choice since it cuts off our outside service as well, but we can't risk this going sideways.

"We're clear," I tell Havoc, who makes his way over to Steel.

They direct everyone into their positions. A few prospects will monitor the perimeter while Legacy and I are sent to squat at the upper level of the warehouse. It's my job to send out a radio signal if anything goes wrong, and since Legacy is the best shot in the group, he needs to be in a position to take out anyone who tries to run.

Legacy wipes a spiderweb off his shoulder as we move to our position in the dusty warehouse.

"Why can't this kind of shit go down somewhere not so grimy." He frowns.

"Scared of spiders?"

"Fuck you." He pulls his gun out, squatting down and getting into position. "Nothing should have that many legs."

I chuckle.

I've seen Legacy run straight at a lineup of Iron Sinners who were shooting at him, so it's hilarious to me that something as small as a spider bothers him.

"Besides..." Legacy brushes dust off his arms. "It's getting harder to explain to Bea why I'm coming home in the middle of the night covered in dirt and blood stains."

I tuck my phone away, watching the front of the warehouse. "Never thought about it like that. How'd King handle it with you?"

"The same way Dad handled everything." Legacy snorts, shaking his head. "He gave me a knife for my sixth birthday and taught me what arteries to cut to take someone down in less than thirty seconds. He didn't hide me from this shit, so I never had any questions."

"Does Bea have questions?"

Legacy frowns, resting his gun on the railing to keep it in position. "Yeah, and I'm not ready to answer them."

I think about Bea running around his backyard in a tutu, kicking a soccer ball, and I get it.

"But you're not moving her off the compound?"

"Fuck no." Legacy glares at me. "It's safer behind the gates."

"Well, then you're gonna have to face this sooner or later. And I'm not saying that to piss you off, brother. But you've got two options in this life, and you know it. Get her out or be honest."

"She's five."

"I'm not saying you have to do it now. But she's a smart girl, and she's gonna start asking questions. If you want to keep her safe, you're going to need to tell her some version of the truth before she starts to think you're keeping shit from her."

Legacy looks over at me, narrowing his eyes. "When did you get so fucking good with this shit?"

"When it's not my life I'm talking about." I drop my chin, raking my fingers into my hair.

"You'll make a good dad, Ghost."

"I'm not having any fucking kids." Whatever doubt I had riding off the compound has only been made clearer through this conversation.

"Okay." Legacy grins.

"Really, okay? You're just dropping it."

"Sure am, brother. And when you realize you're full of shit, I'll be here to point out how supportive I was right now so you can thank me for it."

I open my mouth to tell him that's never going to happen, but movement at the front of the warehouse stops me.

The doors slide open, and five Iron Sinners step through.

They're laughing and bullshitting, and we listen while they wait for their shipment to arrive. I'm on edge until that happens because the in-between is the unknown.

While we know how many guys Titan usually sends on a buy, we don't have the Satan's Reapers pinned down.

Lucky for us, when they back into the warehouse with the trailer full of guns, there are only four of them.

We barely outnumber them, but we have the advantage of surprise on our side.

Watching them, I wait until they're in a better position. I can't signal our men to move in until the best possible moment. When they all turn to face the shipment, distracted by counting the product, it's our time.

Hitting the radio signal on my phone sends a single beep to Havoc below. He motions for everyone to move in, and the Twisted Kings swarm.

Two Iron Sinners try to get the jump on Steel, but Legacy takes them out easily with headshots. I take out one at the side, and Havoc finishes him off down below.

Chaos wrestles with an Iron Sinner, who stabs him in the arm. He flinches, but it doesn't slow him down, and when he manages to get the upper hand, he plants a bullet between the Iron Sinner's eyes.

It takes less than three minutes to put our rivals down, and apart from Chaos's wound, everyone is fine.

Steel and Havoc make sure one Iron Sinner stays alive so we can question him as Legacy and I make our way down from the upper level to meet up with the rest of the group.

Havoc peels back the remaining tarps in the truck, and there are more rifles. "It's at least seven hundred and fifty grand."

Steel nods. "Have the prospects follow you back to storage and pack it up for now. We'll decide what to do with it later. And have Chaos go with you. Patch can meet you there and stitch him up."

"It's just a little cut, Prez. I'm good." Chaos takes a swig from his flask, ignoring the blood trickling down his arm or the knife still sticking out of him.

"That's an order," Steel says. "You're no good to the club if that gets infected. And if you end up in the hospital, your parole officer is going to ask questions."

Chaos grunts, annoyed by being benched, but he doesn't argue. He climbs into the passenger seat of the van, while Havoc and the prospects secure the back.

Steel, Legacy, and I stay behind to question the lone survivor, while Havoc leaves with everyone else.

"We need to make this quick before Titan realizes something is off."

Steel kicks the biker in his side, forcing him to roll over. He's groaning as he comes to, and Steel presses his foot on his neck to stop him from trying to sit up.

"Then I guess we better get started." Steel adds more pressure.

I squat down, pulling my knife from its holster. I thought this day couldn't get any better, but apparently, I was wrong.

"Yeti. Cute." I point the edge of my blade at the name on the Iron Sinner's cut.

"Fuck you." Yeti chokes on his words as Steel puts more weight on his throat.

Steel doesn't stop until Yeti's eyes start to roll back.

Grabbing his T-shirt, I pull it up, digging my blade into his stomach. He tries to flail, but Legacy grabs one arm, and Steel holds onto the other.

"Where's Titan storing the shipments?" My blade slips into him like butter.

Smooth.

Painting a beautiful red river down his side.

"I'm not telling you shit."

"You sure about that?" I drag the blade over his stomach, peeling up a layer of skin and loving the decibel of Yeti's scream. "Usually, I'd take my time with this. Make it special for both of us so you have something nice to remember when you're burning in hell. But fortunately for you, I don't have that kind of time right now."

He grins, showing off his blood-stained teeth. "You think you're doing me a favor? Just fucking kill me. I'm not telling you anything."

"Can't do that." I glance up at Steel. "Right, Prez?"

He shakes his head, and I look down at Yeti. "See, the boss says no. Which means you get me until you give us some answers."

I drag the blade deeper. Still not deep enough to reach an organ because I wouldn't want to lose him now.

"Fuck." He screams, and his eyes get hazy.

"Don't black out." I slap the side of his face. "We're not even at the fun part yet. See this knife? You probably didn't think much of it because it's small, right? But that's all I need. Something sharp enough to make a hole to rip your intestines out. How much of your own guts do you think I can shove down your throat before you choke or bleed out?"

Yeti's eyes widen. They dart around, and he's probably debating whether I'd actually take it that far. Or he's wishing he took a bullet like his friends.

Too bad he didn't. Now he gets me—the man I warned Luna about.

Someone who has made men scream to the brink of death only to bring them back again.

Driving my knife into his side, I find the perfect spot. His screams mute from the pain, but I won't hit anything vital.

"Where's Titan storing his shipments?"

"Boulder City." Yeti groans, and I pull the knife out. "He's storing the guns in a condo at the east end of town."

"He's storing ammunition in a fucking condo?"

"Yes!" Yeti screams when I shove the blade in again.

I look up at Steel. "You believe this shit?"

"It makes sense. Would you have guessed the location?"

Looking at Legacy, he shrugs. Because no, we wouldn't.

"What condo?" I look back at Yeti.

"Boulder Terrace Estates." Yeti groans. "Unit three seventy-two."

"We're running out of time," Legacy warns.

I lean down, looking Yeti in his eyes. "Hear that? We're out of time. Lucky for you."

I drive the knife into his gut, making sure I strike a spot that will be slow and painful. He'll last long enough to suffer while still being past the point of saving.

Pulling the knife out, I wipe the blade on Yeti's cut, standing up to shove it back in the holster.

"A fucking condo." Legacy shakes his head.

"Guess we're going somewhere nicer than a dusty-ass warehouse after all." I chuckle.

We have their guns. And next, Legacy will drain the bank account the Iron Sinners are using to store their excess funds from Zane.

Things are turning around. A win when we've been stacking up losses.

Finally, shit might be going right for the Twisted Kings.

32

Luna

The guys still haven't made it back from their run, so it's quiet around the clubhouse for a Friday night.

Tempe went to bed shortly after Steel left, and the few brothers and patch bunnies who are still awake are playing pool or darts. But I can't sleep, and I can't sit still. There's a pit in my stomach.

I don't believe in things like fate and karma, but I've always had good intuition. I can sense when something is off before I know what it is, and that's what stirs inside me now.

Ghost texted me ten minutes ago that he was safe and just running a final errand with Steel and Legacy, so he'd be back soon, but it didn't settle the bad feeling I've had all day.

Stepping into Ghost's office, I sink into his chair and close my eyes. I breathe in the fading scent of him in the room. I'm glad he doesn't mind me being in here, even after the incident where I found his other phone.

Ghost doesn't believe in setting up walls between us. His space is my space, and I'm still wrapping my head around what that means for us in the long term.

Since the first night I slept in Ghost's bed, I haven't been back to mine. But we haven't discussed if that's permanent or if we're going through a honeymoon phase. I've been taking over his space with clothes and slippers and spending every spare minute with him when he's at the clubhouse, but we haven't defined what we are.

You're my woman.

The statement alone could be taken as him claiming me, and he hasn't corrected me when I called him my boyfriend. But I've also spent enough time with the club to know that it means nothing unless he claims me as his old lady. And I can't help analyzing why he hasn't brought that up.

Does he think I don't want it?

Maybe *he* doesn't.

I'm still learning so much when Ghost seems to already know everything there is to know about me.

Running my fingers over his desk, I focus on a picture frame that sits in the corner opposite his computer. He and Legacy are holding beers, grinning at their patching-in party. Their eyes are hazy, but the smiles on their faces are big and genuine.

I open the top drawer, and the phone Ghost used to message me as Rider is no longer there, but that's not what I'm looking for.

When I picked up the phone, I vaguely remembered a stack of photos sitting beneath it. I didn't pay much attention to them at the time because I was distracted by Ghost's hidden identity, but now I grab the pile of photos and flip through them.

I'm surprised he has physical photographs when most of his life is digital. But as I look through the stack, I see the majority of them are from when he was a kid.

Ghost has always been half a foot taller than all his friends, so he's easy to spot in all of them. His dark hair and chilling blue eyes steal the attention in every photo. He sticks to the background in most of them, but he's all I see as I flip through.

There are a few pictures of him and Legacy. Apparently, Legacy was blonder when he was younger, which must be where Bea gets it.

Some are of club members; others are of the open road.

Near the bottom is a photo of Ghost sitting on the clubhouse steps talking to a girl I don't recognize. They're teenagers, and her dark hair is pulled up in a ponytail. She's smiling at Ghost, who's looking down at his soda can.

Her grin is so big her eyes squint, and as I flip through the photo stack, her grin grows with her laugh.

In the last one, Ghost is smiling back, which is rare for him, so I assume this must be Paulina.

Ghost said they were close since they were young, and whoever this girl is, it's clear he's comfortable with her. In one of the pictures, she hugs his arm, and they look so happy. Whatever hardened in him over the years wasn't quite settled yet.

I continue to flip through, and they get older. Paulina is wiry before her curves change the shape of her figure. The older she gets, the more makeup she wears, and by the time they are in their early twenties, she's no longer that innocent girl on the porch.

She's mature, and her eyes are darker. Something about her feels familiar, but I don't know why.

Leaning back in the chair, I stare at Paulina—the only girl Ghost has loved. It doesn't matter if it wasn't romantic; she had a piece of his heart.

I think about the family he built on this land and how that changed after what he lost. I think about Ghost, the biker, and I think about Marcus Jasper, the man. Paulina was one of the few people who saw both sides of him.

Sides I'm still figuring out.

When I reach the bottom of the stack, I'm surprised by the final picture because it's of me.

I'm sitting in the clubhouse studying. My hair is up, and I'm wearing my glasses. There's not a drop of makeup on my face, and I wonder why, of all the images Ghost must have of me, he chose to print this one out.

One where I'm not even looking up at the lens.

A knock comes at the door, and Venom peeks in. "You all good?"

"I'm fine." I straighten up in Ghost's chair.

"Sorry to interrupt, but they have me doing rounds every hour."

Steel doubled security at the clubhouse after the ATF raid, so I'm not surprised by Venom's orders.

The feds didn't find anything, but the entire club is on edge after they violated their space, and I'm sure they have their reasons.

Venom starts to close the door.

"Hey, can I ask you a question?"

He pauses, and I can sense his hesitation. My evolving relationship with Ghost has really changed my friendship with Venom. Prospects are careful when it comes to things that belong to ranked members—especially their women. Venom probably doesn't want to step on any toes by being too friendly with me.

I don't have a property patch on my back, but Ghost has made it clear I'm off-limits. And Venom respects that by keeping his distance.

"Of course." Venom pauses in the doorway.

He won't turn me down because he wouldn't want Ghost to think he's being rude to me.

"Do you have a family outside of the club?" I ask, tucking the pictures away in the drawer and leaning back in the chair.

Venom shakes his head. "Not anymore. Why?"

"I was just curious."

In all the conversations I've had with Venom, we rarely talked about anything serious. He would flirt, and I would laugh. We talked about whatever trouble the prospects were getting into or the ridiculous bets Soul was making with fellow members.

"Is that why you wanted to become a Twisted King? Because you had nothing else to live for?"

I understand why so many of the men joined when they were young, given this life appeals to anyone interested in operating outside the lines of law enforcement. But Venom doesn't give me that impression. Even if he enjoys himself, I have a feeling he came here for more reasons than that.

Venom props his forearm up on the doorframe. "I guess so. Everyone wants their life to mean something, right? Mine didn't out there. But here, I think it could. Plus, it's as good of a family as any. We outcasts gotta stick together. You get it."

"I'm not a member."

"Member or not, you're part of all this, Luna. I see how you take care of people around here. You were one of the first people to welcome me. You make it feel like a home."

"You think so?"

"I know so." Venom nods. "Ghost is lucky to have you."

"Thanks."

He smiles, grabbing the door. "Open or closed."

"Closed."

"Night, Luna."

"Goodnight."

Venom shuts the door, and I glance in the drawer again. The picture of me is on top now, and I wonder if Ghost feels like I make this place feel like home too.

That's what he is to me.

Not this building or these walls.

But *him*.

Ghost's computer chimes, and I glance up to see a message flash on the screen.

He's always tracking something, so I expect to see coordinates or sensors triggering. But instead, I'm met with a small box in the corner with a message.

Unknown: Time to set things right, Ghost. Turn over what's ours. We hired Luna, but her job isn't done yet. Refuse, and you'll lose a lot more than your whore.

The computer chimes again as a picture comes through. It's an image of Bea running around the compound. Next is a picture of Austin. Picture after picture, images flood the screen, showing the two of them happy before they take a darker tone. The next images are of ATF agents all over the property. Austin in the ambulance, and Bea crying in Legacy's arms.

No one could have taken these shots unless they were here on the compound.

Unknown: Hand her over, or we'll keep going until you have nothing left.

The raid.

The threats.

They're doing this to get to me, and so long as I'm here, I'm continuing to let it happen.

I think about Venom's words. How he said that I take care of the people around me. I've never thought about it because I do it out of instinct, but now that I know I'm the reason these terrible things are happening to them, my heart aches.

I glance down at the picture of Paulina, remembering what Ghost told me the Iron Sinners did to her. What if they did this to one of the girls at the club? Or worse, what if they hurt the kids?

I can't let that happen because of me. I have to try to fight this. Reading the message again, I know there's only one option.

Resting my fingers on the keys, I click into the message. I pull up a window and type a string of code to trace the IP address. But it pings all over the city, changing locations every few seconds.

Unknown: Trying to find me, Luna?

I freeze as I stare at the message.

Unknown: I know it's you. I know how you operate. Come out now. Stop playing games, and they'll be safe.

They could be lying, or this could be my best shot.

The screen lights up with an address and a deadline of two hours. It's not enough time to wait for Ghost, and even if it was, he'd just try to stop me. I got us into this mess, and I need to get us out, whether I survive it or not.

Entering the address on my phone, I see it's only fifteen miles away, so I scribble it on a piece of paper and tuck it in my pocket.

I delete the conversation on the computer and set my phone on his desk. Ghost won't be able to track me without it. Hopefully, it's enough time to face whoever hired me and convince them to stop.

If offering to work for them again will save the club, I have to try. The Twisted Kings protected me. They saved me. I owe them.

Ghost might hate me for leaving, but I love him too much to hurt the people he cares about. So, before he returns, I scribble out a final note and wish I could be here when he reads it.

Marcus,

Thank you for creating a home in my heart.

I love you,

Luna

33

Luna

BEFORE LEAVING GHOST'S OFFICE, I use everything he taught me over the past year to get off the property without him knowing.

He saved me once; now I'll save him.

I send a text message to one of the prospects at the front gate, masking it to look like it came from Ghost's phone, letting them know I'm leaving to see a family member who was just admitted to the hospital.

Ghost will be able to trace back everything I'm doing, but by the time he does, it won't matter. I'll have either made a deal to set this right or gotten so deep that I wouldn't want Ghost dragged down with me.

By the time Ghost returns, I'll be gone.

Maybe in time, after I clean up this mess and give them what they want, I'll be free to come back. If I do, I hope he'll forgive me.

The prospect at the gate checks his phone when I pull to a stop in my car. He reads the message he thinks is from Ghost and doesn't think twice about waving me through. I hope I didn't sign his death warrant by sneaking past him.

It's not his fault.

It's no one's except mine.

I try not to glance at the rearview mirror as the Twisted Kings compound shrinks in the distance. The compound is the first place that ever felt like a home, and with every mile, it aches to leave it behind.

It's not a long drive to the industrial district, but it feels like an entirely different world as I pull up. I abandon my car a building down and go the rest of the way on foot so I can scope out what I'm walking into without them hearing me.

When I finally reach the warehouse that matches the address they messaged, I take a deep breath and close my eyes. This is it. My moment of truth. Ghost has kept me in the dark over what I've done, but it's time I pay for my sins.

I step into the warehouse, and it's dark, except for a path of light that streams from an office to the left.

"Hello," I call out.

The air is dusty and reeks of chemicals.

"I guess miracles do happen." I hear a voice echo from the shadows. "Didn't think Ghost would actually let you out of his hold. Kind of hoped he'd give us a reason to come in for the retrieval."

"Ghost doesn't know I'm here," I yell back to the mystery man.

"That makes more sense." The man chuckles, and it echoes through the walls. "He always had a soft spot for a pretty face that needed saving."

I clench my fists at my sides, wondering if he's talking about Paulina. "I'm here. What do you want?"

A scuffling of shoes on concrete comes from my left, and I spin to face it. The man's boots drag on the warehouse floor with every step until a figure finally forms in the shadows. And when he finally comes into view, my heart pounds in my chest.

"Steven?"

My former foster brother has aged since I last saw him, but he also somehow looks exactly the same. His hazel eyes are distant, and I never could decide if they were warm or cold.

He smirks, and it tugs on the deep scar that cuts through his lip. I remember him getting it when he stepped in and took a beating for his brother.

"Been a while, Luna." Steven pops his knuckles. "But I don't go by Steven anymore, so you can call me Grimm."

It's an unsettling name—the bringer of death. And I wonder if the rumors I heard after we cut ties were true. He might have protected me while we lived together, but there was always a side of him that reminded me a little too much of his father.

A relentless side.

A dark side.

He was impatient and thought he was owed something for what he was forced to live with.

Back then, I wanted to believe him. He and his brother had been through enough that when he taught me how he would hack the school's computer to change his grades to avoid a beating, I understood his reasoning. I even got it when he broke into the city utility billing system and zeroed out the water bill so they wouldn't shut it off when his dad was too broke to pay it.

But looking at him now, I see the ripple effect of those small actions. Of taking and taking, not considering who is on the other end of it.

Grimm cracks his knuckles again, and my gaze drops to the patch on his cut.

"You're an Iron Sinner."

"Thought you were the only one who made new friends after you disappeared, doll?" He smirks, and my spine tingles with the nickname. "Who do you think led you to them?"

"You're the one who hired me to hack the Twisted Kings?"

"Titan asked if I knew anyone as good as I was since we couldn't risk the Twisted Kings chasing it back to my club at the time. So I looked you up. It's too bad you ended up being such a disappointment. I thought I taught you better than to get caught."

His words sting, even if they shouldn't. Steven doesn't know me. What little hacking we did when we were younger is nothing compared to what I was up against in Ghost's system. I doubt he could have gotten in either.

Still, it stings, drawing out the insecurity I had back when I lived with his family. I was a fifteen-year-old girl who didn't know what she wanted or where she belonged. Someone who relied on Steven to help me through it. I thought it was because he cared, but now, I'm starting to think it was manipulation. He weaponized my insecurities to make me compliant, and I fell for it.

"You surprised me with one thing though." He steps closer, wagging a finger at me. "I didn't expect you to follow them back here. Thought you'd wait for me."

"I didn't even know where you were. We haven't spoken since your father kicked me out."

"You mean since you left." He storms forward, grabbing the back of my head and pulling me closer so I'm forced to smell his cigarette breath. "I offered to help you. Remember?"

Steven offered to get an apartment together, but all I wanted to do was get away. And now, looking back, maybe I suspected this side existed in him all along. I considered being his roommate, but it always gave me a bad feeling. Now I know why.

"We needed to move on." I swallow hard.

"Move on? Like I'd ever forget you. You were the only good thing in that hellhole, Luna. You might have disappeared on me after high school, but I was always going to find you again."

He dips his face by my neck and breathes me in. I try to push him off me, but he laughs when I shove him back a step.

"You always were feisty. Happy to see the Twisted Kings didn't beat that out of you."

"They'd never do anything like that."

"They're bikers, doll." He hitches an eyebrow. "Or do you think your boyfriend actually likes you just because right now he's treating you okay? I guess you always were a sucker for someone willing to save you. I'm sure you're a good fuck, but he'll get tired and move on. That's what they all do. That's why you've always belonged with me."

"What are you talking about?"

"I saved you first, Luna. I stopped my dad from beating on you... or doing worse." He steps toward me, and I mirror him with a step back. "You weren't my first foster sister, you know? You should have seen what he did to them. He kept them quiet, but they were thin walls in that apartment. And they felt even thinner in the silence of the night."

Tears sting my eyes when I realize what he's saying.

"You're lucky I was older by the time you came around. And he was drunk more often than not, making him easier to control. I redirected him for you. I took those beatings for you. I kept him in line for you because you were mine. And now you owe me."

His gaze roams over my body, and I process the altered version of the life we shared. Grimm's memory of those years is different from mine, and I see how it could have been worse. But if he thinks he's owed me because of it, he's wrong.

Grimm drags his dark hair off his forehead, and his nearly black eyes have my stomach in knots. Any kindness that once existed in him has hardened.

"You were like a brother to me, Steven."

"Grimm." His frown deepens.

"Grimm," I repeat, stepping back. "You were my brother. That's it."

His fingers wrap around my wrist so hard it hurts, and he's nothing like the boy I remember.

"Don't lie to yourself. We weren't actually siblings. This is okay. You're allowed to like me."

"Like you? I don't even know you. Not anymore." I try to pull away, but he won't let me go. "I'm in love with Ghost."

His eyes flare at my comment, and the invisible band around my chest tightens. I still haven't said that to Ghost, and I don't like that the first time the words are out loud, they were to Grimm. Especially when his gaze darkens with his irritation.

"You only think that because you've been around him, and he's brainwashed you. But I know you, Luna. In ways he never will." Grimm grabs my arm, and I wince from how hard he holds onto me. "You don't belong with them."

"Where do I belong then?" I already suspect his answer, but I need to hear it to wrap my head around what's happening.

"With me, baby doll. With the Iron Sinners. Where you were always meant to be." His face softens as he steps closer. "Think about it; you were always one of us. Helping us out against those assholes."

"I didn't know that. I didn't want to."

"You think you're loyal to them, I get it." He brushes my cheek with his hand. "I let you stay too long. I should have pulled you out sooner."

"You knew I was there?"

"Of course I knew." His eyebrows scrunch. "I didn't want you to go with them, but once you did, I knew you would make it work for me."

My blood chills. I came here planning to bargain with the person who hired me, but that's not what this is at all. This isn't about a job I did or didn't do. Grimm thinks I'm his.

"Titan needed someone on the inside, just in case. And after I saw how the hacker looked at you, I knew he'd trust you enough to let you close." Grimm's eyes flare. "Reyes was prospecting, but he was a little shit. He was bound to fuck it up. I told Titan we could trust you. That when you came home, you'd know enough to help us take down those Twisted Kings assholes."

"I can't." My entire body shakes as I process what he's saying. "I won't."

What he's suggesting is the opposite of what I intended by coming here.

"Oh, doll, they've really broken you, haven't they? You've lost where you belong. Don't worry, I've got you now."

"I'm not telling you anything. You'll have to kill me."

Grimm smiles, and it's filled with so much malice that it makes my stomach turn. "Don't say reckless things, Luna. I waited for you. I trusted you to do what my president needs. If you're not careful, he'll turn you to mulch like that bitch Paulina."

"What do you know about Paulina?" It's nearly a whisper.

"How do you think I met the Iron Sinners, Luna?" He steps forward. "Don't you remember them from back when we were teenagers, always coming and going in the middle of the night?"

I think back to living with Steven and his family. His dad had lots of visitors, and they usually came by late at night, but I never knew what they were doing.

"Your dad was an Iron Sinner?"

"Fuck no." Grimm laughs. "He was a fucking drunk who couldn't be trusted to hold a whiskey bottle upright, much less a gun. But he had connections in Glendale, so he hooked them up with people who could sell product for them. In return, they loaned him one of their girls when they came through town."

I think back to that time—to a night in particular. I woke up for some water and walked in on him and some girl I didn't recognize in the living room. She was much younger than him, with long dark hair. She was the girl in the photograph in Ghost's desk.

My stomach turns, and I wonder how much of that Ghost knows. He seemed to think Paulina was the one being cheated on, but Grimm is saying they were using her as payment.

"She wouldn't do that."

"Are you sure?" Grimm leans in, grinning. "How do you think Titan knew she was going to turn on the club? She confided in dear old Dad that she was done and that she had a friend in the Twisted Kings who was going to help. Who knows, maybe he would have if I hadn't spilled her plans to Titan first."

"You got Paulina killed." A tear slips down my cheek. "They tortured her."

"Don't say it like I'm the villain. She knew what she was getting into when she started letting them pimp her out. She'd do anything for a bump. Girls like that don't give a shit. She wasn't loyal, and she got what she deserved."

"You're sick." I shove at his chest, and he grabs me by the cheeks.

He pulls me so close I almost vomit at the smell of him.

"You're right, Luna. I am sick. Sick for you. If you're smart, you'll remember that, or you'll end up like her. These next few weeks might be rough while you learn your new place, but it could be worse. I promise."

34

Ghost

Luna never responded to my last text message, and it's my first clue that something is wrong.

She's a light sleeper, and she keeps the volume for her notifications turned up so it will wake her if I message her in the middle of the night. I've told her she doesn't need to do that, while at the same time, I love that she doesn't want to miss talking to me when she can. She likes knowing where I am as much as I like keeping tabs on her.

But tonight, I didn't get a response. My message from thirty minutes ago is unread, and I get a bad feeling.

The prospects open the gate to the compound, and I roll up beside Steel.

"Everything good here tonight?" I ask.

"Uneventful." Ricky shrugs. "Everything okay at the hospital? She left right when you asked."

"Who left?"

"Luna?" The prospect answers, digging for his phone.

"What are you talking about?" I snap as my stomach plummets.

The prospect skims through his phone while Steel looks between us.

"Something wrong?" Steel asks.

"We're about to find out."

"Here." The prospect reaches his phone out to me. "You texted that Luna's mom was just admitted, and she needed to get to her right away. You were meeting her there?"

It's more a question than an answer, and every word fogs my head because I sure as fuck didn't say that.

"Luna doesn't know her mom." My teeth grind, and I grab his phone out of his hand.

I read the message, and I know immediately from the tone of the text that Luna was the one who sent it, even if she masked the sender to make it appear like it came from my phone. I abbreviate all my texts, and she spells everything out. And then there's the fact that she was nice.

When I give an order, I don't care how it's received. It's a prospect's job to do what's expected without questioning me.

I look up at Ricky. "You let Luna leave the compound alone?"

"You said—"

"I didn't send you this fucking text." I shove the phone back into his hand. "And you should know better than to let someone leave alone when we're in the middle of a fucking war."

It takes everything in me not to blow his fucking head off. That's a problem for later. Revving my engine, I start toward the clubhouse.

Luna grew up in foster care, never knowing her mom. The text is a bold-faced lie, which means I need to figure out where she really went.

Behind me, I hear Steel and Legacy's bikes following me down the long drive that leads to the clubhouse. I cut my engine when I get there and hop off, storming through the front door.

But Legacy is right behind me.

"Ghost." He jogs to catch up, grabbing my shoulder. "She wouldn't have just bailed, brother."

"I know." I shrug him off, continuing down the hall to my office. "I'm not pissed because I think she'd just fucking leave."

She wouldn't.

She can't.

I won't survive it.

"What do you think happened then?"

"Someone had to have drawn her out. It's the only thing that makes sense. I just don't know why she would listen to them. Fuck."

When I reach my office, the door is cracked, so I know she's been in here. I shove it open, and I can still smell the scent of her vanilla lotion hanging in the air. Legacy pauses in the doorway as Steel comes up beside him.

"Don't tell me to drop this, Prez." I circle my desk and plant my fists on top of it. "I know we agreed she was my responsibility and that if she brought more shit to the club, then that was it. But that's not it."

Steel steps forward, glancing around the room. He looks down at the desk while I watch him approach, but I can't read what he's thinking.

Luna was the enemy when I brought her here, and I've been dragging my feet on claiming her as my old lady, so she doesn't have the same protections as Tempe. Steel could order me to let this go, and I'd have to listen. But he's quiet.

He plants his hand over a piece of paper on my desk, pushing it toward me. "I'm not telling you to let her go, Marcus. I already know she's yours. She's *ours*. We'll get her back."

Steel taps the piece of paper on my desk, and I look down to see it's a note from Luna. The letters swoop and curl. Everything about her is delicate and beautiful.

Picking up the paper, I try to process her words, and what I've done sinks in.

I love you.

I've never said it to her, even if I have felt it since the first time I locked eyes with that girl. The words never felt big enough to describe what I feel.

Clarity, contentment. Overwhelming peace.

She talks about home like we can build it wherever we want, when really, she's home to me.

If I thought losing Paulina ended me, I was wrong. If they hurt Luna, I'll lose all I have left.

"Let us help," Steel says. "Don't shut us out right now. We're only getting her back if we do it together."

He's right.

I've lied for this girl.

Taken a brand for this girl.

Reserved my soul for this girl.

But I can't do this alone.

"Okay." I drop into my chair and find my focus. "I need to figure out why she left and where she was headed. Until we know that, we're dead in the water."

Steel's phone chimes with a text, so he grabs it out of his pocket. "Havoc is heading back with the rest of the crew now. Patch stitched up Chaos, so I should go check on him. We'll be ready to roll once you give the word. Keep me updated."

"Hey, Prez..." I say when Steel and Legacy turn to leave, and they freeze, looking back at me. "Thanks."

"We've got your back, Marcus. She's family." Steel nods. "We'll bring her home."

My brothers leave me alone so I can focus, and I lock myself in my office to search for any clues as to where Luna might have gone. She's no longer here, but she lingers in the air, and it's a unique form of torture I didn't know existed until this moment.

Leaning back, I try to see the room from Luna's perspective. I try to walk it back and figure out why she was in here, and what happened to make her leave.

My desk drawer is cracked, so I peel it open. The stack of pictures inside is out of order from her going through them. The picture of Luna is on top, and it makes me wish I could pull her out of the photograph and bring her back. Beneath it is a picture of Paulina, and it feels like history repeating itself.

Except she and Paulina are different people. While Paulina was similar to Luna when she was younger, she changed. She fell in with my enemies, and she became more like them than I wanted to admit back then. I accepted her lies because it was easier than seeing through them and admitting all the ways I was failing her.

I wanted to believe her, but I knew things were bad. I knew they were feeding her drugs, and I knew what that club did with their women. I should have done something sooner to get her out of there. By the time I acted, it was too late.

I refuse to let that happen to Luna.

Waking up my computer, I start digging through recently opened files.

I've already been through the video footage from my office, so I know that she was on here right before she left. But with the angle, I couldn't tell what she was looking at.

Whatever she saw on my computer is the reason she disappeared.

There's nothing there at first, which means she deleted it intentionally to slow me down. She thinks she's doing what's right because I've kept her in the dark. She has no idea how messy this gets or that I've suspected the person who hired her knew her outside of the job posting. It's possible she thinks she can fix this.

I should have told her more.

It takes me a few minutes to recover what Luna deleted, and once I do, I see a message from the same unknown sender who started threatening me weeks ago, demanding I hand Luna over. The conversation quickly turns to them speaking directly to Luna, confirming they know her well enough to understand how she operates a system.

Whatever she did gave her away.

As I read more, I see why Luna left. They threatened Austin, Bea, the club, her home. She'd never let anyone hurt the people she cares about, so she probably thinks she's doing the right thing.

She isn't considering that we're already at war. They were already coming whether she turned herself over or not.

I type the address they sent her into my phone. Chances are they've already moved her, but it's a starting point.

Leaving my office, I make my way to the bar and see all my brothers gathered. Havoc is organizing the prospects and reassigning who is on patrol as Steel hands out guns and orders.

"Find her?" he asks me.

I shake my head. "Not exactly, but I know where she was headed."

We load up into three vans, with Patch driving the one I'm in. Having a medic on hand is always important in retrieval missions, but I hope we don't need him.

I continue scrolling through my phone while we drive to the warehouse district because something still doesn't sit right. I assumed this was personal from the beginning, but the fact that they knew her style of hacking feels too specific. She's been doing that since she was younger, so they could have come into her life at any point. Not to mention that they're still hanging on after all this time.

Pulling up the address against city records, I look for any ties between the owner and Luna. We know whoever hired her joined the Iron Sinners after Albuquerque, but that's it.

I search permits and ownership transfers until I find the warehouse they lured Luna to. I'm not surprised to see it's in the name of a shell corporation because that's how the Iron Sinners operate. Pulling up that particular business license, I review the names of the associates to see if any stand out. Surprisingly, one does.

Steven Ulysses.

It's an uncommon last name and familiar to me. I've heard it before, but I just can't place where it was.

Ulysses.

My heart hammers as I put the pieces together, and I think back to all the research I did on Luna when she first came to the clubhouse. I looked into every foster family she stayed with, and after the story she told me in the office, I circled back around to one in particular.

Birch and Maya Ulysses. She lived with them from fifteen to eighteen. They had two kids, and one was named Steven.

"Fuck." I tip my head back, gripping my phone.

"What is it?" Legacy asks, but I don't look over at him because that's when it hits me.

This isn't business, it's personal.

He didn't just hire her to do a job; he tested her for his club so he could bring her in. On top of that, Luna said he was the one to protect her from his father.

He thinks she's his, and if that's the case, there's only one place he'd bring her.

I'd know. I did the same thing.

"I know where they're taking Luna." I look over at Legacy. "And we've got a problem."

35

Luna

My wrists ache from being bound behind my back. I try to shift in my seat but can't get comfortable no matter what I do.

Grimm sits beside me in the backseat of the truck. His arm is draped around me, and I have to hold back my desire to vomit every time he rubs the peak of my shoulder with his thumb.

A prospect is driving. They don't talk, and the silence is unnerving.

"Don't worry, doll. Once you learn to cooperate, this will all get much easier for you." Grimm's eyes gleam as he looks at my hands tied behind my back.

He leans in, kissing the side of my head, and my body tenses.

I went willingly because I knew if I didn't, things would get worse, and I needed a chance to figure out a way out of this. But now I think he's misinterpreting it as me being compliant, and his affection has my skin crawling.

"How much longer?" I ask.

His thumb trails up and down the bare skin on the back of my neck, and it sends a chill through me.

"Almost there."

We haven't been driving long, but we're well outside the city, where all the desert looks the same. It reminds me of the road that leads to the Twisted Kings clubhouse, but this one goes in the opposite direction. I don't know what awaits me, but it can't be good.

Finally, a pinprick of lights comes into view up ahead, and then they start to multiply the closer we get. Buildings scatter the desert, and a long fence surrounds the property. It extends so far that I can't see the end of it in the darkness.

Only one thing is clear as the truck pulls to a stop at the gate—the large devil's skull with flames in the center of the iron rods.

Grimm must have brought me to the Iron Sinners compound.

The truck rolls through the gate, and my heart hammers. This is worse than I thought. Of all the places they could have taken me, this is the one place I'll never get out. And one place the Twisted Kings can't go.

It would turn their war nuclear.

As much as my heart aches for Ghost, wishing this had played out differently, all I can do now is hope that I can figure my own way out of this. I thought this was about a job, but Grimm never intended to let me go. I need to fix this before Ghost tries to come for me because he'll just end up getting hurt if he does.

In the dark distance, a gunshot rings out, and it makes me jump. The moment I flinch, I regret it because Grimm pulls me closer. He holds me against him, and it makes the hair on the back of my neck stand on its ends.

Home.

I should have known when he used that word that this is what he meant. A place with no escape, and the one place he knows the Twisted Kings won't breach to save me. A place he belongs because he's turned into someone as sick as they are—someone as disturbed as his father.

I watch the clubhouse get bigger on our approach, and my stomach turns. The Twisted Kings get a lot of crap for the illegal things they do as a club, but they're nothing like the Iron Sinners.

The Twisted Kings have certain moral lines they refuse to cross, and they protect their own. Anyone with them is there by choice. Iron Sinners don't see their club that way. The women here aren't like the patch bunnies back at the clubhouse. Most are brought here unwillingly, and the ones who try to leave are drugged and caged.

Reina lost a friend to this club once, so I've heard all the stories. Women who do walk back out don't leave the same. They're used until they're a shell of who they were.

I wiggle against the handcuffs, but it's no use. My heart races as the truck stops, and Grimm climbs out first.

He grabs me by the arm and pulls me across the bucket seat, not caring that he's rough or that my hands are bound behind my back. Grimm yanks me out of the truck, and I stumble as I land the wrong way on my ankle.

My steps are unsteady, and each one hurts, but he doesn't slow as he pushes me ahead of him to the clubhouse steps.

Grimm shoves my back when I walk too slowly, pushing me inside.

The clubhouse is large but in disrepair, and it smells like smoke and something else awful. Urine, maybe?

The Iron Sinners are partying, but it's nothing like I'm used to seeing at the Twisted Kings compound. To my left, a group of bikers are sticking needles in their arms, and a girl in the corner looks dead or damn near close to it. Eyes follow me as I'm pushed through, and when they skim down my body, there's nothing flirty about it.

They're predators.

The things I know they've done to women send every nerve in my body on high alert.

Looking up at Grimm, I try to wrap my mind around the monster he's become. I always knew his father's blood ran through his veins, but I hoped he'd never actually become him. He looked out for his brother once. He looked out for *me*.

How did that become so twisted?

Grimm guides me into a quieter room, where the music is muffled so it doesn't numb my ears. A man is sitting on a couch with topless women flanking his sides as Grimm pushes me to stand in the center.

"Prez." Grimm nods at Titan, who hasn't taken his eyes off me since I walked in.

Titan's dark hair is buzzed to his scalp. He has tattoos covering his arms and neck, with the Iron Sinners symbol on the center of his throat. I've never met him in person, but I've seen pictures. And now I know they do nothing to capture the unfiltered evil that bleeds out of him.

"You're prettier in person," Titan says, smirking at me. "But I'd prefer you blonde, so we're going to have to wash that shit out of your hair."

I roll my shoulders back, not liking that it even matters to Titan. Grimm made it sound like I was being brought here for him, but Titan insinuates something different.

"You've caused me and my men all sorts of trouble." Titan looks up at me from where he's sitting, narrowing his eyes. "I expect you to make up for that."

"She will." Grimm grabs my arm tightly. "Won't you, baby doll?"

I grit my teeth, not answering.

Nothing I say will do me any good right now. If I'm not careful, my tongue will just get me into more trouble.

"A quiet little mouse." Titan sneers. "I'm going to have fun making you scream."

Grimm chuckles, showing no sympathy for the situation he's put me in. If anything, Titan's threat has excitement flashing in his eyes. I suppose that's what it takes to be one of them.

Heartless.

Soulless.

Disgusting.

The girls sitting at Titan's sides tuck against him. Their eyes are hazy as their eyelashes flutter. Whatever drugs they're on must be intense because they don't seem fully aware of what's going on around them.

"What do you want me to do with her, Prez?" Grimm tugs my arm, and it knocks me off balance.

My ankle twists again, and I wince in pain. The reaction has Titan's eyes gleaming.

"Put her in my room," he says to Grimm. "You know the rules. You can have her once I'm done breaking her in."

Grimm nods, dragging me behind him as I try to resist. But with my hurt ankle and bound wrists, I have no leverage.

Titan's words play in a loop as Grimm tugs me through the party. Everyone is wasted and high. I can barely breathe through the cigarette smoke.

Grimm pulls me around a corner and down a long hall. We pass a door, and I hear a girl screaming, but from the pitch, I get the feeling it's not out of pleasure. She screams again, and my blood chills.

"Please don't do this." I try to resist as Grimm tugs me along.

Grimm chuckles, stopping at a door at the end of the hall. "Don't pretend you don't want this, baby doll. You were their slut for a year. Now you get to be ours."

"That's not what it was." I stumble as Grimm pushes me into the room.

With my hands bound behind my back, I can't catch myself, and I fall face-first onto the bed.

"Not yet." Grimm grabs me by the hair, pulling me up, and tears sting my eyes. "Titan will want you over here first."

Grimm pulls me by the hair. I wince when my weight lands on my ankle as I stumble to follow him. I must have rolled it, and his rough handling of me isn't helping.

But my ankle is the least of my worries when I see where in the room Grimm is taking me.

In a corner is a space where the carpet has been ripped out, so it's just concrete. There's a hook in the center with an iron chain attached to it.

"No." I try to pull back, but it's no use. "Please don't. You don't want this. You wanted to protect me."

"I am protecting you. I'm making you one of us."

Grimm pulls me to the ground, removing my handcuffs, only to replace them with the shackles that attach me to the concrete. My arms are in front of me now, but the chain has no give, so I can't get my hands more than four inches from the ground.

I try to kick him as he grabs my ankles, handcuffing them together. He tightens it so it digs into the one that's swelling, and I wince.

"I thought I was here for you." I think of anything to say that might turn this around.

With Grimm, maybe I have a chance. Maybe I can remind him of the flash of good I remember when we were kids. But if he leaves me at the mercy of Titan, this is over.

"You are here for me, doll." Grimm grabs my waist and pulls me in, licking the side of my neck.

He drags his fingers over my lips, and I try to turn away as bile rises in my throat.

"But this is how it works." Reaching down, he grabs me between the legs, and a tear slips down my cheek.

"You want to be my bitch; you need to show my president you're worth keeping around first. So be a good girl when he and his officers get here. The better you take them, the quicker you're mine."

36

Ghost

We stop two miles away from the Iron Sinners compound. Our vans idle on a desolate road as we stand in a circle.

"It won't take much for this to go to shit." Steel looks around the group. "Even if the Iron Sinners are distracted, it's their territory. They have the upper hand."

Havoc hums, pulling his hair back. "We're outnumbered and outgunned, even with the element of surprise."

Steel nods. "Chances of not walking back out are high, which means we only go in with a unanimous vote."

He looks at me, knowing nothing will stop me either way. But hopefully, when I breach that gate, I'll have my brothers at my side.

"To be clear, killing as many Iron Sinners as we can get our hands on isn't our mission tonight. We go in, and we get Luna. Then we get her out. We take down whoever stands in our way, but that's it. The longer we stay, the worse our chances. We'll deal with the rest of them another day. Understood?"

Everyone nods.

"Let's vote." Steel straightens his back.

"I'm in." Legacy is the first to speak. "We protect our fucking family, or we're nothing."

Havoc nods. "Seconded. And even though Chaos is still getting fixed up back at the clubhouse, he said he'd vote to burn the Iron Sinners to the ground if he could. So, we have his vote."

"You already know where I stand." I cross my arms over my chest, waiting.

"I say let's level those fuckers." Soul grins. "We've been too easy on them."

All around, words of support ring out until the final vote is left with Steel, and I don't know what he'll choose. He has to consider the club as a whole, not just my feelings for Luna. If he agrees to this, he might not come home to Tempe and Austin, and I know that's the last thing he wants.

"We protect our own." Steel nods. "To the grave. If we don't do that, then we don't stand for anything."

He reaches out to shake my hand, and I take it.

Not too long ago, I broke his trust, but his loyalty to me and our club is why he's respected by his men. Why any one of us would easily give up our lives to save his. He would do the same.

"One more thing then." I swallow hard, gripping Steel's hand. "I want to claim Luna as my old lady."

It might not be the best time to bring this vote to the club, but it's important it happens now. Accepting an old lady is just as important as patching in a new member. It offers her protection if I'm gone. It makes her a part of us.

"This can't wait until tomorrow because if I don't come out of this, I need to know Luna will be taken care of."

Steel nods. "Any objections?"

He waits for anyone to speak up, but they don't.

Their silence is the most peace I've felt in a long time. I might not make it out of this alive, but they'll make sure Luna is okay regardless.

"That's settled then." Steel smirks, releasing my hand. "Let's go get your old lady."

Those two words are a balm to my soul, and I wish I'd done it when she could have been standing here to accept that title.

"And let's put a few Iron Sinners in the ground while we're at it." Soul grins.

Everyone is in agreement as we climb back into the vans. The door shuts, and we start to roll forward with the headlights off so we won't be spotted at a distance.

Pulling out my computer, I start jamming all outgoing signals. We're walking into Iron Sinners territory, which means they have the upper hand. In the best-case scenario, some of them are out tonight on runs or at one of their strip clubs. The harder it is for them to call for backup if this goes south, the better.

The vans circle around the compound in a wide arc as we make our way to the north side. It's their most vulnerable border and our only chance.

When we stop at the fence line, I know we'll have to go the rest of the way on foot. It will make it easier to sneak in, but hell getting out. If they figure out we're here, we won't be able to outrun them.

Backup will stay with the vans for a quick getaway, but if they need to intervene, chances are they'll be too late.

Climbing out of the van, I approach the fence. It's impossible to hack the Iron Sinners system remotely, but now that I'm in range of their wireless network, I'm able to find a weak spot to break in.

Once I'm in their system, I search for the security network, shutting down the perimeter alarms. Then, I find the camera feeds and send them in a loop so they won't see us coming. They have half the number we do on our compound, so it doesn't take long.

I'd like to shut down their entire grid now that I have access, but that will just alert them to our presence.

"Done." I shut the laptop and set it back in the van. "If they're keeping her anywhere, it's probably the outbuilding or one of the member's rooms."

It's nearly impossible to process what they'd do to her in either, but I swallow that down for now.

Steel steps forward. "Soul and I will take a few prospects to the outbuilding. Havoc, I want you with Ghost and Legacy to check the main building. Remember, stay out of sight. The second we're caught, we're not walking out of here."

"Then let's not get caught." Havoc smirks.

Legacy chuckles, pulling out his gun. "Good plan."

Stepping through the fence, we slowly split off. I watch Steel and Soul disappear into the darkness as we circle to the main clubhouse.

The Iron Sinners are partying, which is good news because it means they're distracted.

During the van ride here, we studied the layout of the compound from satellite images to give us a vague map to follow. Havoc takes the lead, with Legacy at our backs as we circle until we're at the side where the members' rooms are situated. He finds an empty one and signals us over.

"This is the best entry point." He grabs the cracked window and peels it open.

Legacy climbs through it first, followed by me and then Havoc. Once I'm in, I pull out my phone to scan the network again. Their security feeds are still looping, including the cameras in the hallway. I can't see what's happening live, so I don't know if anyone is out there.

"There's going to be too many rooms to check them all."

"We don't have to." I tap back into the network and go to the surveillance archives.

Pulling up the footage from earlier tonight, I find Luna being brought into the compound in a truck. She stumbles when she's dragged out of it, and it's clear she twists her ankle, but the man dragging her doesn't notice.

He takes her inside, and I watch as she is brought to Titan. They talk briefly before the man pulls her down the hallway, and my chest burns when the bedroom door closes behind her.

"Last door on the left. That's where she is."

I pocket the phone, and Havoc nods, moving to the door. He peels it open, holding his gun to his chest as he looks out.

"Clear."

Legacy and I follow Havoc out of the room and down the hall as fast as we can. Voices and screaming come from behind the closed doors, and I'm tempted to set fire to the clubhouse on our way out.

Rushing to the room Luna is in, we pause at the door, listening for anything on the other side. Then Havoc slowly turns the handle, and we shove our way through.

We sweep into the room one by one. My gun is ready, and I'm relieved there's only one person in here with her. I aim for his head as Havoc shuts the door and locks it.

"Back the fuck up," I say through gritted teeth.

The man stiffens, taking a step back and turning to us, grinning. He has one hand at his side while the other has his gun pointed at Luna.

"Marcus?" Tears spill from her eyes the second her gaze connects with mine. "You shouldn't have come here."

Like there's anywhere else I would be. "I've got you."

The man chuckles at my reassurances. "You must be the man who's been fucking my woman."

I take a step forward but pause when he presses the barrel of the gun to Luna's temple.

"I told you to hand her over, Ghost. You didn't. My baby doll had to find me all on her own. She knows where she belongs."

"Take your fucking gun off her," I command through gritted teeth.

"Why? She's ours now. Our little animal we're going to tame."

Looking down, I see she's shackled to the ground, and my gut sinks. He chained Luna, and the metal is rubbing her skin raw.

"Brave of you to come here. I'll give you that." He sneers.

Luna looks up at him. "Steven—"

He shoves the gun harder against her temple. "I told you don't call me that. I'm Grimm now."

That must be Steven's road name.

"I'm sorry," Luna cries, and I hate that he's making her apologize. "Please don't do this."

"Don't worry, baby. I'm going to set you free from them once and for all."

Grimm reaches into his pocket to get out his phone, and I know we're out of time. The second he alerts Titan to the fact that we're here, they'll storm the room. Havoc and Legacy must think the same because we all move in unison.

Havoc circles the left, and Legacy goes right, but I relax the arm holding the gun and reach for the knife in my back pocket. Shots will tip the Iron Sinners off.

Grimm watches the three of us circling fast and has no choice but to drop his phone as Legacy lunges for his arm.

With Grimm distracted, I make my move, but I'm too late.

His gun goes off, and Luna flinches.

My world stops as I wait for her to fall to the ground, but she doesn't.

I sink my knife into Grimm's jugular, and blood pours over my hand. For a second, I think he missed, and this is over.

But then I see Legacy slump to the ground next to me.

"Legacy?" I call out, but his eyes are dimming. "Stay with me, brother."

Grimm smiles as he watches the scene unfold. As he sees whatever look crosses my face when Legacy falls.

I pull the blade out and drive it into an artery this time, finishing him and shoving him to the ground. Torturing him isn't worth wasting time that needs to be spent helping Luna and Legacy.

"Fuck." Havoc rushes to the door. "There's no way they didn't hear that gunshot."

He grabs a dresser and slides it in front of the door, starting a barricade.

"Marcus," Luna cries, trying to reach for Legacy, but the chains stop her. "He took the bullet for me."

"I've got you. I've got him." My head fogs, and it all feels like lies as everything starts spinning out. "Stay with me, brother."

I grab the keys to the shackles and handcuffs off Grimm and undo Luna's wrists and ankles.

"You okay, beautiful? Did he hurt you?" I tug the shackles from her wrists and grab her tear-stained cheeks.

Her blue eyes blink up at me. "I'm okay. We need to help Legacy."

Releasing Luna, I rush to Legacy, and his eyes blink open.

"It's nothing." He grunts, trying to sit up.

Luna takes one of his arms and I take the other while blood pours out of the bullet wound in his leg. His face pales, and he gets heavier in my grip.

"He doesn't look good, Marcus."

No, he doesn't. But I don't want to say that out loud for Legacy's sake.

Or maybe it's for mine.

I can't lose my brother.

"We have company," Havoc says as pounding starts on the door. "Lots of company."

I pull out my phone, and it barely registers my fingers because they're coated in blood. Opening the network, I shut down the signal blocker so I can call Steel.

He answers on the first ring, out of breath. "Outbuilding was empty."

"We found her, but Legacy got hit. We need Patch."

"Start the van," Steel shouts, and I'm relieved to hear he's already out. "We're gonna drive to you, but I need you to meet us as far out as you can, and we'll pray to fuck nothing takes the tires out."

"Got it."

I hang up and look at Havoc. "We need to get him out of here. Steel's headed our way."

"Let's go." Havoc crosses the room to Legacy. "Ghost, get her out. I've got Legacy."

Luna is in shock as she sits back on her heels with blood on her hands. She doesn't blink until I pull her up into my arms.

"Marcus—"

"Focus on me. I've got you."

"But Legacy—Bea."

"Luna." I grab the sides of her face. "Havoc's got him. We need to get out of here now. Can you do that for me?"

Her entire body shakes as she nods, and I help her stand, carrying her weight as we walk to the window. I jump out first to help Luna climb outside, then assist Havoc with getting Legacy through next.

"I'm good." Legacy hangs weakly at Havoc's side as he finds his footing in the dirt.

Adrenaline is keeping him going, but the second that stops, I don't know what kind of condition he'll be in.

My brother took a bullet for my girl. He's saved my life and now hers. I can't lose him over this.

"I've got him." Havoc steadies Legacy, helping him limp. "Get Luna."

"I'm okay." She shakes her head. "You don't need to help me."

"You hurt your ankle, and we need to run." I don't wait for her to argue as I pick her up.

The four of us rush away from the clubhouse, and beside me, I sense Legacy fading.

Gunshots ring out in the desert, but they miss us in the darkness.

The second the van comes into view, I pick up my pace. A prospect swings the van around, and Steel and Patch jump out to help us. The doors are barely shut when a bullet hits the side, just missing us.

I don't relax until the tires hit pavement, and we disappear into the night, hoping the Iron Sinners are too wasted to track us down.

"How is he?" Steel asks, kneeling over Legacy.

Patch has him spread out on the floor of the van, and all the color has drained from his face. The second we stopped, his adrenaline tanked, and he passed out.

"Not good." Patch applies pressure on the bullet wound. "We're gonna need a hospital."

"They'll ask questions," Havoc warns.

"And we'll figure out how to answer them." Steel's jaw tenses. "We do what we need to do to save him."

Patch nods, yelling new directions for the prospect to take us to the hospital.

Luna starts shaking beside me, and I pull her closer.

"You're safe now." I tip her chin up, brushing her tears away. "They can't hurt you here."

"I'm sorry." Her fingers clench on my cut. "I thought I could stop this. It's all my fault. What happened to Legacy—"

"It's on them, Luna. Not you. They'd have come for you either way. You're safe, and that's all that matters. You're home now."

She curls against me, shaking with her sobs. With one arm, I hold the love of my life, and with my other, I hold my brother's hand.

My family is together.

My family is whole.

So long as Legacy can pull through this.

37

Luna

One Week Later

Ghost has been working nonstop on the perimeter of the compound for the past week, adding additional sensors and cameras. An animal won't get onto the property without him knowing about it. And it's one of the many reasons I know he's stressed.

He keeps busy to stay out of his head, and I wish I could take it all back.

As if he didn't have enough haunting him, that night he rescued me added to it.

Seeing how they chained me down.

Watching his brother take a bullet to save my life.

It haunts me too.

I thought that by taking action, I could save the club from the trouble I was causing. But if I'd known Steven was behind it all along, I would have known that was never possible. He didn't want me to finish a job; he wanted to cage me like his pet.

And I'm thankful every day that Ghost saved me from him.

I'm still working through the nightmares of what happened, but hopefully, someday, I'll be able to move past it.

The only relief I find now is in Steven's death.

He would have let his club rape me, drug me, and abuse me just to bring me into it. That wasn't him caring, and it certainly wasn't him saving me. He was evil through and through, and there was no bringing him back.

I just wish Legacy hadn't been shot in the process. Thankfully, he's on the mend, and Ghost and Steel are finally picking him up from the hospital today. Ghost and I have been helping around Legacy's house, keeping Bea in a routine since Margaret is still struggling with her own health issues.

We're doing all we can to repay Legacy for saving my life. Although, nothing feels like enough.

I pace the kitchen and wait while Bea watches cartoons. I'm the reason she almost lost her father, and I hope he forgives me for putting him in that position.

When the front door finally swings open, Bea jumps up. Legacy limps in, and his jaw tenses with every step, but he won't let Ghost help him. He tries to bury his pain so Bea won't see it.

"Daddy!" Bea runs to Legacy and throws herself against him.

She grabs his leg, and even if it's not the one that was shot, it shifts his weight, and he winces. He plants a hand on the wall to steady himself as he leans down to kiss the top of her head.

"Morning, Honey Bea."

Legacy was born to be a dad. His little girl is his entire world, and even if he's hurting, he reaches down to pick her up.

"Daddy, you're home." She wraps her arms around his neck.

"Of course. Not even the doctors can keep me away from you."

"Is your boo-boo better?"

He taps her nose with his finger. "Almost."

"Did you bring me a pudding cup?"

Legacy tips his head back and laughs. "No, but I heard Uncle Marcus stocked the fridge for you this morning."

"Yay!" Bea cheers, and he sets her down so she can run to the kitchen.

She stole Legacy's pudding every day she went to see him at the hospital, and clearly, she can't get enough.

Ghost stops beside Legacy and grabs his arm. "You got it?"

"I'm good." Legacy shrugs Ghost off, stepping into the house. "Hey, Luna. Thanks for looking out for Bea while I was gone."

"Of course."

He drops into the chair that faces the kitchen so he can watch Bea eat her pudding while she eyes the cartoons from her stool at the counter.

"I'll get the bags." Ghost steps outside, leaving me alone with Legacy.

I circle the couch and sit facing him. While Ghost has gone to see him every day, I haven't seen him since he was bleeding out in the van after taking a bullet for me.

"Don't do that," Legacy says, shaking his head at me.

"Don't do what?"

"Don't feel guilty. It's all over your face."

"I'm the reason this happened to you."

He drags his hand through his hair. "Luna, this comes with the gig. When you're around here long enough, you'll understand that. I'd have done this for any of my brothers because that's what this patch means to me."

"If Ghost had lost you—"

"Then he'd have you and Bea." Legacy looks at Bea. "And she'd have had him. Do I want any of that to happen? No. But that's how this family works around here. You're a part of that now, so you need to understand that."

Tears sting my eyes. "I didn't mean to bring you all into it. But they had pictures of Austin and Bea. If they got hurt because of me—"

"Luna," he cuts me off. "The fact that you put yourself in danger because you were trying to protect them is why I don't regret what happened for a second. You were protecting them, and I was protecting you. That's what we do for family."

"Family..."

Legacy looks to the door, where Ghost is carrying another one of his bags in.

"Yes, family. You may or may not see it, but you saved my brother, Luna. He was a shell of himself until he met you. I couldn't watch him go back to that. And you didn't deserve whatever punishment you were bringing on yourself by turning yourself over."

"So you don't blame me?" Tears sting my eyes. "You don't hate me for what happened?"

"Never." He looks up as Ghost walks into the room. "I'm thankful for you, and so is Bea. You're family now."

My throat burns as I hold back tears because I truly believe what Legacy is telling me. He doesn't trust anyone, but he thinks I'm good for Ghost. And I want to be that.

"Now, get out of here and enjoy your honeymoon phase or whatever the fuck people in happy relationships do."

"We can stay if you need us to," Ghost offers.

But Legacy waves his hand at him. "I'll be fine. I need some time with Bea to talk to her about Margaret."

"Is she getting worse?"

Legacy nods, and my heart hurts knowing how close Bea is to her nanny.

"Don't worry about us. I've got it," Legacy says.

"I'll take care of you, Daddy." Bea runs over and jumps onto his lap, and he smiles through the pain that flashes in his eyes.

"I know you will." He kisses her forehead. "But it's my job to take care of you. So you let me worry about that."

She nestles against him.

"Call us if you need anything." Ghost snags my hand, pulling me up off the couch. "Don't hurt yourself getting better."

"I'll call. All right?"

Something about how he says it leads me to believe he won't, but we don't have much of a choice.

Gathering the last of our things, we leave Legacy and Bea. And when we step outside, Ghost pauses on the front porch.

"Would you ever want to live out here?" he asks, wrapping his arms around me.

I glance at the small street they call the neighborhood. "I've never thought about it. It's quiet."

"It is." He nods.

"And I know you like being in the middle of things to keep an eye on them."

He leans down, kissing the center of my forehead. "I can keep an eye on things from anywhere. But if you want a home, I'd be fine living out here."

"I already have a home, Ghost. I have you."

He brushes my hair off my face when the wind kicks up. "Have I told you lately you're perfect for me?"

"Yes. But that doesn't mean you should stop saying it."

"Don't worry, little owl, I won't." He leans down to kiss me, and I sink into his hold.

I part my lips, and he deepens the kiss, claiming me like I'm not already completely his.

"Ghost," I mumble against his mouth, and his chest rumbles with a growl.

Tempe calls Steel Jameson most of the time, reserving his road name only for when they're at the clubhouse. But I rarely call Ghost Marcus.

Maybe it's because I met him as Ghost. Or maybe it's because I know that's who he is in so many ways. A man who will always be haunted, but he found a way to let me in and love me anyway.

"Let's go home," I say.

He takes my hand to lead me down the porch steps, and that's where I am because home is where Ghost is.

Epilogue
Ghost

Four Months Later

I HOLD MY HANDS over Luna's eyes and guide her into the bedroom.

"What are you hiding?"

"Nothing you won't like." I kick the door closed behind her, removing my hands to free her gaze.

She blinks, taking in the purple glow in the corner of the room before smiling so big her entire face beams.

"You set this up for me?" She walks up to the desk I set up in the corner, grazing her fingers over the keys of her brand-new keyboard. Neon purple lights frame her new gaming station, and I got her a lavender chair that matches her hair. "Kicking me out of your office?"

"Nope, if I'm in there, I expect you to follow." I wrap my hands around her waist, pulling us into the chair with her sitting on top of me. "But with Venom patching in and taking over perimeter surveillance, I don't have to be in there as often. Plus, being in our room gives me the privacy to do this..."

I skate my hand around her stomach, teasing the line of her sweatpants before dipping my fingers in. Grazing them over her pussy, I groan when I find her already slick.

"Play your game for me, little owl. I want to feel your excitement while you do it."

"Ghost." She gasps when I drive a finger deep into her core.

"Game, Luna." I circle up to her clit and toy with it.

She reaches for the keyboard, hitting the key to start the game. Her body shivers as I roll my thumb over her.

"Remember when we used to play?" I ask her as her screen loads. "Before you knew who was on the other side of the computer?"

"Yes." She swallows hard, trying to catch her breath. "But you knew it was me."

"I did." I lick a path up the side of her neck, tasting every delicious inch of her. "And do you know what I'd think about?"

Her lips part as she starts to answer, and I drive another finger in.

"Ghost." My name chokes from her lips.

"Yes, Luna?"

She tips her head back, and her character on the screen runs into a wall.

"Keep playing, Luna. You don't get to come until you kill something."

"You're so evil."

I chuckle against her neck, kissing her. "I'll make it worth it."

Luna wiggles in my lap as she wanders on the screen, presumably looking for something to kill and getting distracted every time I pick up my pace.

When she runs into a wall again, I pause, and she groans in response.

"Something wrong?" I kiss her collarbone.

"I'm just"—she chokes as I drive in knuckle deep—"distracted."

"I can see that." And I'm no help as I nip at her ear and roll her ass over my growing length.

Finally, Luna finds something to fight on the screen, but she's clumsy about it, using all her cooldowns at once and still not getting any good hits in. The boss turns and strikes, and her health takes a hit. She runs before she dies, downing a health potion.

"When we used to play, I'd imagine this." I thrust my fingers deep. "You in my lap, and my fingers knuckle deep in your greedy pussy. I'd imagine you playing your game while I played mine."

"But you aren't playing anything."

"Aren't I?" I roll my thumb over her clit, and she almost dies again on the screen. "Come on, Luna. You want to come; all you have to do is win."

"You're making it difficult." She groans.

"Good."

Luna tries to focus on her game, wiggling in my lap. It's borderline torture, and I'm just as relieved as she is when she kills the boss and shoves her keyboard back.

I laugh. "You're going to break it if you're not nice."

Luna jumps up, spinning around to straddle me and almost sending us toppling in the chair. "I don't care if I broke it. I need you to fuck me."

"Yes, ma'am." I lift her, carrying her across the bedroom and tossing her down onto the bed.

She strips off her T-shirt as I pull her pants down her legs. Unless we're fucking with people around us, I want to see every inch of her, and she knows it.

"You now." Luna scoots back when I start to reach for her thighs. "I want to see you too."

Grabbing the bottom of my T-shirt, I strip it off, shedding all my clothes and climbing over her.

"You shouldn't be allowed to look that good." Her gaze skims down to my cock as I kneel between her legs.

"You're one to talk." I tease her pussy with the tip, nudging in far enough to give her a taste of the pressure.

Her core drips, gripping my dick and begging to take me deeper.

"You want me; you can have me."

"Oh, I know." I shift forward slowly, appreciating her as I watch her pussy swallow every inch. "I've got you."

I work my way in until she's taking my full length. Pausing when we connect before slowly fucking her.

This woman is mine. I don't deserve her, but she is.

Her nails dig into my arms as I pick up my pace.

"Touch yourself for me," I direct her. "Let me see you play with your pussy while I fuck you."

Luna bites her lower lip, sliding her hand down and toying with her clit. Her pussy grips my cock so hard I nearly black out. I'm going to watch this with her later and try to help her understand how beautiful it is to watch her pleasure herself while my cock slides in and out.

I'm resisting every urge to plug her up with my cum because I need her release first.

She glides her fingers over her clit, rocking back and forth as her chest turns red. She tips her head back and searches for air as her breath quickens. Her blue eyes meet mine, and when she comes, she grips me so hard that my vision darkens.

I can't hold back as I bury myself deep, coming inside her.

"Fuck, Luna." I pull out to watch my cum drip from her pussy. "I don't deserve you."

She plants her hands on the sides of my face, pulling me down over her and brushing her lips on mine. "Yes, you do, Marcus. You do."

And when she kisses me, I almost believe her. Because this girl is all I've ever wanted, and even if I shouldn't have her, she's mine.

I leave Luna to get dressed and head out into the bar, where I find Legacy and Chaos both sipping beers.

"Want one?"

"I'm good." I shake my head, dropping onto the barstool on Legacy's right and looking out at the room.

It's still early, so the party hasn't really gotten started, but a few outsiders are already mingling with the guys, shooting pool. Things have been calm since our direct attack on the Iron Sinners clubhouse, and I know Titan isn't going to let it go, which means something big is coming.

We're on the verge of battle, and I sense it hanging in the room.

"Hello." A quiet voice comes from my left, and I look to see a girl slowly circling to stand in front of us.

She's completely out of place in a motorcycle club bar. Her big brown eyes are wide, and her pink cheeks brighten as she bats her lashes. Her wavy blonde hair is down, and she's wearing a white sundress with daisies on it.

"Well, if it isn't the farmer's daughter." Chaos skims her over, being a dick as always. "How old are you, babe?"

She tips her chin up, narrowing her eyes. "I didn't know bikers were so worried about underage drinking."

"Honey, you barely look eighteen, much less twenty-one." Chaos chuckles.

"Well, for your information, I turned twenty-one last week." She glares at Chaos. "Besides, I'm not here for a drink. I'm looking for Jesse King."

Legacy hitches an eyebrow, pausing with his beer bottle at his mouth.

"Do you know where I can find him?" The girl clutches her purse, rolling her shoulders back.

She's got a spine; I'll give her that.

"Sure do." Legacy sets his beer bottle down, not taking his eyes off her.

"Well, are you going to tell me where he is?"

"Depends. What do you want with him?"

She opens her mouth to answer but is cut off by Luna coming around the corner.

"Reagan?" Luna's voice pitches, and she runs over to her. "It's been forever."

Luna pulls Reagan in for a big hug, and I'm confused now because I have no idea how they know each other.

When Luna pulls back, she holds onto Reagan's shoulders. "What are you doing here?"

"I came to see my great aunt Margaret. Mom said she's not doing well." Reagan frowns. "What are you doing here? You hang out with bikers now?"

Luna smiles, looking over at me. "I found my home."

"You always did like getting into a little trouble." Reagan laughs. "Maybe you can help me then. I'm looking for Jesse King."

"Jesse, huh?" Luna looks over at us, her eyebrows pinching when her gaze lands on Legacy.

"Yeah, I told Aunt Margaret I'd help out since she can't get back to work anytime soon. I'm his new nanny."

"Fuck no." Legacy stands up so fast his barstool almost goes flying.

Reagan turns her narrowed gaze on him. "I'd really like to talk to Jesse about this, so if you could—"

"You're looking at him, sweetheart." Legacy takes a step forward, scanning her over. "And my answer is thanks, but no way in fucking hell."

Instead of backing down, the girl surprises everyone in the room by rolling her shoulders back.

"Why not?"

"I have a guess—" Chaos opens his mouth to say more, but Legacy shoves his arm, shutting him up.

"Because I said."

"Jesse—"

"The name's Legacy. Not Jesse. And I don't need your fucking help."

He brushes past her, storming out of the clubhouse, and I faintly hear him start his bike. But instead of leaving, Reagan spins around and crosses her arms over her chest.

"Is he always that charming?"

"On a good day." Chaos laughs. "You need a ride home, honey?"

"Nope." She straightens her spine. "I'm here to help my aunt, and that's what I'm going to do."

"That so?"

She nods sharply. "Anyone have Jesse's number so I can figure out where I'm supposed to be staying?"

Chaos bursts out laughing, and I just shake my head. Looks like Legacy just met his match.

Extended Epilogue
Luna

Two Years Later

THE HOUSE IS STILL a construction site, but it's coming along slowly. We have walls now, and soon we'll have floors. We're in the final stretch, which is a good thing, given we're running out of time.

I plant my hand on my stomach, and the baby kicks. So long as he waits until we can move in, everything will be fine.

Part of me will miss the clubhouse. I like the noise, parties, and the fact that people are always around. But my friends are in the neighborhood, and our little one deserves more space and a room of his own.

That, and the last thing I need is club antics waking up a sleeping baby. If I want to party with my man, I'll just get a sitter.

Behind me, I hear the rumbling of a motorcycle approaching, and I look over my shoulder to see Ghost riding toward me. I miss riding on the back of his bike and can't wait until the baby is born. Then we can get back to our monthly date nights where we just drive and spend time together.

Tempe has already offered to babysit. She says it's the least she can do when I'm always the first to offer to help with Austin and Ember.

Ghost hops off his bike, looking too damn good wearing a helmet and leather. He's a walking distraction as he comes toward me, and I wonder for the millionth time how I got so lucky that I get to call him mine.

"How's our little owl doing today?" Ghost stops in front of me, resting his hands on either side of my stomach as he kisses me on the forehead.

"Rolling around on top of my bladder."

He grins, leaning down to whisper to the baby, "Troublemaker."

"Takes after his daddy."

Ghost smirks. "If it will make you feel better, I'll lie down and you can roll around on top of me."

"I'm sure you wouldn't mind that one bit." I roll my eyes, but I can't bite back my smile.

"Nope." He tucks my hair behind my ear, glancing up at the house. "Did you go inside yet?"

"You told me to wait out here."

"And you listened?" He hitches an eyebrow, and I nod. "Good girl."

"Why are we here anyway?" I ask as he laces his fingers through mine and guides me to the front door. "I thought nothing got done this week."

"Nothing on your long list of demands for the contractor." He kisses the back of my hand.

"You make me sound difficult."

"Not at all, beautiful. I want this to be your dream home."

"So, if it's nothing on the list, what did you do?"

He hums. "You'll see."

Ghost leads me into the house, and it looks the same as it did last time I was here. But I still glance around, expecting something to be different.

He guides me to a room in the back of the house where I plan on setting up my gaming station, and when we step inside, I see all the walls have been peeled back.

"You're *de*constructing?" I laugh when I see the mess.

"Exactly." He spins me in his arms so that I'm facing him.

"Do you realize this is the opposite of what you're supposed to be doing? This baby isn't staying in forever."

"Don't worry, the contractor said it's not pushing back any of your deadlines. And this had to be done."

"Oh yeah? Why?"

"You know the club comes first." He rubs the sides of my stomach. "It's how I'll provide for us and the reason we have the family we do today."

"I know." I rest my palm on his cheek. "I never question that. And I'd never ask you to give any of that up for me.

This isn't an *either-or*, Marcus. I understand what you do for the club, and so will our baby boy."

"You're amazing. Have I told you that?" He grabs the back of my neck and dips down for a kiss. "And I appreciate you for everything you said. More than you know. But that's not why I was saying what I was, Luna. I know you'd never ask me to choose."

"Then what were you talking about?"

"The club already takes me away more than I'd like, so when I'm here, I want to be here with you." He rubs my stomach. "I'm not missing my baby's life or being an absent father. We both grew up with the effects of that, and I swear our baby's not going to suffer for our mistakes like we suffered for theirs. We're giving our children every minute we can. And I'm giving them all my love."

"You're a good man, Marcus. And I already know you'll do everything you can."

"I'm only a good man because I have a good woman." He grins, brushing his lips over mine. "Which is why I had to make a few changes."

"Like removing walls?"

Ghost steps back, waving his arms out. "Exactly. When I'm home, I want to be here. So if I have to be locked in my office doing work for the club, I'd rather it be in our home than the fucking clubhouse."

Glancing around at all the wires, I realize what he's saying. "You're moving your office in here?"

"It depends if you're okay sharing it with me."

I reach for his hands. "I never mind sharing, but how will that work? Isn't it a security issue for the club?"

"It'll be the same as it works at the clubhouse. The system here will mirror the one there, so it won't matter where I am. Plus, I've been passing off a lot of the day-to-day responsibilities to the new guys. They know where to find me if they need me. If Steel can come home every night, then so can I."

"I guess you're right." I've never thought about it that way.

Steel makes sure he's there for his family, and I love Ghost even more for wanting to do the same for us.

"So, what do you think? You going to split the gaming space with me?"

I glance around the room. "Seems like I don't have a choice."

"Walls are still off. I can have them come back and take it out."

Grabbing him by the cut, I pull him to me. "Don't you dare."

He nips at my lower lip, grinning. "I'll make it worth your while."

"Is that so?"

"Yep, now let's get you back to the clubhouse so I can put you to bed and get started."

"Ghost." I squeal as he reaches behind me and grabs my ass. "You're insatiable."

"Because I'm married to you, Mrs. Jasper. I'd have to be dead not to be."

"You're a sight for sore eyes yourself, Marcus." I lift off my heels to kiss him.

And I love that he's mine.

Acknowledgements

Thank you for reading Ghost and Luna's story! I had so much fun writing this one. Their mutual obsession and blistering passion was unmatched. I loved watching them open up to each other and find a home where they least expected it.

I hope you're enjoying this series so far, and I can't wait for you to dive into Legacy next!

To my readers, thank you for embracing this world of bikers. I hope you enjoyed little glimpses of Steel and Tempe in this one. Writing a found family is so special to me, and I hope you are enjoying reading about this group as much as I'm enjoying writing them!

Chris, thank you for listening while I work through the millions of ideas in my head. You are the best sounding board and the most amazing husband.

My boys, I love you both so much! I'm excited to type the end on this one so we can spend some time watching our favorite holiday movies together.

Mikki, I couldn't do this without you. Every time we think we have things nailed down, something inevitably changes. Thank you for being there through all the curveballs and for being as exited as I am for the incredible things to come.

Mom, as I type *the end* on this one, you're about to be here for a visit and I can't wait! I love you and I'm so thankful for your unconditional support.

Alba, thank you for such an incredible friendship. I'm excited for our annual cookie baking, movie watching marathon.

Sam, how many books have we been through together? I dread and appreciate your feedback every single time. You help me see the things I'm usually avoiding, and make sure to challenge me to always do my best.

Kat, thank you for being an amazing editor but also an incredible and understanding friend. I hit a wall before I started writing this one, and I appreciate you helping me find ways to lift the weight off my shoulders so I could get it done.

Vanessa, I'm so thankful to have your eyes on my books to find the little things I inevitably miss. Working with you is such a joy. I appreciate you!

Maggie and Kelly, I keep saying I'm going to take a breather, and never do it. Thank you for encouraging me through the rough spots and always making me laugh. This would be such a lonely profession without you.

To my ARC Team, thank you for the support you show my stories. There are so many incredible books in the world, and it means so much that you take the time to read mine. Thank you for every post, message, and video. You keep me going at the hardest part of the process. Your support in that moment means more than you'll ever know.

Books By Eva Simmons

Series by Eva Simmons

Sigma Sin

Dark Secret Society Romance

Twisted Kings

MC Romance

Twisted Roses

Forbidden, Tattoo Parlor Romance

Reckless

Kinky Mafia/Billionaire Romance

Enemy Muse

Rockstar Romance

Seattle Singles

Big City Romance

About Eva Simmons

Eva Simmons writes dark and dreamy romance with book boyfriends who challenge your morals and hold your heart hostage.

When Eva isn't dreaming up new worlds or devouring every book she can get her hands on, she can be found spending time with her family, painting a fresh canvas, or playing an elf in World of Warcraft.

Eva is currently living out her own happily ever after in Nevada with her family.

Printed in Great Britain
by Amazon